R.I.P.
ELIZA
HART

R.I.P. ELIZA HART

alyssa sheinmel

SCHOLASTIC PRESS / NEW YORK

Library of Congress Cataloging-in-Publication Data

Names: Sheinmel, Alyssa B., author.
Title: R.I.P. Eliza Hart / Alyssa Sheinmel.
Other titles: RIP Eliza Hart | Rest in peace Eliza Hart
Description: First edition. | New York, NY : Scholastic Press, 2017. | Summary:
Ellie Sokoloff is attending Ventana Ranch School in Big Sur, because she
hopes that the wide-open setting will cure her claustrophobia and she was
delighted to find Eliza Hart her childhood friend also in attendance; but Eliza
has changed and for no apparent reason starts spreading rumors about Ellie,
until one day she is found dead-now Ellie must find out what happened to her
one-time best friend, and who killed her, not least because she herself is
everybody's chief suspect.
Identifiers: LCCN 2017022640 | ISBN 9781338087628 (hardcover)
Subjects: LCSH: Claustrophobia—Juvenile fiction. | Anxiety disorders—
Juvenile fiction. | Boarding schools—Juvenile fiction. | Best friends—
Juvenile fiction. | Social isolation—Juvenile fiction. | Friendship—Juvenile
fiction. | Detective and mystery stories. | Big Sur (Calif.)—Juvenile fiction. |
CYAC: Mystery and detective stories. | Claustrophobia—Fiction. | Anxiety—
Fiction. | Boarding schools—Fiction. | Schools—Fiction. | Best friends—
Fiction. | Friendship—Fiction. | Big Sur (Calif.)—Fiction. | GSAFD:
Mystery fiction. | LCGFT: Detective And mystery fiction.
Classification: LCC PZ7.S54123 Raah 2017 | DDC 813.6 [Fic]—dc23
LC record available at https://lccn.loc.gov/2017022640

10 9 8 7 6 5 4 3 2 1   17 18 19 20 21

Printed in the U.S.A. 23
First edition, December 2017

Book design by Maeve Norton

ELIZA

life after death

They say it doesn't hurt when you die.

Dying is easy, comedy is hard.

I know that expression's about acting, but the fact remains that at some point in human history someone started selling the myth that dying is painless: a slipping-off, a falling-asleep. When I was four years old, my grandmother died and I asked my mom if it hurt and she said no quickly, easily, like the answer was obvious.

I don't think she even knew that she was lying.

But now I know she was.

I know because I died recently.

So recently, in fact, that my hair is still wet and my teeth are still chattering and there are bruises up and down my sides and across my back.

I don't think I'll ever heal. I don't think dead flesh *can* heal. But seriously, am I expected to spend the rest of eternity with blue marks dancing up and down the left side of

1

my rib cage, a sick sort of tattoo, a reminder of how much it hurt?

I was never particularly religious, but I did believe in the afterlife. Not in *heaven* exactly, but I believed that something came after. If it was possible for there to be a present—life on earth and all that—I didn't really see why there couldn't be something beyond the present. In physics class last year, when Mr. Wilkins droned on and on about the law of conservation of energy, I'm pretty sure I was the only one who took it as proof of life after death.

The point is, it hurts. Don't let them tell you any different. Pressure on your lungs, heart pounding so fast it feels like it's about to burst out of your chest. Your lungs fight for breath, some breath, any breath, just the littlest bit of breath, surely some air can fit around this weight, no nothing, nothing, all oxygen is denied you.

Your body fights to live, live, live, as though it's been training for this all along.

Your heart is beating harder than it's ever pounded before, reminding you of your flesh and blood and bones.

Your temperature drops.

Your skin is so cold that it hurts when the wind blows.

Your hair is frozen into sharp little icicles that feel like pinpricks against your face.

You're suddenly more aware than ever before that the heart is a muscle, because it's every bit as sore as your legs after a long run, your shoulders after a long swim.

Every heartbeat aches. And then, finally, at last, your pulse slows:

giving up,

giving in,

letting go.

It hurts. Believe me. I know what I'm talking about.

ELLIE

I'm supposed to imagine I'm someplace big.

I try to imagine I'm Julie Andrews flinging her arms open wide on a mountaintop in *The Sound of Music*. Or Julie Andrews floating over the rooftops of London in *Mary Poppins*. But I'm not Julie Andrews. I'm Ellie James Sokoloff and I'm about to drown.

Except that technically, my feet are firmly planted on dry ground. Still, I take a deep breath and hold it. Dr. Allen (therapist number two) always said that would only make things worse. *Don't hold your breath!* she shouted every time she stuffed me into the closet in her office, which wasn't an office at all but just a room in the apartment she shared with her husband and kids on the East Side of Manhattan. (Sometimes I'd bump into her kids after a session and I knew they were laughing at my sweat-soaked, tear-stained skin. At the girl who couldn't even play hide-and-seek without having a panic attack.)

Dr. Allen never understood that I *have* to hold my breath. My brain—well, part of my brain, the conscious part, the logical part—knows I'm not actually underwater, but my lungs have other ideas. Nothing the logical part of my brain says can convince my lungs that they're safe.

I never had all those symptoms you read about (and believe me I read it all): the walls closing in, the sensation that the room is getting smaller. That's what the doctors described to my parents when they explained what my phobia felt like. I've given up trying to explain that it's different for me, that whenever a door closes in a windowless room—an elevator, a closet, a bathroom—my lungs behave like I'm twenty thousand leagues under the sea, with no escape in sight.

I shut my eyes tight and try to visualize a mountaintop, but my mind's eye is blank. Sweat is pooling on the back of my neck and my heart is pounding so hard that I'm surprised I can even hear it when the front door to our suite opens and closes.

I don't want my roommate to see me like this. Even though the door to my room is shut and Sam's never come in without knocking (come to think of it, I'm not sure he's come in *with* knocking), I fumble for the knob and burst out of the closet.

Sam shouts out some greeting I don't really hear because I'm still gasping for breath. Even now, safely in my bedroom, gazing out the enormous window overlooking the ocean, my lungs feel just the slightest bit wet, like if I'm not careful I could still drown from the inside out.

Sam shouts again. "I know you're in there, I hear you breathing."

Not breathing. Panting. God, what must Sam think I'm doing in here? If I were a different girl, he'd think I had someone in here with me. But he knows I'm alone, because I'm always alone. I lean back against the closet door, safely shut behind me.

I was ten when Mom started saying, *You're too old for this sort of thing.* My brother Wes—half brother, second marriage and all that—was five at the time and never had any of my problems, which I think made Mom feel like this was all my fault, or at least my father's. She seemed confident that it wasn't hers now that Wes had proven that she could produce a perfectly healthy and sane child.

After Dr. Allen there was a man named Dr. Grace, and then a woman who insisted I call her Dr. Laura (even though Laura was her first name), who tried to hypnotize me. When that didn't work, she suggested acupuncture, but my parents—who didn't agree on much—agreed that if Eastern medicine was effective, it would have been covered by our health insurance plan.

Sam's still talking from the other side of the door.

"What?" I manage finally. It comes out like a grunt, my voice several octaves lower than usual. I walk to the mirror above my dresser. My dark brown hair is sticking up around my face, my pale skin dotted with freckles courtesy of the California sunshine. I smooth my straight hair back into a ponytail and wipe away what's left of my tears. Sam and I have lived in this two-bedroom suite for almost seven months, and he's never seen me have an attack. So far, no one on this campus has. (Knock wood.)

I open my door and step out into the common area between our bedrooms. Sam's long dreadlocks are twisted into a messy boy bun. He's so tall that sometimes I think he keeps his hair long simply because no one can reach up above his shoulders to cut it. Which is absurd. You sit down to get your hair cut, obviously.

When I first saw his name (Sam Whitker) next to mine on the dorm assignments, I assumed that it was Sam as in *Samantha*, not Sam as in *Samuel*, which is obviously Sam as in *male*. But our progressive little school has no problem with coed living arrangements, it's right there in the catalog. *At Ventana Ranch, we believe in gender-neutral dormitories.*

There was a form you could fill out requesting single-sex accommodations if you weren't comfortable with coed living arrangements. (And another form your parents could fill out if *they* weren't comfortable with it.) I didn't fill out that form because I thought that once I got here I would become the laid-back California girl I was always meant to be.

Sam and I were thrown together because a computer spit us out as compatible. Though Sam told me once that he barely even filled out his roommate questionnaire. He assumed everything would work out because he's the kind of person—smart, handsome, friendly—for whom everything always has. (Sam is the kind of person who never studies but never gets a grade below an A-minus.) So we were randomly paired off like some kind of vicious social experiment or old-school reality show: *Find out what happens when a computer matches you up and you stop being polite and start being real.*

"Someone is stealing the redwoods," he says soberly.

"A person can't steal a redwood tree." I walk over to our itchy dorm-issue couch and retrieve my laptop. I was in the middle of working on a paper when I decided to take a break to test my claustrophobia by locking myself in the closet. "Redwoods are literally the biggest living things on earth." I try to imagine someone sneaking a three-hundred-foot tree off campus.

"Not the whole tree, Elizabeth." I sigh. Sam refuses to call me Ellie like everyone else. Not that anyone calls me much of anything here. "Just the—you know, the knobby, knuckly parts. They're called burls, technically." Sam holds out his phone to show me a picture so that I can see what he's talking about. "I snapped it earlier. One of the trees right next to Hiking Trail C."

The hiking trails that snake across campus are known by letters: A for the easiest, then B and C and so on. Though all the middle letters are missing. (And you'd think A would be the hardest, since we're all students here and As are hard to come by.)

I take the phone and peer at Sam's picture. Someone took an ax and hacked into the side of one of the redwoods, ripping its bark to shreds. I never would've thought the word *butchered* could apply to a tree, but that's what this is. Pieces of rust-colored bark litter the forest floor like drops of blood. The area is ringed with yellow tape, like the scene of a murder in a movie.

There's something about seeing a mutilated tree that makes me realize how *alive* it is. Or was.

I hand Sam his phone back, our fingers almost but not quite touching. (I can't remember the last time I really touched anyone. When my parents hugged me good-bye at the airport before I flew out here?) "Why would someone do that?"

"You can sell the wood," Sam explains.

"There's a black market for wood?"

Sam nods. "Pretty damn lucrative, apparently. I looked it up. It's called burl-poaching. The older trees are the only ones with burls. People use that part to make fancy coffee tables and clocks. The poaching's been happening for years, but it's getting worse lately." Sam reads from an article on his phone. "The trees in this region are known as coast redwoods. These evergreens include the tallest trees on earth, reaching up to 379 feet. Coast redwoods only grow on a narrow strip of approximately 470 miles in the Pacific

Northwest, so their wood is rare and valuable. It's prized among builders not just for its beauty, but also because it's lightweight and resistant to decay and fire." Sam looks up and adds, "Then it says that burl-poaching supposedly got popular among meth-heads looking to make a quick buck."

I shake my head. The damage that was done to that tree was brutal, but it certainly didn't look *quick.* "They think meth-heads are sneaking onto the campus?"

Sam shrugs, sliding his phone back into his pocket. "They don't know."

The sound of sirens fills the air.

ELIZA

sirens

Sirens. Like in the *Odyssey*. Calling attention, drawing eyes. They're coming to find me.

I've decided to amend what I said before. It's possible that dying isn't painful for *everyone*. If you're in a coma and they unplug the machines, it might not hurt because your consciousness is already gone. Or maybe some people really do die in their sleep at a ripe old age after a long and fruitful life.

But to tell you the truth, I don't think life ever slips out of us peacefully. I think it twists and pulls and rips itself away, as violent as being skinned.

I never imagined my life beyond being a teenager. I don't mean I was planning this all along. I just never really saw past what was right in front of me.

In kindergarten, I couldn't see past learning my ABCs to reading actual books.

Third grade, I couldn't see past my multiplication tables to long division.

And sophomore year, I couldn't see anything past filling out the application for the Ventana Ranch School in Big Sur.

On some level, I must have understood that I was filling out the application so that I could actually, you know, *go* there the following year. I just couldn't see that far, like some kind of psychological nearsightedness.

Did I know all along that I'd die young, like a tragic character from a book they made us read in school? Did I know this was coming for me?

The sirens keep wailing, keening, moaning—bringing students away from their dinners and out of their dorm rooms, wondering what's going on.

All because of me.

I thought I would get to sleep. But the sirens are keeping me awake. Not that quiet has ever made it easier for me to sleep.

I've never slept. I mean, I *slept*—but not like normal people sleep. Never through the night. Even as a baby, my mom said they tried everything but I still got up and cried every night. I wasn't hungry and I didn't need to be changed.

I just didn't sleep.

Once I was old enough for a big-girl bed, I climbed out of it. Crept down the hall to my parents' room. Stood on my mom's side of the bed until she woke up. I made her get out of bed and play with me.

At first, she begged me to go back to sleep:

Little girls need sleep to grow up big and strong.
You'll get sick.

I'll *get sick.*

Eventually, she brought me back to my room and sang me lullabies and rocked me back and forth, waiting for my eyelids to grow heavy and close.

After a while, she gave up. Soon, our midnight play sessions became routine.

We were always careful not to wake my dad. *Let him sleep,* Mom would whisper. *He needs his sleep.*

More than you do? I'd ask.

She never answered.

ELLIE

When I was thirteen, my dad moved to an apartment across the street from a hospital. (On the fourth floor of a twenty-story building, low enough that I could take the stairs instead of the elevator even though it meant his only view was of the building across the street.) I spent the night there three times each week, listening to ambulances speeding to the emergency room. But after a few months, I kind of got used to the noise. Within six months, I was sleeping soundly while strangers below me were born and died and everything in between.

But sirens sound different here. Sirens belong in the city, not on a boarding school campus carved into the middle of the woods.

"Maybe they found the guy," I suggest.

"What guy?"

"The tree thief," I answer.

Sam looks out the window and shakes his head. "I don't think that's it."

"Why not?"

"'Cause the Coast Guard just showed up."

Our campus isn't just in the middle of the woods; it's also overlooking the Pacific Ocean. And out of 150 students (75 juniors, 75 seniors), I'm the only one planning to major in English when she gets to college. Literally everyone else is studying the natural sciences. Half of Sam's classes take place on a boat off the coast of Monterey. He comes home smelling like the ocean.

I didn't choose this school because of academics anyway. In a way, the school chose me—in an effort to expand their appeal to liberal arts students instead of students who're only interested in the STEM subjects, they offered a special scholarship for aspiring writers and I won it. I still remember the exact words of my acceptance letter: *You will find a supportive community of artists in the Santa Cruz Mountains.* I didn't know I was the only liberal arts student who said yes to their offer. It never occurred to me to say no. I just wanted to get back to California.

The acceptance letter finished with: *Come to Big Sur, where you will soar.*

I liked the sound of that. Made the place seem positively huge.

When I was little, my parents and I lived in a town called Menlo Park, about two hours north of here. But the summer after first grade, a month after my seventh birthday, my parents got divorced and decided to move back to the East Coast, where they'd both grown up. I'd never actually been to New York before that, not even to visit my grandparents.

My first attack was in an elevator on West Seventy-Eighth Street a few days after we moved. My mother thought it was asthma or anaphylaxis (a word I learned later that afternoon) and rushed me to the emergency room. She seemed disappointed when the ER doctor suggested sending me to a child psychologist and more disappointed still when the therapist (Dr. Shapiro, therapist number one) diagnosed me with claustrophobia a few days later. The attacks kept coming—in elevators, on the subway, once in a restaurant bathroom—so that by the end of the summer, I'd gotten used to taking the stairs and I'd learned to avoid drinking too much water when we went out to eat.

By the time school started, my symptoms hadn't improved and we'd moved on to my first specialist, Dr. Allen, who advised Mom to tell the principal about my condition. My teacher announced it to our class so no one would accidentally shove me in the closet or a locker. (The teacher assumed that no one would be mean enough to do those things on purpose, and—for a while at least—she was right.) My diagnosis followed me through middle school and into high school, but I never believed it was a reaction to the divorce, or some kind of emotional cry for help, the way my parents and all the therapists did.

You know what they say: *location, location, location.* I always thought my body was rejecting moving from the wide-open spaces of Northern California to the narrow streets on the narrow island of Manhattan.

So I hatched a plan—a cure: get back to California by attending Ventana Ranch, a prestigious boarding school for high school juniors and seniors built into the Santa Cruz Mountains on the California coastline.

By the time I tucked myself into a closet the first day of orientation and discovered my claustrophobia had come to California with me, it was too late to go back.

On the other hand, none of the buildings on the campus are more than three stories high, so I haven't had to get in an elevator once since I got here. In fact, the only attacks I've had in California are the ones I've induced in the closet. (Even after more than six months here, I haven't stopped testing my theory.)

Sam's still looking out the window. "Why would the Coast Guard be here?" he murmurs. I cross the room and stand just behind him, careful to stay far enough from him that we're not actually touching. Still, I can feel the heat from his body seeping into the air around him like he's radioactive or something.

It's almost dinnertime and the sun is setting over the Pacific Ocean.

Later, I won't remember exactly when it became clear that the bundle they pulled up from over the cliffs was a body. When it became clear that the body was human. When it became clear that its skin had turned blue.

When I saw its long blond hair and knew they'd pulled a girl up over the cliff.

ELLIE

wednesday, march 16

When I find out that it's *her*, a lump rises in my throat and I'm so surprised that it almost chokes me. I shouldn't care. I mean, I care because caring is the human thing to do, but I shouldn't care *this much* because I didn't really know her. Not really. Not anymore.

We're still standing by the window. In fact, we've barely moved since Sam's phone dinged with a text from a friend outside who heard the dean identify the body.

I wipe my eyes, but that just draws more attention to my tears. Sam offers me a tissue, but I bet he thinks I don't deserve to cry.

"You okay, Elizabeth?"

They put her on a gurney, zip her into a black bag, and wheel her into the back of an ambulance.

"We held hands during recess."

"What?"

I bend my fingers, pressing my nails into my palms so my hands will stop shaking. Like everyone else on campus,

Sam's heard the rumors about Eliza and me. I think even the teachers are wary of me thanks to her. But maybe Sam doesn't remember them, maybe they went in one ear and out the other like my repeated requests that he call me Ellie instead of Elizabeth.

"Nothing," I say carefully. "I don't know."

Sam's phone buzzes with another text. "Cooper says someone called the police when they saw something strange out there."

"I just can't believe it."

She wasn't in Spanish class this afternoon (the one class we have together), but I didn't think much of it. Arden Lin, one of her roommates and best friends, said she had a cold.

"Is she okay?" I'd asked. Stupid. I should've kept my mouth shut. I couldn't help it. It was a reflex.

"Why?" Arden asked. "You wanna bring her some chicken soup? Can't help noticing that when I was sick a few months ago, you didn't seem so concerned."

"*¡En español!*" Señora Rocha admonished, oblivious to the fact that Arden was making fun of me. She made us repeat the whole conversation. Arden didn't know how to say chicken soup in Spanish. While Señora Rocha clucked her disapproval, Arden stared daggers at me.

Now Sam says, "I can't believe it, either." He takes a deep breath, his black T-shirt stretching over the muscles in his chest. "She didn't seem the type."

"What type?"

He shrugs. "I guess you never can tell. I read somewhere that in half of all suicides, the friends and family say they never had a clue. I thought they were just trying to cover up their guilt, you know? But maybe—"

I interrupt before he can finish his thought. "You think Eliza Hart killed herself?"

Looking out the window, the cliff where they pulled her up is across the road and to the left. Directly across the road from our dorm is another dorm (Eliza's dorm), built right up against the edge of the hill. The drop-off is shallower there. You could probably walk down the hill toward the water if you wanted to, though it's all covered in rocks and yellow grass. Not like the sharp, rocky drop where they found Eliza.

"I guess she could've fallen." Sam cocks his head to the side. "But that girl always seemed agile as a cat to me."

Eliza is the kind of girl who inspires even guys like Sam to say things like *agile as a cat*.

(Was. *Was* the kind of girl. She *isn't* anything anymore.)

"Do you think her parents know?"

"The dean probably called them by now."

I nod, backing away from the window.

A fresh round of sirens fills the air. "Police." Sam points to a car coming up the road from the valley down below. It pulls to a stop beside the cliff.

"Would they call police for a suicide?"

Sam shrugs. "Technically, it's illegal, right?"

I nod again. I read once that it's against the law so that they can revive you if you make it to the hospital in time, so that they can force you to get help, so that you won't ever want to do it again.

Of course, all the help in the world hasn't kept me from having claustrophobia.

Anyway, I don't believe Eliza Hart killed herself. I mean, I'm not naive. I know everyone has issues, that kind of thing. But mean girls don't kill themselves. They're too busy making other people miserable.

Or anyway, making *me* miserable. I had no idea just how much this school would be like the one I left behind until I met Eliza Hart. Or, more precisely, re-met her.

We were in kindergarten and first grade together in Menlo Park, but we didn't stay in touch after I moved away. We were too young for Facebook and emails and Snapchat. We were too young for *sleepovers*.

Back then, Eliza's house was Disneyland as far as I was concerned. She had the best toys: an electric car you could sit in and activate by pushing a pedal. I begged my parents to get me something similar for Hanukkah—at Eliza's house there was an enormous Christmas tree, of course—and they finally gave in and got me the one that you moved with your own feet. It was even lamer than a bicycle.

Eliza's Barbie dolls had hair that flowed in ripples down their backs. (My dolls' hair seemed to come out of the box matted and tangled.) She had the best collection of Disney princess movies I'd ever seen. She had picture books with glossy pages that smelled like cologne, and her bedroom was covered in a thick, shaggy carpet that shone when sunlight streamed in through the windows.

Champagne, I remember with a start. Her mother said the carpet was champagne-colored. I used to think the drink was named after the color, not the other way around.

She even had a better name than I did. Just one syllable and four letters different, but so much cooler than Elizabeth.

In kindergarten, our teacher started calling me Lizzy. She said that Eliza and Ellie were too similar, plus there was an Ally in the class, too, and she would get the three of us mixed up if she didn't do something about it.

I hated being called Lizzy. The one good thing about moving to New York was that I got to go back to being Ellie because there was already a Lizzy in our class.

My first day here at Ventana Ranch, I was exploring the campus when I saw her name taped to a door on the third floor of the dorm called Harlan, directly across the road from my own. At first, I doubted it was the same Eliza Hart. What were the odds that after almost a decade my long-lost best friend would end up living across the street from me?

But just in case, I lingered in the hallway, staring at all the girls I thought might be her—blond hair, gray eyes, California tan—waiting for one of them to stop at the door labeled with her name. And then there she was, toting her suitcase down the hall alongside her parents just in time for orientation, not hours early like I'd been. Not exhausted and jet-lagged from taking the red-eye. She was still just as perfect as one of her Barbie dolls.

Maybe I shouted her name too loud. Or maybe I walked down the hallway too eagerly. Perhaps she just didn't remember me—presumably (unlike me), she'd had other best friends since first grade, right? Instead of saying hello, she looked me up and down like she was taking stock of my dark jeans and brown hair (it was blonder when I was little) and gray eyes. (That was the only thing we ever had in common— we both had gray eyes. Though hers had a lot more blue in them and mine more brown. Just another way she was better than me.) She tightened her grip on her suitcase like she thought I might try to take it from her or something. Was I making her *nervous?*

I turned my attention to her parents. I wouldn't have recognized her father. I mean, it had been a long time, but his face was puffed out somehow, even though he looked just as thin now as he had then. I remember that I used to think he was handsome—you know, the way that dads can be handsome—but he looked so old to me now. If I didn't know better I might have thought he was Eliza's grandfather, not her dad.

"Mr. and Mrs. Hart," I said, "it's so good to see you again. I'm Ellie Sokoloff. Eliza and I went to elementary school together."

Her father gazed at me without the slightest bit of recognition, but her mother nodded and said, "How are your parents?"

I sighed with relief. At least one member of the Hart family remembered me. (Or at least she was polite enough to *pretend* she remembered me.) "They're good. I mean, they're not here. We couldn't all fly across the country to move me in, you know?"

I bit my lip, ashamed that I'd just admitted that my parents hadn't wanted to spend the money to fly to California to move me into the dorms. (It wasn't only about the money. They couldn't decide which of them should move me in, and it's not like they could have done it together. They barely made it through my middle school graduation without fighting and they'd been sitting on opposite ends of the school auditorium, not side by side on a plane.)

"I'm glad to hear that they're well," Mrs. Hart answered. "Do you know where the nearest grocery store is? We want to drive into town to get Eliza some essentials."

I shook my head. "I took the bus here from SFO this morning."

Finally, Eliza spoke, rolling her shoulders down her back. She was taller than I was. She'd always been taller. "You don't have a car?"

"I don't have a license," I explained. "You can't get it until you're seventeen in New York." Eliza already was seventeen,

I realized, remembering that she had a September birthday. "Anyway, you don't really need to drive there."

"Well, you need to drive *here*." Eliza lifted her chin like she couldn't believe that a girl who didn't know how to drive had gotten into the same school she had. What had I been thinking, that I could make her nervous? I was pretty sure she was the kind of girl who didn't get nervous. "You're going to be trapped on this campus without a car," Eliza warned.

My heart beat just a little bit faster at the sound of the word *trapped*. The whole point of coming here was *not* to feel trapped. I swallowed hard, hoping the Harts couldn't see my nerves.

"What room are you in?" Eliza glanced up and down the hall.

"Oh, I'm not in this dorm. I'm in Beronda." I gestured vaguely out the window.

Eliza narrowed her gray eyes. "Then what are you doing in Harlan?"

Until then, I hadn't known it was weird that I was there. Of course it was *weird*. I should've been back in my own room, waiting for my own roommate to show up. "Just exploring." I looked at my shoes. Black boots with zippers up the sides. Out of place next to Eliza's flip-flops. "Well, I better go unpack." I gave a little wave and turned on my heel, heading back toward my own room, where every single thing I'd brought from the East Coast had long since been put in its place.

"We didn't go to elementary school together," Eliza said to my back. "Just kindergarten."

"First grade, too," I corrected, spinning around with a smile. I was happy that she actually remembered me. "I moved to New York after first grade."

"That's hardly elementary school," Eliza said, and I stopped smiling.

Later, I saw Eliza driving her car out of the student parking lot. A cream-colored SUV with automatic everything. It probably knew how to park itself.

The ambulance they put her in starts to drive away, without sirens this time.

Jumping off the cliffs is one way out of here that doesn't require a car.

Not that I think Eliza jumped.

ELIZA

there's no place like home

I can't remember what it felt like to fall. Falling never frightened me, even as a little kid. Before swimming took over, I used to do gymnastics and I laughed when I fell off the beam.

Not like the other girls. They all cried.

When I was little, the only thing that made me cry was waking up in the middle of the night. It meant that I would have to try to fall asleep again, the hardest thing in the world.

I stopped sneaking into my parents' room by the time I was seven. I spent my restless nights alone, tossing and turning and begging my body to turn off the way other girls' did.

Sometimes I tiptoed to my door and considered walking down the hall.

Imagined waking my mother.

My father slept all the way on the other side of their big bed, and anyway he had pills to help him sleep by then, pills that made it nearly impossible to wake him up. Sometimes I worried there would be a fire or an earthquake in the middle of the night and he'd sleep right through it.

And then I'd imagine what life would be like with just Mom and me. It didn't look so bad.

And then I'd feel awful for imagining that, for thinking that, and I'd be even more awake.

Just like I am now.

The other girls called their mothers *Mommy* all the way through elementary school. Not me. I graduated to *Mom* early.

My mother never wore perfume. When the other moms came to pick up their little girls after school, the air was thick with the scent of Chanel and vanilla, jasmine and apricots. Coconut from the moms who spent their days by the pool at the country club and mint from the mothers who'd had a drink at lunch and tried to cover up the scent by brushing their teeth. But my mother was decidedly odorless. I went into her bathroom once, smelled her shampoo and her soap—they had a scent just like everyone else's. But somehow the smells all disappeared after they hit her body.

When I was ten, my mother asked my pediatrician if she should be concerned that I had trouble sleeping. He said I was just a healthy, energetic child. I wasn't the least bit hyperactive during the day, so he didn't diagnose me with ADHD or anything like that.

When I was thirteen, they tested my thyroid—apparently, an overactive thyroid can keep you from sleeping. But my thyroid was perfectly normal.

At least some part of me was.

Now I wonder how my mom took the news, when they told her I'd died.

Did she let them see her cry?

Did her hair fall out of its tight bun, and did her shoulders slump? She always hated the way I slouched. One of our biggest fights ever, I swear to God, was about posture.

Although that might have been a metaphor for something else.

I'm getting distracted.

But then, it was always like this when I couldn't sleep. My thoughts would bounce one to another all on their own, no matter how hard I tried to ignore them.

Did Mom tell my dad herself, or did she make someone else do it? Did he even understand what had happened, or is he still medicated into oblivion like he was at Christmas?

I never knew which dad was going to be waiting for me when I came home.

Medicated Dad,

Dark Dad,

Fun Dad.

I hated all those dads, even though Fun Dad and I had some good times. But once in a while there was Normal Dad, even though *normal* wasn't the right word for it since his appearances were so few and far between. But I really loved Normal Dad.

Mom used to tiptoe around Normal Dad, like she thought maybe he would stick around a little bit longer if she just did the right thing or avoided saying the wrong words. She knew full well that remission didn't work that way, but knowing wasn't enough to keep her from tiptoeing, wasn't enough to keep her from hoping (at first) that this time would be different,

this time would last,

this time he would be the man she fell in love with,

the man she chose to marry,

the man she decided to have a child with,

the man she could leave that child home alone with without worrying what might happen.

I used to tiptoe around Normal Dad, too. I can't remember exactly when I realized it didn't make a difference.

You know, it's true what they say: There's no place like home.

But just because there's no place like it doesn't mean it's so great.

Personally, if I were Dorothy, I would have stayed in Oz instead of trying to get back to Kansas.

ELLIE

I'm in bed trying to read, but I can't concentrate on the words on the page because I can't stop thinking about Eliza's hair. It fell in a perfect blond waterfall of waves down her back. It even looked pretty when they pulled her up from over the cliffs, blowing in the breeze. A totally irrational, nonscientific part of my brain believes that if I'd grown up in California, my hair would be wavy and blond, too.

Even though it's warm under the covers, I shudder. I shouldn't think things like that. It's disrespectful. Even though it's actually a compliment. Just another way she was perfect. Just another reason not to be suicidal.

Don't be ridiculous, Ellie. People don't kill themselves over their hair. Or anyway, they don't *not* kill themselves because they have perfect hair.

I narrow my eyes and hold my book closer to my face, trying to focus on the words swimming across the page in front of me. A person isn't supposed to need reading glasses till she's at least twice my age. (Which is sixteen, by the way.

Sam already turned seventeen, but my birthday isn't until the end of April.) Back in the city over the summer, my doctor told me that I was reading too much—it was weakening my eyes.

I toss my copy of *The Complete Short Stories of Ernest Hemingway* aside, throw my blankets back, and walk to the window. It's so foggy that I can't see the stars, but it's not dark because they've set up floodlights around the place where they pulled up her body. Sam said that it was lucky she hit that ledge. If she'd made it down to the open sea they probably never would have found her. We probably wouldn't even know that she was dead.

I thought that was a strange thing to call *lucky*, but I kept it to myself.

Sam says they'll do an autopsy to determine the cause of death. He listed the possibilities: Trauma from the fall. Exposure from lying out there for so long. Drowning when the tide rose. I thought it sounded like the options on a multiple-choice test, and then I thought that no one in her right mind would think about the SATs at a time like this.

It's cold but I don't close my window. I always keep it open at least a crack. (Open windows make a room feel bigger.)

If she didn't jump, she might have fallen.

But if she didn't fall, then the only logical conclusion is that someone pushed her, right?

The police must think that's at least a possibility. Why else would they have wrapped the ridge of the cliff with yellow crime-scene tape and lit it up with floodlights?

I hear music playing. Everyone's down in the student center in the valley for Wednesday Reading Night. (The administration decided not to cancel the evening's activities. Wednesday Reading Night is a Ventana Ranch tradition, rain or shine; it says so in the catalog.) Sam invited me to walk down there with him tonight, but it's two days before spring break, so it's not like I have a ton of studying left to do. And anyway, I'm not taking half the classes that everyone else takes, so I don't exactly need a study buddy. (Sometimes I wonder if I actually love reading and writing or if they just became habits because they're good hobbies for a girl who hasn't had a real best friend since around the time she started reading chapter books.)

Judging from the sound of music coming from down the hill, no one is really studying tonight.

I'm pretty sure the entire dorm is empty. Everyone else is down in the valley. I think maybe no one wanted to be alone.

And I think maybe they were right. You'd have to be an idiot to choose to be alone at a time like this.

Right?

I get dressed fast. It's cold here at night—the average temperature drops into the forties, but this week it's even hit the thirties—so I layer a sweatshirt under a wool coat.

When I get outside, I realize the flaw in my plan. I won't be alone once I get down to the student center, but I most certainly will be on the walk from here to there. I consider turning back, but in the shadows from the floodlights, the dorm looks smaller than usual, the sort of place that makes you feel trapped.

So I start walking.

There are two ways to get down to the valley from the dorms. Turn right, and head toward Hiking Trail D, which weaves through the woods and down the hill until it opens out into the valley. (Nothing like a school gathering that requires hiking.) It's the fastest way down, but I don't exactly feel like trekking through the woods tonight, jumping in surprise every time a pine needle so much as snaps beneath my feet.

So I turn left instead, onto the narrow road that borders the dormitories and leads to the dining hall. Just before the dining hall is a long staircase that leads down to the parking lot. Then I'll just need to walk through the parking lot to reach another staircase that goes straight down into the valley. No woods, no hiking, no pinecones crunching beneath my feet. The only problem is that directly across from the top of the stairs, right next to the dining hall, is the spot where they pulled Eliza's body from the cliffs.

I keep my head down and count my steps. One, two, three, four. One, two, three, four. Left, right, left, right.

The sound of a car coming up the hill makes me look up. It stops beside one of the floodlights, so that its paint gleams and glitters when the light hits it. Someone gets out of the driver's seat and holds open the backseat door.

"I'm sorry we couldn't get you here sooner, Mrs. Hart, Mr. Hart."

"Yes, well. All that traffic in Santa Cruz."

I recognize Eliza's mother's voice immediately. Not just her voice but the tone, just as no-nonsense as when she asked me for the nearest grocery store.

"Are you sure you wouldn't rather come back tomorrow when it's light? There's really no need to do this here. I can ask you my questions back at the station."

"Here will be fine, thank you."

The man who apologized lifts the crime-scene tape so that Eliza's parents can walk right up to the edge of the cliffs.

"I'm sorry, but I do have to ask whether Eliza showed any signs of depression?"

"Your colleagues already asked us that when they came to our home, Detective Roberts." Detective Roberts doesn't say anything. His silence must prompt Mrs. Hart into answering, because she quietly adds, "Eliza was a perfectly normal girl."

I'm not trying to eavesdrop. But I can't possibly keep going down this road without bumping into them and if I bumped into them I'd have to think of the right thing to say and I'm the kind of person who can't think of the right thing to say even under the best circumstances, let alone the worst.

So I keep still.

"Of course," Detective Roberts murmurs, his pencil making scratching sounds as he scribbles something onto his notepad. "And, Mr. Hart." He turns to the tall man silhouetted behind Eliza's mother, who takes a step backward, like he's scared if he gets too close, he'll go flying over the edge of the cliffs, too. "Did you notice Eliza acting . . . unusual recently?"

Eliza's father doesn't answer. George, I remember. His first name is George. Not that I ever called him anything but Mr. Hart.

He was usually still at work when Eliza and I had our after-school playdates. I can't remember what he did, though. Something businessy, like a lawyer or an accountant. He's wearing a suit without a tie and a button-down shirt. He squints as the brightness from the floodlights hits his face.

Mrs. Hart is wearing a camel-colored coat and her blond hair—just a shade darker than Eliza's, like maybe she didn't spend as much time outside in the sun as her daughter did—is twisted into a low bun at the nape of her neck.

"Mr. Hart?" Detective Roberts prompts.

"Can't you see he's too upset to talk?" Mrs. Hart interjects, but she doesn't reach out to take his hand or rub his shoulder or pat his back. Her husband turns his head from side to side like he's looking for something. I duck behind the nearest tree before he can see me. *Great idea, Ellie. Hide from the police like the weirdo you are.*

"Of course, Mrs. Hart." Detective Roberts's voice is deep and gravelly. I wonder if he sounds like that all the time or only when a seventeen-year-old's body has been pulled from the sea.

"Yes. When can we go home?" Mrs. Hart asks as though the detective didn't already say they didn't have to do this here tonight. "There's a lot to arrange. We still haven't had time to contact the rest of our family and I have to reserve a church for the funeral. I'm not sure our usual church will be large enough."

Eliza's grandfather was the mayor of Menlo Park before we were born. I think he even ran for governor once. Her family knows half the state.

"Of course. However, I must tell you that it may be some time before we can release Eliza's body to you."

"She's my daughter."

"Of course." How many times has Detective Roberts said *of course* tonight? More than he's said *I'm sorry*? "But her body is all the evidence we have at the moment. She might be able to tell us—"

"Detective Roberts, my daughter isn't about to tell anyone anything anymore."

The detective pauses before answering, like maybe he thinks Mrs. Hart is about to start crying. When she remains dry-eyed, he says, "I appreciate how badly you must want to bury your child, but we need time to conduct our investigation. We don't even know the exact cause of death yet. I assure you my colleagues will take good care of her."

At this, Eliza's father gasps, like until just this second, he forgot that he needed to breathe.

"George—" Mrs. Hart begins, but before she can say anything more, someone else walks up to them, stepping over the tape. Alan Carson, the dean of students.

"Here he is," Dean Carson begins. Another, slighter, person trails behind him. "Julian Alvarez." Julian stands in front of a floodlight so he's just a silhouette. He's a junior, like me, and he lives in Eliza's dorm, Harlan. When Julian doesn't say anything, the dean adds, "Tell the detective what you told me."

"I saw Eliza." Julian looks at the ground.

"When?" Detective Roberts asks.

Julian shrugs. "About a week ago."

I can sense the detective's disappointment. He thought Julian was talking about the night Eliza fell. (Was pushed? Jumped?)

"Go on, Julian," the dean presses.

"She was fighting with someone."

I swear my heart skips a beat.

The detective stands up a little straighter, his disappointment receding. "What do you mean?"

"It was the middle of the night and I was working on a paper. I mean, I don't usually put off papers until the night before they're due, but I got an idea on relating dolphin behavior to human behavior—" He stops himself, as though he's just realized that's not the part of the story anyone here is interested in. "Anyway, around two a.m. I looked out the window and I saw Eliza out after curfew. She was with someone on the path outside our dorm."

"Did you recognize that someone?"

Julian shakes his head. "It was dark and I was looking down on them from the third floor." There are little footlights lining the path, but they aren't bright enough to do much more than guide you up and down the path at night, and they dim them after curfew anyway. "And there's a tree"—he turns around and gestures up the path to his dorm, pointing at a redwood—"blocking most of the view from my window."

"Then how did you know it was Eliza?"

"Her hair," Julian answers. Eliza's hair is unmistakable, and light enough that you can see it in the dark.

No one else at Ventana Ranch has hair like Eliza's. I'm not sure anyone anywhere has hair like Eliza's, except maybe celebrities who have a team of stylists whose entire job is to make their clients' hair look like Eliza's hair looks naturally.

"Can you tell me anything about the person she was talking to? Was it a male or female?"

"I couldn't tell. He—or she—was pretty well hidden beneath the branches."

I look around, like I think I'll be able to magically see what Julian missed that night a week ago.

"How can you be sure they were arguing? Did they raise their voices?"

I already know the answer to the second question: No. Julian's room faces the path in between Harlan and Beronda, just like mine. Which means that if Julian could see them, Eliza and her companion were somewhere below my window, too. Which means I would've heard them, if they were being loud. Open window and all that.

I wish they'd been loud. I wish they'd woken me up. I wish I'd seen whoever it was so that maybe I could add something to Julian's story. Maybe I'd have seen something he missed. Something that would help the police find this person now.

"No, but I could tell that he—or she—grabbed her at some point. Grabbed her arm. She tried to pull away but whoever it was wouldn't let go."

Eliza had strong arms, lean and toned because of her swimming. She always looked so powerful to me. Whoever was holding her against her will would've had to be even stronger.

Strong enough to push her over the cliff? My breaths are shallow, my heartbeat quick. Despite the chill in the air, my palms are sweating. I tell myself that nothing bad can happen to me now, not with the police just a stone's throw away.

"Did you do anything? When this person grabbed her?"

Julian doesn't answer. Dean Carson says gently, "No one is saying that you did anything wrong," but even I

40

can tell his heart isn't in it. He's thinking what I'm thinking—maybe if Julian had said something then, had shouted out, had run down to help her—things might be different for Eliza now.

Finally, Julian says, "After a while, she twisted her arm away and stomped back toward the dorm."

"And the other person? Did that person go back to the dorms as well?"

Julian shrugs. "I don't know."

I shake my head in frustration. I wish Julian were a better witness.

The dean offers, "It must have been a student. Students need to show their IDs to get on and off campus. An outsider wouldn't have been permitted on campus at that hour." He sounds desperate to believe this, desperate to think that our security is tight enough to protect his students.

The detective nods but he doesn't seem entirely convinced. Dean Carson didn't mention that it's only at the front gate that we have to show our IDs to the security guard who sits in the booth all day. There are other entrances along some of the hiking trails, gates that have magnetic locks that grant access to the parks around the school. No one uses them, but apparently our IDs have magnets in them that open the doors.

The detective tells Julian he can go and turns back to Dean Carson. "I understand that the students are about to go on spring break?"

"Correct." Dean Carson rubs his hands together like he's trying to keep warm. "Friday is their last day. Of course, given the circumstances, we're considering canceling tomorrow's classes as well, but—"

Detective Roberts interrupts, "I'm afraid we have a bit of a problem, Dean. I can't conduct a thorough investigation if half my witnesses leave to party in Cabo."

"I'm sorry?" Dean Carson sounds bewildered.

"This young man seems to think Eliza might have had a problem with someone on this campus. I need to know who that person is."

"Surely you're not suggesting that one of the students had something to do with Eliza's accident?" Mrs. Hart interjects.

But if one of the students had something to do with it, it wasn't an *accident.* I shiver.

"I'm afraid I have to consider that, given what we've just been told."

"Teenagers argue all the time." Mrs. Hart sounds exasperated. "You can't just cancel spring break. Tickets have been purchased, hotel rooms booked."

If Detective Roberts thinks it's odd that Mrs. Hart is worrying about reservations at a time like this, he doesn't say so. (I guess you never know what kind of details people will focus on.) Instead he continues, "I'm afraid I must insist that we try. On such a small campus, everyone is a potential witness."

Or suspect, I think.

"Yes, yes," Dean Carson answers. "We always keep the dorms open over spring break, keep the cafeteria up and running. For students who need to stay."

Students like me. Scholarship students who can't afford the flight home. And who don't really want to go home anyway.

Mrs. Hart opens her mouth but I don't hear what she says next because someone grabs me from behind, his arms over mine.

And all I hear is my own heartbeat.

ELLIE

wednesday, march 16

I twist my neck to see who's holding me.

"What the hell, Sam?" I disentangle myself from my roommate angrily, but my skin tingles beneath my clothes where he held me. Inwardly, I beg my lungs to behave themselves. Someone's arms are not the same as a small room, no matter how tightly they hold you. Anyway, Sam didn't really *grab* me—he just kind of squeezed my arms so I would know he was there. So far, my lungs seem to know the difference. Or maybe Sam just didn't hold me long enough for panic to set in.

Did Eliza panic, when someone grabbed her arm and wouldn't let go?

"I should ask you the same thing."

"Huh?"

"What are you doing hiding behind a tree next to a crime scene?"

"I wasn't hiding. I was on my way to Wednesday Reading Night." How can the truth sound so much like a lie? Trying to make my explanation more convincing, I add, "I didn't want to be alone," but it just makes me sound desperate.

"I figured as much." Sam kicks the ground. "That's why I was coming home."

I can't hide my surprise. "Really?"

Sam shrugs. He's standing so close that I can smell his breath: peppermint. "It's not like it was a fun scene down there. Everyone's pretty freaked out."

"Do they all think she killed herself?" I ask softly.

Sam shrugs. "Julian saw—"

"I heard."

"It's all anyone can talk about."

I nod. It's all I can *think* about. A movie is playing in my mind: someone wrapping his hand around Eliza's arm and refusing to let go.

Sam reaches up to adjust his boy bun. "I guess the police aren't going anywhere anytime soon." Neither of us moves to go back to the dorm or down to the valley. We turn to face the floodlights, Sam just behind me.

"You don't consider the students suspects?" Dean Carson asks the detective. A few moments ago, he seemed so certain that no one who wasn't a student would be on campus in the middle of the night. Now it sounds like he's hoping it was a stranger.

"I'm afraid I can't rule anything out at this juncture."

"Why would there be suspects when something was so clearly an accident?" Mrs. Hart says it like it's a statement, not a question. It's the second time she's referred to Eliza's death as an accident.

"We'll start with the students and teachers who knew Eliza best," Detective Roberts answers, which isn't exactly the same thing as saying *No, of course they're not suspects* or *Yes, this was just a tragic accident.* "The students who would have seen her soonest before . . ." He pauses like he's struggling to find the find word. He can't say *accident* because it might have been intentional and he can't say *fall* because someone might have pushed her. "Before the incident," he finishes finally.

"Some parents might not want their children to stay here over break," Mrs. Hart points out. "Surely you can't force the entire student body to stay."

For the first time, Mr. Hart speaks. "Whatever the detective thinks is best." His voice sounds nothing like you'd expect, coming from such a tall man. It's high-pitched, the kind of voice that you might even mistake for a woman's if you weren't paying attention. A voice I haven't heard since I was seven years old, one I didn't realize I'd remembered. Like a song whose lyrics you didn't forget even after years without singing it.

"We'll secure the campus," Detective Roberts promises, once again not really answering the question he's been asked. "We'll monitor everyone who comes in and out."

When Sam speaks, I feel his breath on the back of my neck. "Yeah, but what if the murderer is already on campus?"

I shudder.

Dean Carson gestures toward the dining hall. "Why don't we head inside?" The cafeteria is usually closed at this hour, but I guess the dean has keys. "Get you some coffee. You must be exhausted."

Mrs. Hart nods. "Thank you."

Sam grabs my hand and I swallow a gasp at the feel of his palm—paper-dry and pleasantly warm—against my own. As far as I can tell, Sam doesn't own a single scarf or a winter coat other than the ski jacket he uses for weekend trips to Lake Tahoe. In fact, a few days ago he laughed at me when I left the dorm wearing a hat and gloves. "You're not in New York anymore, Sokoloff," he said.

Now, he pulls me toward the dorm, lacing his fingers through mine. "Let's get out of here," he says. "It's almost curfew."

None of the other students are rushing up from the valley to make it back to the dorms before our 11:00 p.m. curfew. No one's worried about getting into that kind of trouble tonight. They're probably more worried about walking around campus alone.

When I don't budge, Sam adds, "Elizabeth, come on."

I twist my hand from his and stuff it in my pocket, but I follow him down the road, careful to keep to the shadowy edges.

I can't help looking back. Dean Carson places his hand gently on Mr. Hart's elbow. "Mr. Hart? Won't you join us inside?"

"I'm coming," he answers in his strange, reedy voice. "I'm coming."

I'm coming. I'm coming.

Suddenly, I'm in Eliza's champagne-carpeted room at five years old, and her dad is shouting her name from the front door.

"I'm coming to get you, little girl!"

Eliza squealed with delight. "Daddy's home early!" She pulled me out into the hallway, started dragging me toward the front door of their sprawling house.

"Where's your mother?" Mr. Hart asked.

"Not home! Just us and Cassie." Cassie was the babysitter.

"I'm sending Cassie home." He knelt and lifted his daughter overhead. At the time, he was the tallest person I'd ever seen in real life, well over six feet tall. When he threw Eliza into the air above him, it looked like flying.

When he looked down and saw me gaping up at him, he winked. "Let's redecorate." He led the way into Eliza's room and pulled out Eliza's watercolors and finger paints.

"I'm only allowed to color in the kitchen," I said cautiously. My mom thought I'd drip paint all over our house. It was fall—not even Thanksgiving yet—and Eliza and I had only been best friends for a couple of months. I didn't want to ruin anything.

Mr. Hart winked again. "Not today," he said.

When my mother came to pick me up later, my hands and arms and legs and clothes were covered with every color from Eliza's paint box. Mom apologized profusely to Mr. Hart as she led me to our car. She yelled at me the whole ride home, mortified that I made such a mess of myself at the Harts' expensive house. I never got to tell her that Mr. Hart helped me paint a horse right over the wallpaper on Eliza's bedroom wall, picking me up so I could make it as tall as he was.

When we got home, Mom tried to wash the paint out of my clothes, but they were beyond saving. She put me into the bathtub and scrubbed my skin so hard it hurt. I tried to tell her that Mr. Hart said it was okay to make a mess, but the words wouldn't come.

ELLIE

thursday, march 17

In the morning, the fog is so thick that it condenses on the trees and drips down. It sounds like rain on the roof of our dorm. I'm still in bed when I hear voices outside.

"Rest in peace, Eliza Hart. Rest in peace, Eliza Hart."

On my phone is an email from the dean addressed to the whole student body, letting us know that today's classes are canceled. I get out of bed, my bare feet slapping against the linoleum floor, and raise the wooden blinds to look out the open window.

There are three of them. Girls still in their pj's, standing with candles outside Eliza's dorm, probably right where Julian saw her arguing a week ago. Any other day, some professor would be running up the road, scolding them to blow out their candles, reminding them of the risk of forest fires.

But today, no one stops them. In fact, when another student walks by (I recognize her as a senior who probably never talked to Eliza), they hold out a fresh candle to her, inviting her to join them. She does, and soon her voice is part of their chorus.

"Rest in peace, Eliza Hart. Rest in peace, Eliza Hart."

They gaze up at the dorm, the building that houses the room where Eliza Hart slept and dressed and studied and snacked.

Suite 308, on the third floor, a two-bedroom suite for three people to share. Eliza had the single (of course), a coveted corner room with views of the ocean on one side and the redwoods on the other. If this campus were a hotel, that would be the honeymoon suite. The girls outside knew exactly which window to gather beneath. But no one's going to call *them* stalkers just because they know where she lived.

I only saw the inside of Eliza's room once. In January.

Even at the time I knew it was a terrible idea, but I tried it anyway. (Desperate times calls for desperate measures, right?) Maybe I was frustrated after spending winter break at my mom's, in an apartment that was always overflowing with my little brother's friends, not even in high school and already cooler than I'll ever be.

Or maybe I'm just an idiot.

Whatever the reason, in late January, I knocked on the door of room 308. Unlike me, Eliza's roommates were girls, and they were her best friends, the kind my parents said you were supposed to make in high school, the kind you'd keep your whole life. (I was tempted to point out that *they'd* met in high school and it hadn't exactly worked out so well for them, but I kept my mouth shut.) Eliza and her two roommates had known one another before coming to Ventana Ranch, and rumor had it that they coordinated their roommate questionnaires to be sure that the computer would spit them out together. (I thought it was more likely that one of their parents had asked the administration for a favor, but I kept my theory to myself.)

Eliza probably would have ended up being best friends with whomever she lived with. Who wouldn't want to be her best friend?

Eliza could probably find friends in her sleep. She wouldn't have known how hard it is to make friends when you can't go to crowded parties or sneak rides on your school's elevator (meant for faculty only) or gossip in the bathroom or even grab food from the pantry in the cafeteria when the teachers weren't looking. I couldn't hop on the subway and head downtown to go shopping after school (even though the trains have windows, I can't take being inside the tunnels), or make plans with a classmate who happened to live above the tenth floor—as high as I could climb the stairs without becoming a breathless, sweaty mess. (In a miserable irony, claustrophobia actually made my world smaller, because there were so many things I couldn't do and places I couldn't go.)

Eliza's roommate Erin made me wait in the hall while she checked whether Eliza was busy. I twisted my arms across my front and shifted my weight from one foot to the other. At least the hallway had enormous windows on either end, flooding the place with watery January sunlight. (I'm okay as long as there are windows. It's why I can manage on a plane, but I don't drink water for a full day before a flight so that I won't have to use the restroom.)

Not counting Christmas break, I'd been living at Ventana Ranch for four months, and I hadn't made any friends. I'd barely made a single friendly acquaintance, other than Sam, and we only talked about the technicalities of living together. *(Can I use the bathroom now, or were you gonna shower? Is there any cereal in the kitchen?)* I didn't think I had anything to lose by trying to reconnect with my old friend. Maybe we could grab a cup of coffee. Go for a walk. Even have lunch together down in the valley where everyone could see us. If my classmates saw that *Eliza* didn't think I was that bad, surely they'd have to give me a chance.

"Are you hugging yourself?" Eliza asked when she finally came to the door. She had one hand on her hip, cocked to one side like she was posing for something. But Eliza Hart never posed for anything. She naturally looked like that. I can't believe I thought I made her nervous the day she moved in here, even for a second. Eliza was the kind of girl who made *me* nervous, not the other way around.

I untwisted my arms.

"What do you want?"

"May I come in?" Inwardly, I groaned because I should've said *can* I come in. Technically, *may* I come in is more correct, but no one actually talks like that.

Eliza sighed but turned around and led the way inside. Her roommates—Arden Lin and Erin Smythe—sat on the couch facing an enormous flat-screen TV (a gift, I'd heard, from Eliza's parents), and they giggled at the face Eliza made as we walked through the common area toward Eliza's bedroom. I looked the other way. I told myself that they might not be laughing at *me*. Maybe they were laughing at something they saw on TV.

And I tried to ignore the knot of jealousy in my stomach. How could I be jealous that these three girls had inside jokes when those jokes were so clearly about me?

Erin had wavy brown hair, and Arden had straight black hair that fell like a curtain down her back, but all three suitemates wore leggings and tank tops like they'd just gotten back from the gym, and their skin was golden tan. The whole campus knew that Erin and Arden had spent winter break on a research boat in the Galápagos Islands after winning an internship contest. Eliza won it, too, but she chose not to go because of family obligations. Her uncle had won reelection to Congress in November—she'd interned for his campaign the previous summer—and she spent winter break helping out in his local office. It would look just as good on her college applications as the Galápagos internship. Better, maybe.

Eliza closed her bedroom door behind us and leaned against it, like she was scared the other girls might try to come in. "What do you want, Ellie?" she repeated, quietly this time.

The words came out faster than I meant them to: "I thought we could have dinner together or something."

Dinner was served in the dining hall between six and eight each night. I usually grabbed food to bring back to the dorm. But Eliza always sat front and center in the cafeteria.

"Dinner?"

"Or lunch," I stuttered, wringing my hands like a nervous old lady. "Maybe coffee." Students could always get coffee in the student center. My palms were sweating. I hadn't meant to just dive right in. I was going to ask her how her Christmas was. What classes she was taking this semester. I tried to direct the conversation toward something more innocuous. "I mean, how are your parents doing?"

She folded her arms across her chest. "What's *that* supposed to mean?"

I blinked, taking a step backward. Since she was leaning against the door that meant I was walking even farther into her room.

Before I could answer (it wasn't *supposed* to mean anything), a wave of understanding passed over Eliza's face. "You want to be *friends*?" She was speaking loudly now.

I exhaled. "Not just you and me." I tried to keep my voice down, even though surely Erin and Arden had heard the way Eliza made *friends* sound like a dirty word. "Erin and Arden could sit with us. At dinner. Or coffee. Or whatever."

"I'm not about to expose my roommates to you. They already know what you're like."

I shook my head so hard it hurt, shocked speechless. *No one* here knew what I was like—that was the whole point!

"What are you doing at Ventana Ranch, anyway?" she continued. "No one comes here to learn how to write stories."

"They offered me a scholarship—" I began, but she didn't give me a chance to finish.

"Why did you even apply here?" She narrowed her eyes. "I got in early admission, you know."

"I didn't know."

"*Sure* you didn't. I was probably accepted before you even sent in your application. It was all over Facebook."

"I'm not Facebook friends with you—"

"Oh, come on, Ellie. Tell the truth for once. Did you *follow* me here?"

Eliza's window was closed behind me, the shades drawn despite her enviable view. I took a deep breath, begging my lungs to behave. *Not here. Not now.* "What are you talking about?" I croaked.

"It's bad enough that you're a liar, now you're a *stalker*, too?" Eliza was practically shouting.

A *stalker*? It was so absurd that I couldn't stop the laughter from building up in my throat. Even if I was, what kind of danger could I possibly pose to a girl like her? I was at least three inches shorter than Eliza, and unlike her, I didn't start my mornings with swim practice or a rigorous hike on Trail F. I tried to swallow the sound before it came out of my mouth, but that just made it worse: It came out sounding like a cackle. I can't really blame Eliza's roommates for thinking I was some kind of maniac when they heard it.

Eliza stepped aside just as the door flew open. "You okay, Eliza?" Arden asked.

Eliza nodded but didn't say anything.

"I think you should leave," Arden said to me.

I started to say, "This is all just some big misunder-standing—" but then Erin came into the room, too. She tapped her foot against the floor, silently communicating *Get out of this room or else.*

Eliza stayed in her room with Erin, but Arden followed me to the door.

"I'm so glad Eliza warned us about you," Arden said as she closed and locked the door behind me. "She told every-one on day one."

I shook my head, blinking back tears. Eliza had *warned* them about me?

The strange thing about rumors is that when you're at the center of them, you're usually the last person to know what they are. It was October before I knew why no one sat with me at meals, why no one wanted to be my conversation partner in Spanish class. (The class had an odd number of students, so I always ended up paired with Señora Rocha.)

It was Sam who finally told me, the week before Halloween. He said word had gotten out that I was a pathological liar, that my parents had moved me from California to New York not because of their divorce but to send me to a special school for troubled kids, and that the strain of taking care of me had caused them to split up.

I was so shocked I couldn't even ask him how the rumors got started, or whether he believed them, too. And since then, I hadn't wanted to mention it, like I thought maybe if I ignored the rumors hard enough, they'd just go away.

But until that January day in the hallway outside suite 308, I never guessed that Eliza had actually *started* the rumors. Sure, she was the only person on campus who knew me before, but the stories were so untrue that I didn't think whoever started them *needed* to have known me.

Before I knew what I was doing, I was banging on the door Arden had practically slammed in my face.

"Wait!" I shouted. "I don't understand." The wooden door hurt my hand, but I kept on knocking. Why hadn't I figured it out sooner? "Please!" I said. "Let me back in. I just want to talk—"

The sound of someone sniggering to my left stopped me. Up and down the hall, people were coming out of their rooms, watching me.

"Freak," someone muttered, and was met with a chorus of laughter. Normal laughter, nothing like the cackling sounds I made in Eliza's room.

They thought I was obsessed with Eliza Hart.

A *stalker*, just like she said. Now they'd all be saying it by the end of the day.

They thought I was crazy.

"Why did you do this?" I shouted at the door, but no one answered me. I ran down the hall, down the stairs, and out the front door without making eye contact, but the damage had been done.

———

The voices outside my window grow louder. More students have joined the chorus. They must have run out of candles because some of them are holding up their phones with the flashlights turned on.

Now I'll never know why Eliza hated me. Was I just an easy target from the very first day, when I told her I couldn't drive? Or maybe she was just *mean*.

Erin and Arden separate from the group. They stand just below my window, their arms around each other.

"I shouldn't have covered for her," Arden cries.

"It's not your fault," Erin reassures her, patting her back. "We both covered whenever she cut class."

Wait a second—perfect, straight-A student Eliza Hart cut class? In Spanish yesterday, Arden said Eliza was sick.

"I should've known that something was different yesterday when we woke up and she wasn't there," Arden says.

"How could you have known? Eliza was always off hiking or swimming at all hours."

Arden sniffs. "Yeah, she never cared about curfew."

Eliza snuck out after curfew?

"There's no way we could we have known yesterday was different." It sounds like Erin is trying to convince herself, not just Arden. Arden nods slowly.

"Do you think *he* knows?" Arden asks.

"It's on the news."

"What a terrible way to find out your girlfriend died."

"Well, if she'd told us *anything* about him, we would have tracked him down and told him ourselves."

"She always said she had her reasons for keeping him to herself," Arden says, and Erin sighs as if to say *isn't it romantic?* Arden continues, "Are you gonna tell the police that Eliza had a boyfriend?"

Erin shakes her head. "Eliza would kill me if I told!" Erin claps her hand over her mouth, like she can't believe what she just said. "You know what I mean," she mumbles.

"I know," Arden agrees. "I'm not going to tell, either. What good would it do anyway? We don't even know his name."

"Did you see the email from the dean?" Erin asks.

Arden nods. "I think it went out to the whole student body."

I turn away long enough to grab my phone and check my email. Sure enough, there's a note from the dean asking whoever it was who fought with Eliza last week to come forward.

He assures us that (if it's you) you're not in trouble; they're just trying to piece together the final days of her life.

Arden tilts her head, gazing upward. I step away from the window before she can see me.

"Maybe *he* was the one she was fighting with." Erin says exactly what I'm thinking.

"He didn't sound like the kind of guy who would grab her like that," Arden says. I agree. Not that I have any idea what Eliza's boyfriend was like, but I can't imagine her being with anyone who didn't treat her like a princess.

"But who else would have a reason to fight with Eliza?"

"The police will figure it out," Arden answers finally. I inch closer to the window so I can see Arden tugging Erin back toward the other students, who hold out their arms to welcome Eliza's roommates.

Eliza was a model student. I'd never have guessed she cut class and had a secret boyfriend whose name her best friends didn't know.

Then again, I never guessed that she wanted to hurt me, either.

The voices continue their chorus:

"Rest in peace, Eliza Hart. Rest in peace, Eliza Hart."

"Rest in peace, Eliza Hart. Rest in peace, Eliza Hart."

ELIZA

sharing means caring

Still cold. But very quiet. The pain has shifted: It still hurts but it's more of an ache than a spasm. Is that progress? Can a person get *more* dead? I thought it was an absolute thing: dead or alive.

No in-betweens.

No ifs ands or buts.

Ellie Sokoloff used to beg to drive my electric car. Not the hybrid they gave me for my sixteenth birthday, but the miniature convertible they gave me when I was five.

I was an only child. I didn't really get the whole sharing thing. I only let Ellie drive it because my nanny, Cassie, made me.

I remember thinking that my mom wouldn't have forced me to share,

being angry while Ellie rode around the backyard,

her grin so wide it looked like her face might split in two.

Part of me was always glad when Ellie went home at the end of our playdates and there was no one I had to share with anymore.

I wonder whose decision that was. The whole not-having-another-kid-after-me thing.

No. There's no need to wonder whose decision it was. Of *course* it must have been hers.

Dad always went along with her decisions. He deferred to her, even when he should've known better. He'd shoot me an apologetic look across the room when she said no to something he would've said yes to. Like an unspoken apology was enough to make up for his failure to stand up to her.

Maybe that was why she didn't want another kid.

Maybe she already felt like she had two.

Or maybe she just didn't want to keep spreading these genes around.

She tried to leave him once. I was nine. She packed a bag for both of us. She even made it to the driveway, was lifting the bag into the trunk when he came running out of the house, sobbing so loud I covered my ears. My mother glanced around; we had a long driveway but maybe the neighbors could hear. My father begged and my mother gave in.

I never asked her why she stayed. Was it because she loved him and couldn't stand to see his pain, or was it because she thought it might actually be worse for me if we left?

Once, Ellie took one of my Barbie dolls home with her. Cassie told her she could. I was so angry I didn't talk to Cassie for days and begged my mom to fire her. I declared I'd never invite Ellie over again, but on Monday, Ellie brought the doll to school and gave it to me before lunch.

I'd thought she was going to keep it.

I would've kept it.

I asked if her parents made her bring it to school. Her parents were the type of people who thought the Hart family could afford to buy their princess a million Barbies, what did one more or one less matter? But Ellie said no, her parents didn't even know about the doll.

She just gave it back all on her own.

Barbie's hair was even smoother than it had been before.

Ellie told me she'd spent the whole weekend brushing it with her own hairbrush.

Ellie told me once that she wanted a little sister, but her parents said no every time she asked.

I remember everything about her.

It's ironic, when you think about it. She's the one who was stalking *me*, isn't that the way it was?

Or anyway, the way I said it was.

ELLIE

friday, march 18

Classes are still canceled. Would they have canceled classes if it had been another student who died? Someone less popular, less beloved?

I guess it's not fair of me to think like that. This is a small, tight-knit campus. It says so in the catalog.

My old school was a lot bigger, but there wasn't a single student or teacher who didn't know about my phobia. I'd gone there starting in second grade, and there were kids I was friendly with, but no one I was so close to that it seemed worthwhile to stay in touch after I came here. Sometimes I got invited to study groups and sleepover parties, but I never had a best friend because a best friend is someone you can whisper your secrets to when no one's looking, and someone was always looking at me because they all thought I might freak out at any second.

I couldn't blame them. I *had* freaked out a few times over the years. Not that many, when you think about it—just six times between second grade and sophomore year. (Six times at school, that is.) It didn't take much: Once, someone accidentally knocked me into a tight corner as he rushed to the head of the lunch line; another time, a taller girl pushed me into the closet when she was getting her own coat before recess. In eighth grade, a teacher once caused an attack: She sent me to get the basketballs from the closet beside the gym. It was an enormous room, and she undoubtedly thought I'd be fine. *I* thought I'd be fine. But there were no windows and the balls for each sport were divided up by chain-link fences that looked like cages, and when I didn't come back after fifteen minutes and they all came looking for me, I was curled up into a ball on the floor, rocking back and forth and gasping for air, unable to even move the three feet to the door.

Outside of school, I did my best to avoid crowds and rooms without windows, which isn't exactly convenient when you live in the most populous city in the country, where real estate is at such a premium that people turn closets into bedrooms.

So last spring, I came up with my Ventana Ranch plan. This place is so prestigious (according to the catalog, 85 percent of the student body attends top-tier universities after graduating) that I knew if I got in and won a scholarship, my parents wouldn't say no.

It's easy—or anyway, easier—to get straight As when you don't have any friends to distract you. There's plenty of time to spend your weekends working on your application, crafting a packet of short stories to submit to the admissions board.

Ventana Ranch was going to be my chance to make all the friends I'd been missing out on. No one here knew about my phobia. But I'd barely been on campus a day before the other students were looking at me the same way they had at my old school. Like one wrong move could send me over the edge.

By the time I understood *why* they were looking at me like that, it was too late to do anything about it.

The problem with classes being canceled is that there's nothing to do. (Well, there's a makeshift memorial service in the student center, but I don't know if I should go.) I had an English paper that was due today, but I'm scared that if I email it to her, Professor Gordon will think I'm callous for worrying about grades and due dates at a time like this. I'm still in bed when my phone rings.

"Hey, Mom."

"Hi, honey. How are you?" She's speaking in her special Ellie tone, the one she used for talking to my teachers, my therapists, and me over the years. Concerned, but also exhausted. She tries to cover up her reluctance, but it's obvious she'd rather be doing anything other than worrying about how her already-fragile daughter is going to handle an actual tragedy.

"I'm fine," I assure her, knowing that the administration sent emails to all the parents, alerting them to the situation on campus.

"I'm glad." I can hear the relief in her voice. She probably had to psych herself up to call me, steeling herself to hear all about her daughter's latest crisis.

She's not a bad mom or anything. When my claustrophobia started, she was really concerned but full of hope, certain that we just needed to find the right therapist who could cure me. But then I failed to get better.

I change the subject to something I know will make her happy. "Wes has his basketball finals next week, right?"

I can practically hear her face break into a smile. When she speaks, her voice sounds completely different—*brighter* somehow. It's not like I don't know that my little brother is her favorite. Wes—unlike me—is cool and popular and athletic. (I never tried out for a team, not even sixth-grade basketball, when the teachers admitted everyone who wanted to be on the team. A team huddle is a bad place for a claustrophobic.) Wes is tall, like his dad. Even his name is cool: Wes isn't short for anything. His actual full first name is Wes. And his last name is Ross, not Sokoloff. Wes Adam Ross.

A few years ago, Mom tried using Wes to cure my phobia. "Set a good example for your brother," she'd say, as though he actually looked up to me or something. Wes never looked up to anyone, least of all me. As far as he was concerned, I was the lame big sister who was to blame for his getting the smaller bedroom, who ruined every rare family vacation by insisting we stay on low floors in hotels. On our last trip—to Florida, over a year ago—the bellman was walking me past the elevator toward the stairs when a woman in a wheelchair crossed our path.

Wes shook his head. "I can't believe you need as much special treatment as someone with a *real* disability."

He had a point. Sometimes I used the bigger stall in public bathrooms, set aside for people with disabilities, and when I emerged looking fully abled, people often gave me dirty looks. The strange thing about claustrophobia is that even though I don't want people to know about it I also wish I had a sign around my neck so that people would know without my having to explain. They'd walk me past the elevator to the stairs without asking a single question or needing any explanation.

Wes rolled his eyes as the bellman opened a door that said *For Emergencies Only* and pointed to the stairs: dingy and gray, nothing like the brightly decorated hotel lobby. Mom used to insist on taking the stairs with me, because she worried about me being alone. I don't remember exactly when she decided I was old enough to be by myself.

"Wish Wes luck for me," I say now, imagining him making slam dunk after slam dunk.

Mom's voice slips back into her Ellie tone. "You sure you're okay?"

I shrug, feigning nonchalance even though she obviously can't see me. "It's not like I was friends with Eliza Hart anymore, Mom."

I imagine Mom nodding, trying to decide whether to say what she says next. "If you start to feel . . ." Mom pauses. "*Bad* about it, you know you can call Dr. Solander."

Bad is Mom's code word for claustrophobia, and she says it as though the word itself tastes bitter and weighs about a thousand pounds. Dr. Solander is a friend of a friend of a friend of my stepdad's. He works in San Francisco, and my stepdad gave me his contact info before I started school. "I told him all about you," he said stiffly. "Anytime you feel the least bit stuck, you can just go in for a session."

I looked Dr. Solander up online. He doesn't specialize in claustrophobia, and he doesn't usually work with teenagers. Plus, San Francisco is at least a two-hour drive from Big Sur. But I didn't point any of that out because it's not like I wanted to go to therapy anymore. I was sick of therapy. It had never done me any good.

Anyway, Mom didn't want to go searching for *another* specialist. I heard her complaining to my stepdad once: "If I could get back all the time I spent searching for specialists," she said, "I could have learned a new language. Gotten my master's in psychology and cured her myself."

Now she says, "The dean's email said that the school is going to have on-campus grief counseling." I nod, even though she (still) can't see me. "Not that you're grieving," Mom points out quickly. "Like you said, you barely knew Eliza."

That's not exactly what I said, but there doesn't seem to be any reason to mention it.

It's the least of the things I haven't said to my mother. I never told her about the rumors. Never told her I haven't made any friends here. I don't want to give her another reason to be disappointed in me.

I wasn't the only one who wanted Ventana Ranch to be a fresh start.

Someone knocks on my door. Probably Sam.

"Mom, I gotta go. My roommate wants to talk to me."

"Good, that's good." We hang up without saying good-bye.

"Come in," I call out. Sam opens the door and leans against the doorframe. He's almost always leaning on something, so he always looks casual and comfortable.

"You're not coming?" he asks.

"What makes you say that?"

"You're still in your pajamas."

Sam's dressed in black jeans and a black sweatshirt, like he's going to a very casual funeral. Though a memorial service isn't a funeral. Eliza's body still hasn't been released from the police.

"Everyone's going to be there," Sam says.

I shrug. I'm used to not being wherever everyone else goes.

"It'll look strange if you don't come."

It's the closest Sam's ever come to mentioning the fact that Eliza Hart hated me. Or maybe he means I had plenty of reason to hate her.

"It'll look strange if I *do* come. Everyone knows Eliza hated me."

71

They all *hate me,* I think but do not say. In January, not long after I pounded on Eliza's door, we had a school-wide trip to an aquarium in Monterey. There was a tank with two dolphins who'd been rescued from one of those swim-with-the-dolphins places in the Caribbean. The aquarium was rehabbing them in the hopes of eventually setting them free. I made the mistake of asking why the dolphins had needed to be rescued. "Aren't those places nice?" I asked. Arden answered before the tour guide could. Some of those places bought dolphins who'd been kidnapped from their families. Dolphins in captivity have shorter life spans than dolphins in the wild. No matter how big the tanks, they aren't nearly big enough or challenging enough for animals as athletic and intelligent as dolphins.

"I thought dolphins liked humans," I said dumbly.

"Would you like the species that had hunted and imprisoned you for hundreds of years?" Arden answered back.

"But I've heard stories about people who were rescued from sharks by wild dolphins. Dolphins playing in the wake of a boat."

"Have you also heard stories about dolphins being herded into coves for slaughter?"

I shook my head. I hadn't.

"Figures you'd be the kind of person who thinks it's okay to keep animals in cages," Arden said.

I spent the rest of the trip trailing behind the group, missing most of the tour. When we got back to school, I did a little bit of research. Arden was right. (Of course Arden was right.) There was even an award-winning documentary about the cove she'd mentioned. That's the problem with studying the world inside a book when everyone else was studying the world around us.

Eliza didn't even have to say a word. She'd set the stage back in September, and that was all it took. The other students—teachers, too—looked at me like I was a monster. I never got to explain that I just hadn't known, that of course I didn't want to slaughter and imprison animals.

Now Sam peels himself off the doorframe and steps inside. He pulls out my desk chair and sits on it backward. He looks perfectly at ease, like he's sat there a thousand times before, like this isn't his first time inside my room. I sit up, bending my legs so I can rest my chin on my knees. My hair falls across my eyes, and for a second I think Sam is going to reach out and brush it aside to get a better look at me. My heart starts beating faster, anticipating his touch.

But instead of fixing my hair, Sam tightens his boy bun even though (it looks to me) it's already tighter than usual. "Elizabeth . . ." He sounds uncharacteristically hesitant.

"Why do you do that?"

"Do what?"

"Insist on calling me Elizabeth instead of Ellie? I tell you almost every day that I like to be called Ellie." I flip my phone over and over on my bed just to have something to do.

Instead of answering, Sam says, "I know how hard this must be for you."

I shake my head. "It's not hard. I barely knew her." Like my mom said. I look away from the concern in Sam's eyes. Quietly, I add, "I'm not crazy like she said I was." (Not *as* crazy, anyway. Or anyway, not the same type of crazy. *She* said I was a stalker and a pathological liar. Which is ironic, come to think of it, since *that* was a lie. If only she'd known about my phobia, she would've had a real reason to tell everyone I was nuts.)

Sam stands up, tapping his fingers against his thighs. "I just don't think you should give them another reason to wonder about you."

"To wonder what?" None of them ever seemed the least bit uncertain about me. As far as I can tell, they believed everything Eliza said from day one.

"Just get dressed. I'll wait for you in the other room. I'll tell them it was my fault we were late." Sam is already out the door, quietly closing it behind him.

I swing my legs over the side of the bed, gazing at my pale feet sticking out of the bottoms of my plaid flannel pajamas. I wonder what color Eliza's toes were painted when they found her. Like a lot of California girls, she wore flip-flops whatever the weather and she had a different color on her toes every week.

I saw Eliza sitting in the meadow once with Arden and Erin, passing around nail polish. She painted each toe a different color, giggling over their silly names: light pink was called Ballet Slippers, and tan was called Sandy Toes, and there was a creamy color she claimed was called Starter Wife.

I wasn't eavesdropping. Or anyway, I didn't *mean* to eavesdrop. It's just that she and Arden and Erin looked exactly like what I thought life at Ventana Ranch would be: sitting in the grass, laughing with my friends. They looked so beautiful and happy, so at ease with one another. It was impossible not to want to join them.

When Eliza saw me staring, she leaned in and whispered something to Erin, who laughed. Arden lifted up her hand like she was trying to shoo a bug away, but I knew the gesture was meant for me.

I walked away. Into the woods where no one would see me cry.

Now I cross the room and open my sock drawer. Then my T-shirt drawer. Then my jeans drawer. I don't take anything out. What are you supposed to wear to a memorial service for a girl who hated you? I look out my open window at Eliza's dorm. What would she have worn, if *I* was the one who'd died and it was my memorial service being held in the student center? She probably would've had just the right outfit. It's probably hanging in her closet right now, alongside all her other perfect clothes. I wonder what they'll do with her clothes now that she's gone. I wish I could wear what she would've worn.

I shake my head. Maybe I *am* as crazy as she said I was. Longing to wear a dead girl's clothes doesn't exactly sound like the wish of a sane person.

I swipe on some lip gloss.

"Come on, Elizabeth!" Sam shouts from the other room. I swallow, then decide on black pants and a blouse. It doesn't matter what I wear. Whatever I wear, it won't be right.

Whatever I wear, it won't be nearly as perfect as what Eliza would've worn.

ELLIE

friday, march 18

Sam and I stand in the back. All the seats have been taken by students who actually got here on time.

"Took you long enough, Whitker," someone whispers to Sam from the row of chairs in front of us. I've never actually spoken to him but I know it's Sam's friend Cooper.

"No clue what to wear," Sam returns with a shrug. I wonder if the lie is obvious to someone who doesn't live with him. Sam's the kind of person who can walk out the door just minutes after his alarm goes off, and I'm pretty sure he's never worried about what to wear.

I'm wearing the wrong clothes, just like I knew I would. Everyone else is in pj's or yoga pants, greasy hair pulled into messy buns, not even a hint of makeup on their tear-stained faces, like their grief was too raw to take the time to care about how they looked. I rub my lips, but it only brings attention to the lip gloss. I don't know what I was thinking with these black slacks, like I'm thirty-six instead of sixteen.

My dressier outfit doesn't look respectful. It doesn't even look like I'm trying too hard. It looks like I care more about how I looked than I care about Eliza, unlike everyone else here. It's just another way I don't fit in, another way that they're all in this together and I'm standing on the outside wishing they'd invite me in.

(Get a grip, Ellie. You shouldn't be jealous that they're mourning together and you don't feel like you're part of it.)

Cooper leans over to whisper to the girl sitting next to him, loud enough so I can hear. "I heard someone threw her over the cliffs."

She gives him a dirty look and clutches a wrinkled piece of paper to her chest. It's a sign that says *We'll miss you, Eliza.* "Don't be ridiculous. If someone threw her, she wouldn't have been found so close to the edge. She *must* have fallen."

On the other side of her someone else says, "If she fell, why do the police practically have the campus on lockdown? It's *obvious* they think someone pushed her." She's holding a single white rose. I look around and notice that a bouquet is being passed around like a packet of worksheets in a classroom: *Take one and pass it down.*

"My mom wants me to get the hell out of here," someone else chimes in. "I said not before midterms." He waves his rose like a magic wand.

The girl beside Cooper shushes him. "Show some respect." She straightens her arms so that she's holding her sign high overhead. The student center is round, and the chairs are arranged in circular rows curving around an open space in the middle. Across the room, someone else is holding up a piece of poster board that reads: *Gone But Never Forgotten*. It's decorated with glitter, ribbons, and a smiling picture of Eliza: blond, beautiful, golden. That still photograph looks somehow more alive than half the people in this room.

At least a half dozen other students are holding signs that read: *R.I.P. Eliza Hart.*

Cooper and his friends fall silent, but my brain is going a mile a minute, silently continuing their conversation all by itself.

Maybe she died at the instant of impact, the very moment her body struck the cliff.

Maybe the fall only injured her, and she was trapped on the cliff and drowned when the tide came in.

Maybe the fall caused internal injuries, and she slowly bled out, bleeding internally where no one could see.

I shake my head, willing my thoughts to shut up already. *Freak,* I think to myself. Eliza even has *me* calling me names.

Dean Carson stands in the center of the round room and clears his throat. "You may have noticed that the police are still on campus," he begins. "Once again, I urge the student who argued with Eliza Hart last week to come forward and speak with us." He pauses. "Let me assure you that whoever you are, you're not in trouble. We just need to know exactly what happened."

He doesn't say, *So that we can rule you out as a suspect,* but it's clear that's what he means.

Or rule you in, I guess.

Silence. Someone coughs, and everyone's gaze follows the sound. A senior whose name I don't know looks at the floor, tries to swallow her next cough. After a few seconds, we return our focus to Dean Carson.

"I'll be in my office for the rest of the day. Come forward whenever you're ready."

He continues, "Until we get to the bottom of this, the police will remain on campus. They will be questioning students and faculty alike." He sent out another email last night explaining what will happen next, and now he repeats it: The police will conduct interviews. Parents and teachers can be present while we're questioned, and no one is required to stay. The police can only *request* our cooperation at this stage. "As a precaution, an officer will be stationed at the front gate to sign students in and out."

A precaution against what? I wonder. Someone making a break for it?

Or someone trying to get in?

"Thank you again for your help," the dean finishes finally, though I don't know why he says that since so far no one has actually been all that helpful. "I'll be in my office if anyone would like to talk. The rest of the staff and I are here for you during this difficult time." He leaves us alone. This memorial service is for the students, not the teachers.

A group of girls take the dean's place in the center of the circle. Each of them holds a single rose and they're singing a song they claim was one of Eliza's favorites. It's a cheerful love song and its high-pitched bubbly notes sound totally out of place. Didn't Eliza have any more appropriate favorite songs? Maybe she never had a reason to listen to sad music.

The singing girls cluster together like they're trying to keep warm. Erin Smythe is at the center of the group, but she's not singing. She's crying. The group tightens around her.

(Sometimes I have to remind myself that other people don't have problems with small spaces. It seems like such a miracle to me that most people don't drown when the world gets too tight.)

I shift my gaze to the window across from me. The student center is down on the meadow in the valley, and the walls are floor-to-ceiling glass. This room is usually flooded with constant sunlight, but today the fog that usually stays put at the top of the hill is rolling down, blanketing the valley. It looks like a wave, like a flood rushing down the hill and soaking us momentarily before it rushes past. It's like the tide coming in, one wave after another after another.

When the singing stops, Arden Lin runs to the center of the room to embrace Erin. They're both crying so loudly I can hear each individual sob. I pull the sleeves of my sweater down over my wrists and duck my chin into the tan scarf wrapped around my neck like I'm trying to hide.

Soon, everyone (well, not everyone: not me, and not Sam) is hugging each other and crying.

The entire student body is here. Seventy-five juniors, seventy-five seniors.

Seventy-four juniors, I correct myself.

Is one of us the person Julian saw fighting with Eliza that night?

Is one of us the person who killed her?

Sam pushes his long, lean body off the wall. "I think we can go now."

We've barely taken two steps toward the door when a hoarse voice calls out, "What are *you* doing here?"

I don't realize the voice is talking to me until Sam answers, "She's leaving, Erin. It'll be okay."

"It'll be *okay*? My best friend just died, and her stalker came to the funeral."

I hear myself saying, "It's not a funeral." That didn't come out the way I meant it to. I wanted to say that I wouldn't go to her funeral if they didn't want me there.

"What?"

I look at my shoes. Black leather boots. Perfect for walking around on New York City sidewalks. Pointless here. Why am I wearing these? "Idiot," I mumble.

Arden puts her arm around Erin. "What kind of psycho are you?"

"I didn't mean—" I meant *I* was the idiot.

Sam tugs at my sweater. "Let's go."

"What the hell, Sam?" Arden shouts. "How can you take her side?"

"I'm not taking anyone's side—"

"What do you call showing up here with that girl?" She spits the words *that girl* like they taste sour. I don't think anyone's ever looked at me with as much hate as Arden is looking at me with now. I swallow the lump in my throat. They'd hate me even more if I cried. I have no right to cry for myself when they're all crying for Eliza.

Sam yanks on my sweater, leading the way toward the door. But before we get outside, Erin shouts, "I'm going to tell the police about you. Just you wait." I turn around as Erin collapses into tears.

"Everyone knows it was you fighting with Eliza that night," Arden hisses, tightening her arms around Erin.

"What?" Butterflies flutter across my belly.

Yesterday morning, Erin asked, *Who else would have a reason to fight with Eliza?*

And *I'm* the answer Arden came up with.

Arden continues, "You were her only enemy on campus. The only person who hated her."

"I didn't hate her—"

"Well, you liked her a little too much."

Sam tugs on my sleeve again. "Come on." Sam's voice is stern. I follow him out the door and up the hill like an obedient puppy.

Earlier, Sam said, *It'll look strange if you don't come.*

When I didn't want to go, he said, *I just don't think you should give them another reason to wonder about you.*

When I took my time getting dressed, he added, *I'll tell them it was my fault we were late.*

I stare at my roommate's back as he leads the way up the hill. The fog rolls through one more time, then disappears, leaving nothing but bright sunshine. Sam takes off his sweatshirt, revealing a white T-shirt that's practically soaked through with sweat. Was Sam actually *nervous* in there? I watch his muscles as he rolls his shoulders down his back and nods his neck from side to side like he's trying to release his tense muscles.

He knew they thought I was the one who fought with Eliza last week.

He knew they were going to blame me.

ELLIE

friday, march 18

"Is that why you didn't answer me the other night?" My voice sounds small, like I'm scared of hearing the answer.

Sam flops down hard on the couch in our suite's common area. "What are you talking about?"

I fold my arms across my chest, standing over him. "When you came back from Wednesday Reading Night—I asked if they all thought she killed herself, too, and you didn't really answer me."

"Julian's story just has everyone on edge." Sam's trying to look nonchalant, but he's not very good at it—which is saying something, because he's usually nonchalant about everything.

"You should've let me stay in bed this morning."

"I just thought if they saw you . . ." Sam sighs. His back curls into a giant C when he slouches. "I didn't know they'd react like that."

I gesture toward the crowd down in the valley. "They're your friends." I imagine them trudging up the hill with pitchforks and torches, coming to get me like I'm the target of an old-fashioned witch-hunt.

Sam reaches up and undoes his bun. "They're my *class-mates*," he corrects firmly.

I shift my gaze, looking for something to focus on other than my roommate's earnest face. I settle for staring at my feet. I'm so sure Sam is *friends* with those people. At least, he acts like he is. He eats with them and parties with them and even occasionally hooks up with them.

Softly, Sam asks, "Did you ever think that maybe it's just easier to be friendly, whether they're really your friends or not?"

"Of course it's easier," I concede, still studying my shoes. "But only if being friendly comes easy to you."

"You can be friendly," Sam offers.

I shake my head, dropping my arms to my sides. "I don't mean friendly like nice or polite. I mean friendly like, like—" I bite my lip. "Like knowing how to make friends." I collapse onto the couch beside him. "Not everyone fits in as easily as you do."

"Believe me, that took years of practice." We're sitting close enough that I feel it when Sam takes a deep breath. "When a kid from the East Bay moves to Marin halfway through middle school, he learns a thing or two about fitting in."

"I thought you grew up in Mill Valley." Mill Valley is a town in Marin County, north of San Francisco.

"My *dad* lives in Mill Valley," Sam explains. "But I mostly grew up with my mom. I didn't move in with my dad until I was thirteen."

"Why'd you move?"

"My mom died."

I lift my fingers to my lips. "I'm sorry."

"Not your fault." He leans back, stretching his long arms above us. "I really did think it would help, you know. You going to the memorial service."

It's hard to breathe around the lump in my throat that's been there ever since Arden called me *that girl.* "They hate me."

"They don't hate you. They don't *know* you, Elizabeth."

I've never liked the sound of my full name. Elizabeth is not a cool girl's name. Elizabeth can be smart and she can grow up to be powerful (see Queen Elizabeth I). She might even be well-liked and popular if she's lucky, but she will never be *cool.* Erin, Arden, and Eliza—those are cool-girl names.

"Anyway," Sam continues, "in a few days, the police will have interviewed you and it'll all be over."

"Why would the police want to talk to me? They said they were going to talk to the students who knew Eliza best."

"They said they were going to *start* with the students who knew Eliza best. Eventually, they'll want to talk to anyone who knew Eliza. Which is pretty much everyone on campus, right?" He doesn't add the real reason they'll want to talk to me: Erin's promise to tell the police about me.

"I didn't have anything to do with what happened to her."

"Of course you didn't." Sam reaches out to take my hand, but I pull away. I don't want him to feel how my palms are sweating. Maybe the police already believe I had a motive; I had every reason to hate her, right?

"You should ask them to do your interview here," Sam suggests gently.

"Here?"

"I heard the police are using Professor Clifton's old office for their interviews."

"So?" Professor Clifton retired at the beginning of the semester. He taught AP Chemistry, so I never had a class with him.

"You've never been up there. There's a window, but it's tiny, and last time I was there, it was covered up by a stack of books they hadn't cleaned out yet. It might still be blocked." Sam's Adam's apple bobs up and down.

"How did you know?" I breathe.

Sam knocks on the wall behind the couch. "These walls aren't that thick. I've heard the speeches you give yourself before you step inside your closet."

I feel myself blushing, and I bury my head in my hands.

"It's okay, Elizabeth. You don't have to be embarrassed."

I groan. All this time, I thought I'd at least succeeded in keeping my phobia a secret from everyone here.

"I'm scared of heights," Sam says suddenly.

"What?"

"I'm scared of heights."

I look up at him. "We literally live on the top of a hill."

"Don't remind me," Sam moans. "Haven't you ever noticed me looking away from the cliffs when I walk to class?"

I can't help it; I burst out laughing. Sam folds his arms across his chest, pretending to be offended. "I thought you'd be more sympathetic."

"I'm sorry, but you have to love the irony."

"What irony?"

"Someone as tall as you are being scared of heights." Now Sam can't keep a straight face, either. His laughter just makes me laugh more.

"Do you realize that's the first time I've ever heard you make a joke?" he asks.

"Am I really that dull?"

"Let's just say living with you isn't exactly a barrel of monkeys."

"Let's just say anyone who uses expressions like *a barrel of monkeys* is in no position to judge." Sam grins, but my own smile falls. Like Sam said, the walls are thin. "If they hear me laughing, they'll just hate me more." I swallow a few times, like I think I can undo our laughter.

"They only dislike you because Eliza told them to and it never occurred to them not to listen."

I look at Sam's enormous hands when I ask. "Why did it occur to you?"

"*Judge not, that ye be not judged,*" Sam recites.

"What's that from? Shakespeare or something?"

"It's the Bible."

I look at my roommate with surprise. "You know the Bible by heart?"

"Parts of it."

"I didn't know you were so religious."

"I'm not."

"So you just memorized the Bible for fun?"

"My mom sent me to Sunday school every weekend."

"My mom sent me to Hebrew school, but I can't recite the Old Testament."

"Maybe your teacher wasn't as good as mine."

"Apparently not." I pause. "So that's why you're not judging me—because of God?"

"I'm not really sure if I believe in God."

"Spoken like a true Sunday-school grad."

Sam shrugs. "I went to church because my mom went to church, and I went to Sunday school because she needed an afternoon off when I was a kid." He smiles at the memory. "She used to say that I didn't have to believe in religion or God, but she expected me to be a good student and to listen to the lessons of charity and humility and kindness."

"Do you still go to church?"

"When I'm staying at my dad's, I'll drive into Oakland on Sundays. I like walking where she walked, sitting where she sat."

I nod.

"And the reason I'm not judging you is because I've lived with you since September and I've never seen any evidence of the girl Eliza warned us about. Granted, you've said more to me in the past forty-eight hours than in the past six months . . ." Sam trails off and grins. Finally, he finishes, "It's too bad they all believed her instead of finding out for themselves about you."

"Yeah, well, I never had a chance." Who would, up against the beautiful, smart, popular girl who always said the right thing and wore the right clothes and looked the right way?

When they pulled her over the cliffs, her tan skin was tinged blue. She was wearing a long dress, and it flapped against her legs in the wind.

I thought she was beautiful even then.

I wonder if Eliza was still wearing that dress by the time her parents got to see her. Maybe she was on a slab in the morgue, covered up with nothing but a sheet. Maybe they'd cut the dress off her body and filed it away as evidence. Or maybe they gave the dress to her parents to take home.

Suddenly, I realize: I've seen that dress before. Years ago. On the first day of kindergarten. That was the dress that Mrs. Hart was wearing when she dropped Eliza off. Cream-colored and covered in pink and yellow flowers, it rustled when she moved. My own mother was wearing slacks and a blouse, rushing on her way to work. I wished she dressed like Eliza's mom. Eliza's mom was so much prettier than my own. It was the first time I was ever jealous of Eliza. Maybe the first time I was ever jealous at all.

"Elizabeth?" Sam prompts. "You okay? You look like you're a million miles away."

Not a million miles. Not even a million years. Just back to being five years old and wishing my life looked more like Eliza's.

ELLIE

saturday, march 19

The next day, the police start calling students and teachers into Professor Clifton's office for interviews. No one seems to have any other plans, since most people would normally have left for spring break by now.

"They haven't called my name yet," I say hopefully to Sam over breakfast. I have a box of stale cereal (but no milk) in the dorm, so there's no need to go down to the cafeteria and face everyone's angry stares.

Sam shrugs. Fresh from the shower, he's wearing nothing but a towel, and I'm carefully *not* staring at the muscles on his chest and abdomen. His torso is shaped like an enormous V, wide shoulders and a slim waist. (I will *not* develop a crush on my roommate. I mean, I'm not blind, but what would be the point of my having a crush on anyone? I could have an attack anytime they leaned in for a kiss.)

"So far they're only interviewing the students whose parents insisted on getting them off campus as soon as possible." Sam grabs a handful of cereal and plops onto the couch.

"Oh," I say, my little bit of hope deflating. I thought maybe the police had dismissed whatever Erin told them as meaningless teenage-girl gossip. "That makes sense, I guess."

All morning, the campus has been crowded with parents who wanted to be there when the police question their children. I guess it's the law that for anyone under the age of eighteen, their parents have to be there, unless they give the police permission to proceed without them. Like my mom did when they asked her (she texted me this morning to tell me), and like Sam's dad did. In his email to the parents, the dean said he'd attend any interviews parents were unable to attend, and I guess my mom thought that was good enough. I guess it never occurred to her to insist on being here when she's so confident I had nothing to do with anything and barely knew Eliza. And it's not like she'd fly across the country for what might be a five-minute interview. (About 80 percent of students here are from the West Coast, so it's not as much of a trek for their parents.)

"Did you hear Coop on the phone with his mom before?" Sam asks, and I nod. Over the past twenty-four hours, we've heard lots of arguments through the thin walls of our dorm. Kids whose parents wanted them to leave, even if that meant they weren't cooperating with the police.

What if I remember something that can help the investigation? I'd never be able to live with myself if I left. (What could you possibly remember, I wonder. I'm pretty sure if you'd been a witness to either her murder or her suicide, you wouldn't have already forgotten about it, right?)

I want to stay here. You can still feel her presence in the air. (That from someone I'm pretty certain never even had a conversation with Eliza.)

Eliza would have wanted me to stay. (Like you have any idea what Eliza wanted. Not that I should judge because I have no clue, either.)

When else will I get to see a police investigation like this in action? (That particular kid sounded way too excited about all this, like it was the first time anything interesting had happened and he was too dumb to realize it had happened *around* him, not *to* him.)

Now I close the box of cereal. It tastes like sawdust, and not just because it's past its expiration date.

Sam presses the heels of his hands into his eyes. "You wanna get outta here?"

"Where can we go, though?" They're showing movies down at the student center, but I don't think I'd be any more welcome there than in the cafeteria. And neither would Sam, thanks to me.

"Hiking Trail Y," Sam suggests, and I swallow a groan. The Y trail is the least popular trail on the property, and for good reason. Enormous redwoods are right smack in the middle of the path, and you practically have to climb them to make your way around.

Sam grins. "It's not *that* bad." He doesn't add that it's the one place on campus (other than this suite) where we're least likely to bump into anyone else. He doesn't have to. I'm already putting on my sneakers and heading for the door.

Just ten minutes into our hike, and I'm panting. "Hiking Trail Y, as in *why the heck am I doing this to myself*?"

Sam laughs. "I had no idea you were in such crappy shape."

"My classes don't exactly pack the same punch yours do." Sam literally got course credit for working on a fishing boat last semester. He'd come back to our room reeking of dead salmon and covered in fish blood.

The path narrows, slanting upward, and Sam moves ahead of me. "Watch where I put my feet," he instructs. "Try to step exactly where I do."

I'm too out of breath to say anything, so I just nod even though Sam can't see me. Sam's strides are so long that I struggle to follow his footsteps. At least looking down at the ground is easier than looking up at the path ahead.

Around us, the forest hums and cracks. The breeze knocks pinecones down from their branches, and the pinecones smack against the trees as they fall to the ground. A pack of wild turkeys gobbles from somewhere among the bushes. The pine needles crunch beneath our feet. We startle a doe into trotting away, her hooves nearly silent against the ground. It's almost noon, and the sun is bright overhead. Still, there are puddles in the shadiest spots, patches that the fog drenched overnight. We're deep in the forest now.

Sam stops walking to take a long drink from his water bottle, then passes it to me. For the first time in days, the temperature is climbing to the upper sixties, and Sam's forehead is covered in a sheen of sweat. He rubs his forehead with a bandana he pulls from his pocket, then ties it around his dreads.

"Is there any place on earth more beautiful than Big Sur?" he asks suddenly.

I shrug. "I haven't been very many places." Per the terms of my parents' divorce agreement, I spent most school vacations at my dad's apartment.

"Well, I have. My dad loves to travel. Trust me. Nothing compares to this." He holds his arms out wide.

I take a swig from the water bottle. If you had to die, maybe Big Sur wouldn't be such a bad place to take your last breath. Especially up along the cliffs where they found Eliza. But I guess I shouldn't think things like that, as though there's a bright side to Eliza's death. *I'm sorry you had to die, but at least you had a nice view.*

I pass the bottle back to Sam and pull the sleeves of my sweatshirt down over my wrists. I expect Sam to resume walking, but instead he stays exactly where he is, and when I open my mouth to ask him why, he holds a finger to his lips, signaling that I should stay quiet.

Soon, I hear it, too. Voices. Two of them.

"I really thought there wouldn't be any chance of bumping into anyone on the Y trail," Sam whispers.

"I'm sorry." Sam's reputation will never recover from being seen with me two days in a row.

The voices are getting louder; they're coming closer.

No, they're getting louder because they're yelling.

And they're coming closer.

And then another sound fills the air. The ugliest sound I've ever heard. It's so loud that I push my hands to my ears, trying to drown it out. It takes me a few seconds to realize what we're hearing.

It's a buzz saw.

Quick as a snake, Sam reaches out and grabs me, pulling me into a hollow at the base of a redwood tree just off the path. I shake my head frantically, but Sam's dark eyes are stern. He tightens his grip on my arms, turning me so that my back is against his front.

"What are you doing?" I hiss. Sam doesn't answer.

"Turn that thing off!" one of the voices shouts harshly. The noise stops. "This one," he says, and I imagine he's pointing.

Finally, I understand why Sam pulled me in here. It's the tree thieves. It has to be. Who else would have a buzz saw out here on the trails? My heart's pounding, and I'm not sure if it's because of the small space or the fact that we're just a few layers of bark away from a couple of criminals.

Sam steps back, pressing himself against the side of the cave to hide us. I don't know why some redwoods grow like this, with bottoms that open up into little triangle-shaped caves. It looks almost like the tree has a mouth open in mid-yawn. Sam has to slouch to fit in here, curling over me.

Invisible water gathers at the base of my lungs, threatening to rush in and drown me. I know my skin is turning pink and blotchy beneath my sweatshirt. The cave is as stuffy as a closet.

I try to breathe, just like every therapist I ever had told me to. I remind myself that I've actually been in one of these caves before. When I was five years old, my dad and I spent a day in Big Sur. I didn't like it at first: It was cold and dark in the woods, and the hills were too steep for me to climb. But when I saw one of these hollowed-out redwoods, I ran toward it. It looked like the kind of place a fairy princess would live.

I wasn't afraid back then.

Now I open my mouth, but my lungs refuse to take in any breath. My mom once said I look like a fish out of water, and I didn't have the patience to explain to her that the way it feels is exactly the opposite. I feel sweat pooling under my arms and at the base of my bra, feel my hands grow clammy, my pulse get faster. I try to close my eyes so that I won't see the wood surrounding me, but my eyelids won't cooperate, won't let me imagine I'm someplace else, someplace big, someplace safe. Without enough oxygen, I'm getting light-headed. I slump against Sam and lift my hands to my throat like a choking victim.

Sam shifts so that his hands are just over mine, and I'm surprised that his palms are cool. I want to pull his fingers off mine, but instead I twist my fingers through his and hold on tight, like I think he can save me from the rising tide.

"You're okay," he whispers, his voice as quiet as breath. "I've got you. You're safe."

Sam must feel my heart beating faster, faster, faster. "Breathe," he instructs.

I had a therapist who tried to talk me through an attack. She shouted the word *breathe* at me like she thought the louder she said it the better. I burst from the closet with tears streaming down my face, and later I saw that I'd scratched up her bare arms on my way out the door. After that, she always seemed mildly scared of me, the way a person who's been bitten by a dog is never quite comfortable around them again.

But when Sam says *breathe*, it sounds like a question, not a command. His voice is quiet and even. And for some reason, that makes it easier to inhale.

I look up; the tree is hollow for several feet above us. Pieces of wood hang down like stalagmites. Inside, the wood is even redder. I try to make myself think about how old this tree is, how deep its roots. It's survived storms and earthquakes and forest fires. I try to think about anything but the size of this space and the voices growing closer.

My eyes finally close.

I tell myself: *There's plenty of room.*

Silently, I repeat: *There's lots of air.*

You're not going to drown, Ellie.

And finally: *Hiding here is better than coming face-to-face with the men carrying the buzz saw.*

A gruff voice says, "Told ya her ID would still work."

ELLIE

saturday, march 19

Another voice answers. "We couldn't have known for sure. News said the campus was on lockdown."

"Yeah, but it's just a magnet, remember? She told us this place never updated the security system."

"So much for the police guarding the entrance," Sam mutters into my ear. His breath tickles. Apparently, the police are only stationed at the main entrance.

"How did you get her ID anyway?" the gruff voice continues.

"She gave it to me."

The gruff man laughs. "*Sure* she did. Things were so warm and fuzzy between you two in the end."

The other man doesn't answer.

I've never been in a confined space with another person for this long before. I've never been this close to another person before.

"Breathe," Sam whispers in my ear again, so quiet that I'm not sure he really says it at all. I lean against him and feel the rise and fall of his chest against my back, begging my lungs to follow his lead.

In, out. In, out.

"She shoulda listened to you, huh, Mack? Maybe she'd still be alive."

"Maybe."

Oh my God, are they talking about *Eliza*? Is it *her* ID that's still working?

My pulse quickens. I squeeze Sam's hand, wondering if he's thinking the same thing. I feel him nod.

I concentrate on my breathing: *In, out. In, out.*

Instead of a mountaintop, I imagine that I'm back in my room, safe and sound. I try to picture my pillows and my dresser drawer, but instead all I can see is Eliza's body suspended over the cliffs with a string, someone flying her just like a kite.

I open my eyes. Visualization never works.

"Let's get to work," the first man says.

The buzz saw starts up again. The noise the saw emits shifts from a buzz into a hum as they start cutting into a tree. (Thankfully, not the one we're hiding in.)

Sam loosens his grip on me. Cold air rushes to fill all the places he'd been squeezing tight.

Over the sound of the saw, one of the men—Mack, I think—shouts, "It's gonna be a bitch lugging this back down to the truck."

"That's what I have you for," the other man answers. "You're the muscle; I'm the brains of the operation."

"I know, I know," Mack answers, like he's heard these words dozens of times before. His breaths come fast, like he's working hard. "Course, I don't think my muscles will make much difference if I break my back dragging a hundred pounds of wood down a mountain."

The gruff man laughs. "You're nineteen. Pretty sure your body can take it."

Mack breathes heavily in response. "Next time we're picking a tree closer to the truck."

"We had to pick one of the paths she said would be empty this time of day. We had more options last time." *Last time.* He must mean the tree they cut up on Hiking Trail C. They must have done it in the middle of the night. "At least now we don't have to split the profits with that girl, right?" He says *that girl* the same way Arden said it about me at Eliza's memorial service. Like he chewed up the words and now he's spitting them out rather than swallow them. "It's not like she needed the money." Mack must shrug or something because the other man explains, "Dude, it was on the news. She's Edward Hart's *niece.* Her grandfather used to be the mayor of Menlo Park."

I swallow a gasp. They're *definitely* talking about Eliza.

The gruff voice continues, "She ever tell you why she bothered with us when her family was so rich?" Abruptly, the saw switches off.

"Doesn't matter now, does it?" Mack answers. "Are you sure it's a good idea to be here so soon after . . ." Another pause. "This place might be crawling with police."

"We've got an order to fill," the other man answers. "And clearly the police aren't crawling around here. This is as far from where they found her as you can get, right?"

I don't hear Mack's answer, but he must agree because the saw roars back to life. In my mind's eye, the tree explodes with blood when the buzz saw makes contact. "Sam . . ." I beg.

"I know." He doesn't have to whisper anymore. Even with his mouth next to my ear, I can barely hear him over the sound of the buzz saw.

Sam unwraps himself from around me, but laces his fingers through mine. He peers out of the cave, then looks back at me and nods; the men must not be looking in our direction. Slowly, Sam leads the way up the hill and away from the voices below us. He's careful to keep off the path, hidden by the trees. I'm so relieved to be out of the cave that I almost start to cry. The buzz saw is so loud that we don't have to worry about keeping quiet.

My breath comes a little easier now that we're out in the open. Still, my heart is beating fast—I'm not sure if it's the effort of hiking, or the fear that one of those men will turn around and see us. Once more, I keep my gaze trained to the forest floor, trying to put my feet exactly where Sam puts his. It's harder now because I'm shaking so hard.

Sam leads the way off the path and into the woods, even though there are signs everywhere warning students not to do just that. (Rattlesnakes! Mountain lions! Poison Oak! Ticks!) The forest is so dense that it muffles the sound of the saw.

By the time we make our way back to Hiking Trail D, I can't hear it at all.

Sam drops my hand and turns around. "You okay?" He puts his hands on my shoulders, slouching so that we're face-to-face. They give drowning victims CPR after they pull them from the water. It never occurred to anyone to give me mouth-to-mouth after pulling me from a small space. Now Sam looks like he might actually try it.

I keep my eyes focused on his chest rising and falling at a steady pace. After a few moments, we're breathing in unison, like I've fallen into step beside him.

Finally, I manage to say, "Do you think that guy—Mack—is the one Julian saw fighting with Eliza?"

Sam nods. "Sounds like it might've been."

"Do you think those men killed Eliza?"

"I don't know. But they just rocketed to the top of my suspect list."

I can still hear the gruff voice saying *She shoulda listened to you, huh, Mack? Maybe she'd still be alive.*

And I can still hear Mack's answer.

Maybe.

Maybe *what?*

Maybe Eliza refused to hand over her ID. Maybe they wanted it so they could get on and off the campus whenever they wanted to, ripping into the redwoods without having to split the profits with her, like that man said.

But then, why was she working with them in the first place? It's not like she needed the money. She was *Eliza Hart.* Her parents gave her everything she wanted.

Didn't they?

"We have to go to the police." Sam drops his hands from my shoulders and starts pacing. "I didn't see them, but one of them was called Mack, did you hear that?"

In the pocket of my sweatshirt, my phone buzzes with a message. I pull it out to take a look, expecting a text from my mom, maybe a picture of Wes's latest slam dunk. Sam reaches for it—he thinks I want to call the police, too.

But when I see the message on the screen, I step backward, out of the reach of his long arms. My ponytail is falling out of its elastic, and strands of hair stick to my forehead.

I hug the phone to my chest and shake my head. "We can't go to the police. Like you said, we don't even know what those guys looked like."

"So? We *heard* them. We have a *name*. Mack. I mean, maybe it's just a nickname, but c'mon, it's something, right?"

Sam takes a step closer to me, and I back away again, tripping over a root on the ground and falling hard onto my bottom. Tears spring to my eyes.

Sam crouches down beside me, but I crab-crawl away from him frantically.

"Elizabeth, you're freaking out."

"Of course I'm freaking out!"

107

"I know." Sam keeps his voice low, like I'm a wild animal he doesn't want to startle. "I was scared, too. But we got away from those men. They're not going to hurt us now." He holds his arm out for my phone. "We have to call the police."

Without loosening my grip, I hold up my phone so Sam can see the message I just got from Dean Carson: *Ellie, can you please come to Professor Clifton's office at 4 o'clock this afternoon? The police have some questions for you, as do I.*

As do I. I imagine Dean Carson typing up that message, taking the time to type those last three words.

Dean Carson is my academic advisor. I spent hours in his office at the beginning of the semester figuring out my independent study program. He joked about the fact that no one else had accepted the school's liberal arts scholarship. Now I wonder if he was just pointing out that no one else had been as desperate as I was.

As do I. He didn't have to add those words. He wanted me to know he's suspicious, too.

"Even the dean thinks I did it." I can't bring myself to say the word *killed*. I put my phone back in my pocket like I'm trying to hide it from myself. "*Everyone* thinks I did it." I brush the tears from my eyes, smearing dirt all over my face.

Sam shakes his head. "You just have to explain—"

"What? That from the day I showed up here Eliza hated me for reasons I never understood? That Eliza was the liar, not me? It'll be my word against a dead girl's. And not just any dead girl. *Eliza Hart.*" Even the tree thieves were impressed by her. The niece of a congressman. Granddaughter of a mayor. Princess of Menlo Park. Queen of the campus.

Sam's voice remains calm. "But now you can help them. You'll tell them what we saw, what we heard about Eliza working with those guys. They're definitely going to be more suspicious of two men sneaking onto campus than they will be of you."

"They won't believe me! Who would believe that Eliza was involved in something like that?" Those men sounded like they could barely believe it and they were the ones working with her.

"You have a witness." Sam sets his jaw and swallows, his Adam's apple bobbing up and down. "Me."

I push my hair off my forehead and yank at the collar of my sweatshirt, hotter than I've been all winter. "The entire campus practically attacked you just for bringing me to the memorial service. They already think I got you on my side somehow."

"This isn't about sides. We'll just show them the tree those guys cut into—"

"The wood was getting stolen before Eliza died. It'd look like I was trying to connect two completely different crimes." Just the fact that I was hiking on the most difficult trail will be enough to make them suspicious. It's not like I'm known for being athletic around here.

Sam lowers himself onto the ground. His legs are so long that when he folds them up it reminds me of a daddy long-legs spider. "So what do you want to do?"

I close my eyes, squeezing out what's left of my tears. I *want* to go back to our suite and lock the door behind me. I *want* to close the shades and climb into bed and pull the covers up over my head to block the world outside.

But I would never do that because it's too much like being in a small space.

I take a deep breath in, sigh it out heavily.

I want to go back to a few days ago, when Eliza Hart was the living and breathing mean girl who made my life so miserable, when I didn't know that trees could be butchered, their parts stolen and sold.

I want to go back to last spring, when I could've chosen to stay at my old school instead of coming here. My claustrophobia may have kept me from making friends, but no one hated me. No one spread lies about me. And no one suspected me of *murder*.

At least in a couple years, I'll go to college. Another chance at a fresh start.

I wonder just how many fresh starts a person like me gets to have. It feels like I'm already running out.

I open my eyes and stand, brushing the dirt and pine needles from my pants. Sam's right about one thing: It will help if I can offer the police another suspect (or suspects). But telling the police *I heard these scary guys in the woods talking about Eliza* isn't nearly enough. I need to know what they look like. I need to know how they got into business with Eliza—or how she got into business with them. I need to offer the police names and descriptions and cold hard facts that point away from me.

It's the closest thing to a fresh start I can think of right now.

"Elizabeth?" Sam prompts. "What do you want to do?"

I roll my shoulders down my back, trying to make myself taller just like Eliza did on our first day here. I have until four o'clock.

"I guess I want to find some burl-poachers."

ELIZA

buzzing

This is what I know:

It hurt when I crashed onto the ledge.

My wrist folded beneath me.

I heard something in my leg *pop*.

After that, the only thing I was aware of was the pain.

So cold that it hurt.

So wet that it hurt.

It still hurts. Maybe it always will.

Did I try to get up? I always got up. Even on mornings after yet another restless night when the last thing I wanted was to get out of bed, to go to school—I still found the will to get up. It would've made my father sadder if he knew I wanted to stay in bed all day every day, not sleeping but not actually functioning, either. It would've led to another one of my epic fights with my mother.

He's the sick one, how can he be expected to take his meds on time? Why don't you manage him better?

It's not my job to be his caretaker—

Of course it is. No one made you marry him.

I didn't know—

Spiky and sharp, I never let her finish a sentence.

Now I wonder what exactly she didn't know. What she might have said if I hadn't stopped her.

Did he really manage to hide his illness from her before they got married?

Or did she just not understand how bad it would be?

I didn't have the patience to listen, and now I'll never know. Maybe in some families confiding in your parents makes things better, but in mine it just made things harder, and harder was the last thing I wanted.

I must've bled when I hit the ledge. A gash above my eye? Maybe I was bleeding internally. Would I have known if I was bleeding internally? Can you *feel* it?

How strange that I don't know exactly what killed me.

I guess it doesn't matter. Dead is dead, however you ended up that way.

I miss Mack. I never really missed him when I was alive. He was always just *there* when I wanted him: He would come get me or I would sneak off to meet him. He was so available that I never had to miss him.

Until that night.

He was so angry.

He said he never wanted to see me again.

He said this was getting dangerous.

I didn't expect to be so *awake*. Isn't that what they tell little kids when they ask about death, that dying is like going to sleep? Or maybe you're not supposed to tell them that anymore. It would probably give them nightmares.

I'm so awake I'm practically buzzing.

I wish there were a book to explain all of this. They could give it to you seconds before you die, just enough time to skim it, just long enough to fill in the blanks. They could call it *What to Expect When You're Not Expecting Anything at All*.

If Mack were here, he'd be quick to point out the holes in that particular plan.

He'd say that if there were a book that told you what to expect when you died then you wouldn't be expecting nothing; you'd be expecting all the things the book told you about.

Mack wasn't like Erin and Arden and the rest of the kids at Ventana Ranch. They took what I said as the gospel truth, even when it was a blatant lie. Like the things I said about Ellie Sokoloff.

I always thought they believed me because they liked me.

But now I think they might have been worried I'd start rumors about them next.

Mack never had any problems standing up to me.

Mack wasn't scared of fighting with me.

He wasn't scared of me at all.

In the end, *I* was scared of *him*.

ELLIE

Eliza was right, that very first day: Without a license or a car, I'm trapped on this campus.

When Sam offers to drive, I have no choice but to say yes.

We pass the makeshift memorial beside Eliza's dorm on our way to the parking lot. Someone has taped the signs from the service (*R.I.P. Eliza Hart*; *We'll Miss You*; *Gone But Never Forgotten*) to the brick wall. They've switched from real candles to the battery-operated kind. Now that the grief and shock isn't so fresh, my classmates are back to worrying about forest fires like they used to.

Sam lets me into his car—an old Toyota Camry he says used to be his mom's—and drives toward the gate. I hold my breath: I imagine the cops guarding the main gate have been given pictures of me, just like in the movies, with words like *High Alert* and *Wanted: Dead or Alive* emblazoned across the top. They've been instructed not to let me leave, to drag me in for questioning kicking and screaming if they have to.

There's a line of cars ahead of us, and a policeman standing with a clipboard at the front gate.

"We have to sign out," Sam explains, as if I don't already know. I mentally count the cars ahead of us. Four.

"How long do you think this will take?" What if Mack and his partner finish while we're waiting in line? They could drive away and disappear, and we'd never find them.

Sam shrugs. "I think we have enough time," he says, as though reading my thoughts. "I don't think dismantling a redwood tree is quick work."

Two more cars pull up behind us. They have beach chairs and towels in the backseat. They can't make it to Cabo this week, but at least they can go to the beach in Monterey. *They* probably don't have to be back by 4:00 p.m. to talk to the police.

"Are you sure you want to do this?" Sam asks. "We can just go to the dean with what we know."

The car at the front of the line gets waved through, and we move up. The driver of the following car passes the cop his ID. We wait.

Highway 1 is just on the other side of the front gate, a straight line going north and south. Beyond those gates are total strangers who've never heard of me or even of Eliza. Strangers who don't think I killed or stalked anyone.

"I'm sure," I answer finally, even though the only thing I'm sure of right now is that I want off this campus.

"Did you write back to the dean?" Sam asks.

I shake my head. "I don't know what to say."

Another car gets waved through, and Sam eases off the brake. We roll forward.

I glance at my phone. The dean's message stares back at me. *The police have some questions for you, as do I.*

"Maybe they're looking for me." I picture the police pounding on the door to our suite. Bringing in a battering ram to knock it down.

I shake my head. The administration probably has an extra key. If they wanted in, they wouldn't have to knock the door down. And my appointment isn't for hours. If they wanted to find me now, the dean would've asked me to go to Professor Clifton's office right away.

"Why do you think Eliza was working with those guys?" I ask. Sam said that meth-heads steal redwood burls to make a quick buck. "Do you think she was using the money to buy drugs?"

Sam shrugs. "Didn't the girls on the swim team get tested for that kind of thing?"

"I guess. Maybe." The truth is, I have no idea how being on a sports team works. If I were actually athletic, I'd have sought out a sport that didn't require much teamwork. Maybe running. You have to join a team, but you mostly get to compete on your own.

I guess the swim team is kind of like the track team that way.

"Anyway," Sam continues, "she didn't seem the type. Squeaky clean and all that."

There's only one car ahead of us now. "It's not like she seemed the type who'd be involved in illegal tree-poaching, either."

When it's finally our turn, the cop asks for Sam's ID first, then mine.

"Samuel Whitker," he mutters, looking at a list of names on his clipboard. "Elizabeth Sokoloff."

I hold my breath, but he just puts checkmarks and the time of day next to our names on his clipboard and lets us go.

I exhale.

Sam turns left on Highway 1 and starts to circle the campus perimeter. Our plan is simple: find the truck Mack mentioned and follow it. Sam thinks he knows which entrance they hiked up from (a rarely used gate that abuts the park beside the campus, for students who want even more of a challenge than Hiking Trail Y). We guess the truck is parked as close to the entrance as possible so they won't have to carry the wood any farther than absolutely necessary.

"What if they're already gone?" I ask.

Sam shakes his head. "Even with the buzz saw, it'll take them a while to cut through that tree."

I spot a green pickup truck parked on the shoulder of the highway. "That must be it." Sam pulls over and parks, his small Camry partly hidden by some branches that hang over the road.

"Now we just have to wait," Sam says. He drops his hands from the steering wheel and leans back in his seat. "How did the claustrophobia start?"

"Huh?" I ask dumbly.

"Just trying to distract you. You seem agitated."

"And you thought bringing up my phobia would calm me down?" The words sound meaner than I intend them to. I shake my head. I shouldn't be mean to the one person at Ventana Ranch who doesn't hate me, especially when he's willing to follow men with chain saws to God-knows-where with me. "Sorry," I mumble.

"No worries."

"It started in an elevator on West Seventy-Eighth street the summer before second grade." Every therapist I ever had opened our first session with this question. At one point, I considered prerecording the answer to save time.

"No, I don't mean where. I mean . . . *how*? Why do you think small spaces scare you so much?"

"You know, there's a school of argument that says that claustrophobics are actually right."

"How's that?"

"I read an article about it once. Small spaces *are* potentially dangerous. Elevators *do* plummet to the ground sometimes. Trains *do* get stuck. Tunnels flood." I once read about a now-defunct underground train in London without windows and with doors that could only be opened from the outside. They wouldn't have gotten rid of it if it was perfectly safe, would they? "Maybe claustrophobics are the rational ones and everyone else is crazy."

Sam cocks his head to the side. The ends of his dreadlocks tap against the glass of his window. "Do you really believe that?"

Sane people don't think they're drowning when they're on dry land. "Not even a little bit." I grin.

Sam laughs. "My therapist would say you're using humor to keep from answering my question."

I look at my roommate with surprise. "You have a therapist?"

"I did. After my mom died, my dad insisted. I always thought it was his way of getting out of having the tough conversations with me himself. But without having to feel guilty about it, you know?"

I nod.

"This way, he could still feel like he was doing the right thing—" Abruptly, Sam stops. "Look," he whispers, pointing.

The two men emerge from the woods, struggling to carry a bumpy slab of wood between them. It's just one burl, but it's enormous, perhaps big enough to be carved into a tabletop.

Their backs are to us, so I can't make out their faces in order to give the police a description. They load the wood into the flatbed of the truck. They're working so fast that they don't bother glancing around to see if anyone's watching.

They scramble into the front of the truck and start driving north.

Sam shifts from park into drive and starts to follow, careful to keep a few car lengths between us and the truck.

We head north on Highway 1. Traffic slows as we get closer to Carmel, and I give thanks that California is a state with more bridges than tunnels. (The constant risk of earthquakes makes tunnels too dangerous.) I don't think I could stand sitting in traffic inside a tunnel. In Manhattan, just knowing that the ground beneath my feet was filled with tunnels where the subway sped along was enough to make me shudder.

I'm pretty sure I'm the only person in the state of California who actually takes comfort in the fact that the ground here is unreliable.

"I know what you mean," I say as we slow to a crawl.

"About what?" Sam never takes his eyes off the green truck.

"About how your dad expected therapy to cure you. My mom—" I take a deep breath. Sometimes I think my mom wished that my mental health was something she could just check off a to-do list. "I mean, she wasn't like that at first, you know? But after the fifth or sixth therapist—"

"How many therapists have you had?"

I don't even have to think about it. "Eight."

"Eight?" Sam echoes.

I nod. I got a new therapist with almost every school year, the way other kids got new teachers. (Of course I got new teachers, too.) It felt like every September there was a fresh recommendation from the school nurse or my pediatrician or even sometimes from the last therapist, after his or her form of therapy didn't fix me. After a few months, Mom would start asking why I was still avoiding elevators and subway cars—hadn't the new therapist helped at all? Eventually I'd give a small space a try, have an attack, and we'd move on to someone else.

"Why aren't you still in therapy?" Sam asks. "Couldn't you have found someone out here?" I don't answer right away, and Sam rushes to apologize. "I didn't mean that you, like, needed a new therapist. I wasn't calling you crazy."

I fold my arms across my chest and put on an authoritative voice. "Didn't your therapist ever tell you that therapy wasn't just for crazy people?"

Sam laughs again. He has a deep, throaty laugh. I like the sound of it. "Yeah, she said it the very first day. That I shouldn't be worried about the stigma of therapy, or whatever." My first several therapists told me the same thing. (Not that I ever believed them. I was crazy, and we all knew it.)

There are a few cars in between us and the truck now, but traffic is moving so slowly that I'm not worried about losing it.

"Anyway, I think my parents lost faith in therapy after the last specialist didn't work out."

"Why?"

Things did not get off to a good start with therapist number eight, whom I started seeing right before the start of my sophomore year. She insisted that I call her by her first name, which was Cami with an *i*, and I think my mom gave up on her the day she introduced herself. *Cami*, in my mom's silent opinion, was not a therapist's name. *Cami* lacked gravitas. *Cami* wasn't going to save me.

But Cami was the latest on a long list, so I went every week—Wednesdays at three-thirty, right after school let out—for seven months. Mom didn't give up on Cami until last April, when a particularly severe attack at my old school made it painfully clear that I wasn't getting any better.

I don't really blame the kids at school for picking on me. I mean, I wasn't weird in the traditional sense—I didn't wear weird clothes over my uniform skirt or make disgusting concoctions in the cafeteria. My oddity didn't really show on the outside. In fact, I always tried to wear the right clothes and say the right things in class. But no matter what I said or wore, I would never blend in. Everyone at school knew about me.

I may as well have been wearing a sign that said *Class Freak*.

There were mean girls at my old school, cool girls who made our uniform look stylish, unlike mine, which had been fitted when I was thirteen. I'd long since grown out of it, but my mom didn't seem to notice.

The mean girls didn't tease me the same way they teased the girls who wore the wrong things and had the misfortune to be born with the wrong hair. They didn't pick on me when I got the answer wrong in class because I was a straight-A student who almost always got the answer right. In fact, more than halfway through sophomore year, I thought they'd lost interest in me altogether.

I was wrong.

Afterward, I remember thinking that *this* was the cruelest thing anyone would ever do to me.

Of course, that was before Eliza.

ELLIE

"Earth to Elizabeth, earth to Elizabeth."

I blink. "Huh?"

"Whatcha thinking about?"

I don't want to lie, but I also don't want to keep talking about my phobia. I train my gaze on the truck in front of us. "I was thinking that we might be about to get ourselves killed." The school catalog promises *a world of unexpected adventures awaits you* here. I don't think this is what they meant.

"Huh?"

"You know, following the guys that we think might have murdered our classmate?"

"What does that have to do with why your parents gave up on therapy?"

So much for changing the subject.

"I had a really bad attack last spring," I answer finally. "Worse than any I'd ever had. I couldn't catch my breath even after I was out in the open again. They had to bring me to the hospital. Sedate me. After that, my parents figured therapy hadn't really been helping."

"Wow." Sam whistles. "What brought that on?"

"Being in a small space, obviously."

I expect Sam to laugh or at least roll his eyes at my lame joke, but he stays serious. "No, I mean, why was that attack so much worse than the others?"

I tuck the hair that's fallen out of my ponytail behind my ears.

That time, I wasn't just imagining that I was trapped. That time, I really was. That time, they were holding me captive, and they wouldn't let me out.

"These girls at my old school thought it would be funny, I guess. They locked me—" I take a deep breath. Shrinks always want you to talk about what's bothering you. But sometimes talking about it makes it worse. Sometimes talking about it takes you back to that terrible day, to the tears streaming down your face that your lungs took as further proof that you were drowning. To the lump in your throat so huge that it was choking you. To the feel of the bathroom tile growing hot beneath your knees.

"They thought it would be funny?" Sam echoes incredulously.

I nod, but I'm only half listening.

There were certain places in my old school that I avoided. The elevator, obviously. The darkroom in the basement

(I took ceramics instead of photography). And most of the bathrooms. The two bathrooms where I felt safest were on the fifth and sixth floors—they had windows just outside the stalls. Most of the other bathrooms weren't that bad, actually, but I still avoided them for the most part. They had large enough stalls but no windows.

There was one bathroom I never set foot in. On the third floor, beside the junior lounge. It was one of those individual-size bathrooms—no stalls, just a door and a toilet and a sink. It was so small that the taller girls could literally touch the sink with their knees while they sat on the toilet. I mean, they said they could. I wouldn't know.

I don't know what made these girls—Sascha, Stacy, and Katie—decide to do what they did. They must have planned it, because Sascha asked me to meet her by the junior lounge so she could take a look at my chemistry notes after lunch. Maybe I should've seen it coming because Sascha and I weren't really friends. We weren't even juniors, so why would she want to meet in the junior lounge? I shake my head now, just thinking about it: How could I have been so clueless?

Sascha had made fun of me before—giggling the word *freak*, whispering about me loud enough so that I could hear: *weirdo, wimp, has to leave Field Day early for therapy*—but the teasing died down after middle school. I honestly believed that my phobia was too lame—old news and all that—to interest her anymore.

There were three of them on one side of the door and only one of me on the other. Tears were streaming down my face before the door even clicked closed.

Later, one of the girls told the headmaster that they'd been trying to help me. Claimed she'd read an article about immersion therapy. You just had to get someone to face her fears in order to force her to overcome them. I could've told her that therapist number five had already tried immersion therapy, to no avail. But the excuse was enough to keep the girls from getting expelled.

If those girls had really been trying to help me like they claimed, maybe they'd have shouted words of encouragement. *You can do it! It's okay! Hang in there!*

I tried. I wanted my brain to work like theirs. I wanted a normal brain and normal lungs.

I still do.

Later, I was shocked to hear that I'd been locked in the bathroom for only nine minutes. I honestly thought it had been at least a half hour, maybe longer. But they let me out in time to make it to their fifth-period classes.

I guess I should be grateful they didn't just run off when the bell rang. They actually got a teacher instead of leaving me on the floor alone, barely breathing. I hate to imagine what I must've looked like when they finally opened the door: eyes bulging, skin blotchy, gasping because I was trying to get some air in, any air in, just a whisper of air in.

By the time my mom got to the hospital, the sedatives had kicked in and I was breathing normally. I'd even washed my face so she wouldn't see how much I'd cried.

"I can't believe we're here again," Mom said. An attack had sent us to the hospital only once before: that first one, when I was seven years old. "All this time, and nothing has changed."

She paused like she was waiting for me to say something. I could've pointed out the things that *had* changed: I'd gotten older, Mom had gotten married, Wes had been born—but that wasn't the kind of change Mom was talking about. She didn't even want to hear how good I'd gotten at avoiding small spaces, so that I hadn't had an attack in months. Avoidance wasn't the same thing as getting better.

"We sent you to the best therapists. To every single person that your teachers and doctors recommended."

For years, every time someone suggested a new doctor, a new mode of therapy, my parents acted like the cure was just around the corner. I'd been through everything from hypnosis to immersion therapy, been put on antianxiety medication and even a special macrobiotic diet that made Wes gag.

That day at the hospital, Mom didn't sound angry, just tired. "Do you know how much your therapy has cost over the years?"

I didn't.

She sighed. "How is it possible that you're still not over this, Ellie?"

I shrugged. I was tired, too.

"You *know* the walls aren't really closing in. You just have to try—"

She stopped herself then, but it was too late. My mother was sick and tired of having a daughter with a Problem with a capital *P*. And she blamed me for not *trying* hard enough to be normal.

Now, I open my window. The air in California is so different from the air in New York: It smells like the ocean, and even though the state is famously dry right now, there's moisture in the breeze coming off the Pacific. California air is thinner somehow, like it doesn't hold on to all the smells and sweat and sounds the way Manhattan air does.

I tell Sam, "Anyhow, after the incident with the other girls, it seemed like the Ventana Ranch School would be a good idea."

Mom was so proud of me when she found out I applied. Like it was proof that I was *trying*. "A change of scenery will do you more good than a dozen therapists," she said. She had no idea how close her logic was to my own. If she knew what it was like here—how miserably I'd failed—she'd be disappointed in me all over again. And she'd never understand if I told her that what Eliza did was worse than what those girls did that day. At least what those girls did was based on something *true*. At least I understood why they hated me.

Sam says, "My dad thought so, too."

"Huh?" I ask dumbly.

"That Ventana Ranch would be a good idea. I mean, we came to the decision together, at least that's what we tell ourselves, but the truth is, living with him just wasn't working out. He has a whole other family—did I tell you that?"

I shake my head.

"Yeah, he got married when I was six years old. They have two kids who've lived in Mill Valley all their lives."

"Why did you choose Ventana Ranch?" Sam is the only African American boy at our small school. There are two African American girls in the senior class, and a teacher and an administrator, but that's not the same thing. "Isn't it just as bad here?"

"You mean just as white?"

I feel myself blushing. "I didn't mean—"

"Sure you did," Sam interrupts. "And you're right. But it's different because these people aren't my family, you know what I mean?"

"Not really," I admit.

"Every time my dad introduces me to someone as his son, I can tell there are a dozen questions dancing around that person's brain. Am I adopted? What happened to my mother? Where was I born? That kind of thing. They're usually too polite to ask, but it doesn't make a difference because I know what they're thinking." I nod. "And whenever they *do* ask,

I have to explain what happened to my mom, and I don't exactly feel like discussing her with a stranger, you know?" I nod again, realizing that it's not entirely my own antisocial fault that Sam and I have lived together for months and I only just found out that his mom passed away. From the look on his face, I can see it's something he prefers to keep to himself. "Plus, I have this younger brother and sister who look nothing like me—Dad's second wife is white like he is. Which leads to another ton of unasked questions." Sam takes one hand off the wheel and fidgets with the bandana wrapped around his dreads.

"My mom remarried, too. She doesn't even pretend that my half brother, Wes, isn't her favorite child anymore." (Not that I can really blame her.)

"How about your dad? Did he get married again?"

"I think he thought one failed family was enough."

Sam nods. I take a deep breath and roll my window up.

Traffic is picking up. Sam changes lanes, barely holding the steering wheel, just sort of resting his palms against it. Boys in New York never look this grown-up hailing a cab.

"Ellie was my mom's name," Sam says suddenly.

"What?"

"My mom. Her name was Ellie. Short for Elise, not Elizabeth like you. And it's not like I called her Ellie, I called her Mom. So I don't know why it's hard for me—"

I reach out and put one of my hands over his on the steering wheel. Without taking his eyes off the road, Sam turns his hand so that his fingers are twisted through mine and squeezes.

At once, Sam drops my hand like it's hot and curses. He tightens his grip on the wheel. The green truck is changing lanes, cutting across traffic to get to the right side of the road. Cars honk as it forces its way across the highway.

"They're getting off at the next exit." I point.

Sam curses again, turning his blinker on. I don't know if we'll be able to make it over to the right side in time. The truck is already picking up speed on the exit ramp, where there isn't nearly as much traffic as there is on the highway. Sam leans on the horn.

"What are you doing?" I shout. "They'll hear the horn and know we're following them."

Sam glances at me. "It's either this or risk losing track of them altogether."

I shift in my seat, feeling my phone in the pocket of my sweatshirt. It feels like it weighs a thousand pounds.

The police have some questions for you, as do I.

"Don't lose them, Sam. Please don't lose them."

He nods and presses down on the gas pedal.

ELLIE

saturday, march 19

According to the signs on the side of the road, we're driving through a town called Capitola. Most of the cars and trucks here have surfboards sticking out the back. The streets narrow, becoming more residential as we turn away from the ocean.

If this were a movie, we'd be heading toward a seedy bar, or maybe an enormous warehouse piled high with stolen wood, drugs strewn everywhere, with big dogs snarling from behind a chain-link fence.

(I'd be okay with a warehouse. At least it would be big.)

But this isn't a movie and they're pulling into the driveway of a small one-story house, the kind of place that my dad would call a bungalow. They get out of the truck and go inside, leaving the wood in the flatbed like it's no big deal. Sam rolls right past the driveway and pulls over a few houses later. But when he puts the car in park, neither of us makes a move to open our doors. I don't think either of us can believe that we just followed a couple of criminals (murderers?) for ninety minutes to a town we've never heard of.

"Maybe you should ask for a lawyer," Sam suggests suddenly. "The police can't talk to you without one, right?"

I shrug. "I'm not sure. Do Miranda rights—you know, the whole, *you have the right to remain silent* stuff—apply when you're not actually being arrested?"

"I don't know." Sam unties and reties his bandana.

"My mom already gave the police permission to talk to me anyway."

"I'm sure if you called her and explained—"

I shake my head. My mom isn't interested in another Ellie crisis. "None of the other students asked for an attorney, right? It'll just look suspicious if I do."

Sam pulls the keys from the ignition and fidgets with his key chain. "If it makes you feel any better, I'm not exactly looking forward to being questioned by the police, either."

Apparently, both of us would rather be here, just a few houses away from the men who maybe/probably killed Eliza, than back on campus where the police are waiting to talk to us. I twist in my seat, glancing at the truck in the driveway down the road. "Eliza got herself killed and it's going to ruin my life," I mutter.

Ruin my life.

I've heard someone say those words before. My mom? Maybe I overheard her talking to my stepdad about my phobia. No; it's not her voice that I hear. This voice is deeper

135

than my mother's. More even-keeled. When my mom gets upset, she shouts. This person was quiet, almost whispering. Calm even as she spoke about serious things.

A woman's voice, low and hoarse: *You're going to ruin my life if you keep this up. All our lives.*

I heard that voice again recently, deep and dry. Eliza's mother.

All our lives. She didn't know I could hear her. We were playing hide-and-seek and Eliza was it. I was under the table in the dining room.

The memory comes rushing back: They *did* fight at Eliza's house. Not like they fought at my house before my parents split—not with raised voices and slamming doors—but in harsh whispers they thought no one could hear. I heard someone start to cry—was it Mrs. Hart?—but then Mrs. Hart was saying, *It's okay. I'm not leaving,* in that same dry whisper. I realized it must have been Mr. Hart who was crying. It was the first time I ever saw a man cry, though technically I didn't really *see* it, I heard it. He wept. I watched Mrs. Hart's feet cross the floor so that she was standing next to him. I guessed she was hugging him and rocking him back and forth like my mom did when I cried.

I curled up into a little ball, scared that they would find me and I'd be punished for eavesdropping, even if it was an accident.

Ready or not, here I come!

The two grown-ups broke apart at the sound of Eliza's voice. I heard the clinking of glass as Mr. Hart poured himself a drink. Mrs. Hart began, *You shouldn't*, then stopped. From my hiding place, I watched her suede moccasins walk away, followed by Mr. Hart's loafers a few seconds later.

Eliza found me in seconds, just like she always did. I decided I'd have to choose a better place to hide next time.

Now I rub my hands together, clammy with sweat. "What should we do?"

Sam pulls his phone out of his pocket and offers it to me.

"We can't call the police!" I protest.

"Why not? Now we don't only have a name, we have an address, too."

"Yeah, but Mack and his friend could deny they ever worked with Eliza Hart. They could say they just found her ID somewhere. They might get arrested for stealing the trees, but how do we tie it to what happened to her?"

Sam shrugs. "I don't know."

"I wish we could somehow replay what we heard them saying this morning."

Sam's eyes light up like he just thought of something. "Maybe they're *still* talking about her."

"What do you mean?"

"They were talking about her on the trails this morning, right?"

We've already been over this. "We can't prove it."

Sam holds up his phone. "But if they talk about her again, we can."

Sam and I crouch beneath an open window.

"This is crazy," I whisper. My heart is pounding. Sam holds his finger to his lips, shushing me. He holds his phone up above us, his finger poised above the record button.

"We should get out of here. I don't hear anything anyway." My voice is shaking.

That's not entirely true. I hear the sound of the TV— some daytime talk show is on. I hear the sound of a can being popped open and the hum of a car driving past; I turn around and see that it's a bright shiny Lexus. In the distance, I can hear waves crashing against the beach. We're not that far from the water.

I wasn't expecting a place this *nice*. (I guess the kind of people in the market for these particular stolen goods— architects, artists, furniture designers—wouldn't want to go to a creepy warehouse to buy their burls any more than I would.)

I try to self-soothe just like one of my therapists (number five? Number six?) used to encourage me to do: I tell myself that Mack and his partner can't be that bad, not if Eliza was working with them. Eliza was smart. Smart people don't get involved with dangerous people. Smart people know better than to get in over their heads.

But then I remember that however smart she might have been, Eliza got herself killed.

Plus, Sam and I are supposed to be smart—straight A-students at a prestigious school—and here we are, doing what's probably the stupidest thing I've ever done.

So much for self-soothing.

"We should get out of here," I repeat. My breath is so shallow that I can hardly get the words out.

Before Sam can answer, I feel a hand on my shoulder, pulling me up to stand.

The hand snakes around my neck to cover my mouth before I can scream.

Sam springs to his feet. The hand on my mouth squeezes, pushing me so that I turn around to face the person attached to it. He's wearing a faded blue baseball cap pulled down over his eyes. His muscles are so big they bulge out of the sleeves of his T-shirt.

He's not as tall as Sam, but he's still taller than I am, just like Eliza was. Julian said the person he saw was about her height. I imagine this man picking up Eliza and tossing her over the cliffs. For a guy who cuts into decades-old trees every day, it was probably easy.

"Who the hell are you?" I recognize his voice from the woods. This is Mack.

"Concerned citizens," Sam practically spits. He gestures to the truck in the driveway. "We know where you got that wood."

"What's going on out there?" the gruff voice shouts from inside the house.

Mack pulls me closer, wrapping his arm around my neck, his hand pressed so tightly over my mouth that I can't move my lips.

"Nothing, Riley," Mack calls back. "Just a coupla kids who don't know what they're talking about." He says the last words slowly, looking over my head at Sam. "I'll get rid of them."

I feel myself start to shake beneath Mack's grip.

The other man—Riley—emerges from the house. Riley isn't as muscular as Mack, but he looks older. And he's tall, almost as tall as Sam. He can't have been the man Eliza was fighting with. I shift my gaze back to Mack.

"This is a citizen's arrest!" Sam shouts suddenly. He looks around, like he's hoping someone will come out of the surrounding houses when they hear the commotion, but the neighborhood stays still. "For illegal . . ." Sam pauses, struggling to find the right words. "Wood-chopping," he finishes finally. His shoulders slump. He knows how ridiculous he sounds. Sam's height looks less like of an asset next to Mack's muscles.

Without loosening his grip on me, Mack reaches out with his other arm and grabs Sam's phone, slipping it into his own pocket. Riley laughs out loud. "Why don't you invite our guests inside?" He nods at Mack, who pulls me backward. He doesn't lay a hand on Sam. He seems to know that if he drags me into the house, Sam is going to follow.

The bandana falls out of Sam's hair, onto the driveway. His dreadlocks fall across his face, but he keeps his eyes locked with mine.

I'm not going to leave you, his eyes seem to say. *We're gonna make it out of here.*

Alive.

ELLIE

saturday, march 19

Mack pulls me toward the door of the bungalow. Was it this easy for Mack to hold Eliza against her will? Surely she fought back. She probably kicked and screamed and scratched and bit.

But it wasn't enough to save her.

Will it be enough to save me?

Mack's arm around my neck feels like it's made of steel. I reach up and dig my fingers into his flesh, trying to loosen his grip. He barely seems to feel me pulling at him.

Mack's hand smells like redwood.

What's he going to do with me once he gets me inside? What if Riley tells him to lock me in the closet?

I hear the front door slam shut behind us. Mack says, "If I let you go, will you keep quiet?" but I can't answer because I'm starting to choke.

One of my therapists swore by visualization (*picture Mack letting you go*), but when I close my eyes, I can only imagine Mack locking me up someplace small and leaving me there forever.

I try to open my eyes, but they stay shut as stubbornly as they stayed open inside the tree with Sam this morning. Mack loosens his grip, but I'm still choking. Hot tears drip out from under my eyelids and land on Mack's arm, wedged beneath my chin.

"What's wrong with her?" Mack asks. His voice is surprisingly gentle. "She have asthma or something?"

Mack loosens his grip and the sound of my wheezing fills the room.

"Shut her up!" Riley shouts.

"Elizabeth," Sam says. "Elizabeth, open your eyes and look at me." I shake my head, eyes still shut tight. "Look at me," Sam repeats.

Mack lets go of me and I fall hard onto what feels like an old couch.

"Open your eyes," Sam repeats, placing one hand protectively on my knee. Finally, my eyelids open.

Sam keeps his gaze even with mine and breathes in and out, in and out, in and out, silently instructing me to follow him. I press my feet into the wooden floor, feeling bits of sand on the hardwood beneath my sneakers. The faded orange couch is fuzzy beneath my fingers.

After a few breaths, I nod. I can breathe again. I ball my hands into fists, trying to stop their shaking.

Mack plants himself in front of us, looking every bit as solid as the trees he destroys. After ninety minutes staring at the back of his head on the road, I'm surprised to see that he doesn't look anything like I imagined: no sinister expression, no five o'clock shadow covering his features. He takes off his baseball cap, revealing dirty-blond hair and bright blue eyes. He's startlingly handsome. He looks like he should be out on the water catching his next wave. He even has those tan lines that surfers get around their eyes from squinting in the sun.

Like Mack, Riley is wearing cargo pants and work boots and a sweat-stained T-shirt. Neither of them are the skinny, shifty meth-heads/heroin addicts I'd been expecting.

"So," Mack begins once I'm breathing relatively normally, "where did you two come from?"

"Ventana Ranch," I answer softly. A flicker of something— recognition? disgust? hope?—passes over Mack's face. Too late, it occurs to me that maybe it would've been better if I lied about where we came from. My hands are still trembling, so I slide them beneath my thighs to hide it.

I look around, trying to imagine Eliza in this house, running deals with these men. She surely held herself with confidence, acted tough, never showed fear. I force myself to sit up straight and answer again, louder this time. "Ventana Ranch," I repeat. I hate my voice for shaking. "We saw what you did this morning."

"I already called the police," Sam adds. "They're on their way."

I glance at Sam hopefully: Did he really call the police? No, I've been with him this whole time. He's just hoping he can scare them into letting us go.

Mack hands Sam's phone to Riley, who looks at the screen and (apparently) checks Sam's recent calls. "Doesn't look like you called anybody, Citizen's Arrest." He slides the phone into his pocket. Slowly, I reach for my own pocket, but Riley sees me move and shakes his head. "Tsk, tsk, tsk." I drop my hand back onto the couch, and he nods at Mack. "Take care of 'em." His eyes dart to the window, as though part of him thinks that despite what he saw on Sam's phone, the police might really be on their way. "Do it quickly."

"I've got it," Mack answers with a shrug. "You've got calls to make."

He almost makes it sound like Riley is a normal business-man, running late for a meeting. Except for the fact that he just stole Sam's phone. And that his calls are surely about the black market goods in the back of his truck. Riley walks out the front door, and I hear the sound of a car starting; he's driving away with our evidence.

My heart is pounding. What exactly does *take care of 'em* mean?

"Are you going to take care of us like you took care of Eliza?" I'm shaking so hard—not just my hands, but my whole body now, like I'm freezing even though it's warm in here. I barely manage to get the words out.

Mack narrows his icy eyes. He doesn't look handsome anymore. "What do you know about Eliza?"

I open my mouth to answer, but no words come out: My teeth are actually chattering. I'm not sure I know the first thing about Eliza anymore. The girl she grew up to be is nothing like the friend I remember. But the girl I saw painting her nails in the valley didn't look like the kind of girl who'd be working with men like this, either.

All I know for sure is that she hated me. And now I'm in danger—*real* danger—because of her. Because even after she died, the rumors she started swirled around our school like a hurricane.

Finally, I mutter, "I can't believe I'm going to die for a mean girl."

Mack's eyes narrow further. He balls his hands into fists. "Eliza wasn't mean."

"What?" I ask dumbly. Sam tightens his grip on my knee, steadying my shaking. I can feel his pulse through my leggings. His heart is beating almost as fast as mine.

"Eliza wasn't mean," Mack repeats, louder this time. "She had her mood swings, I'll give you that, but . . ." Mack pauses, his face softening. "You know she used to visit the trees afterward, like visiting a patient in the hospital or something." He glances at us, then sets his jaw and swallows. The softness in his expression vanishes. "Did she send you here?"

"Send us here?" I echo. "She's dead."

"I know she's dead," Mack answers bitterly. "I just thought— I dunno, maybe she left a message for me or something."

"A message?" What does this guy expect, a thank-you note for killing her? "How about *you're not going to get away with what you did*?"

Mack takes a step back. For a second, he looks less solid, like a breeze could knock him over.

"You think I hurt her?"

"You butchered those trees."

Mack looks like he thinks I'm an idiot for not knowing the difference between a girl and a tree. He lowers his muscular body into a chair across from Sam and me and buries his face in his hands. Sam glances at the door. He raises his eyebrows: Should we make a run for it?

I try to stand, but my legs are still shaking.

This is what being trapped is really like. It's not a closed door to a closet or a bathroom.

Trapped is a strong man between you and your escape.

Mack looks up. "You know she never slept?" He sounds almost impressed, like sleep was for normal people, weaker people, and Eliza couldn't be bothered with it.

It takes me a second to realize that there's probably only one reason why Mack would know her sleeping patterns. "*You're* her secret boyfriend? She came *here* when she snuck out after curfew?"

"Eliza had a boyfriend?" Sam asks, just as Mack says, "How did you know about me?"

I answer Mack. "I didn't know about *you*," I explain. "I just heard Erin and Arden talking about *someone*." I don't explain who Erin and Arden are. If he's her boyfriend, he probably already knows.

Mack nods. "She told them she was seeing a college student and she had to keep it a secret because her parents wouldn't approve of her seeing someone older." He wrinkles his nose at the lie.

Sam jumps in. "Listen, Elizabeth and I don't want any trouble. We're just—"

Mack cuts him off. "Just accusing me of murder." He laughs bitterly, then looks at me. "Your name is Elizabeth?"

"Ellie," I correct automatically.

"Ellie Sokoloff?"

My heartbeat speeds up again. Beneath my sweatshirt, goose bumps rise on my arms. "How do you know my name?"

Instead of answering, Mack whistles, looking me up and down. "Ellie Sokoloff," he repeats. I fold my arms across my chest like I think I can block his view of me. "Man, was she scared of you."

I squeeze my hands into fists. It's bad enough that the kids at school think I had something to do with her death, but here I am standing across from an *actual criminal*, and *I'm* the one she was scared of?

"I was scared of her, not the other way around!"

Mack laughs his joyless laugh. It sounds like he's coughing up something sour. "Looks like she did a number on both of us," he says finally.

Sam grabs my hand but keeps his gaze trained on Mack. "You loved her." It's not a question.

Mack's face hardens. "Not that it mattered much."

"You knew who she was," I add quietly. "This morning, in the woods, you told Riley you didn't know about her family. You were lying, weren't you?"

Mack stands and springs across the room. He crouches so his eyes are level with mine. I shrink against the back of the couch.

Did he look at Eliza like this, the night he killed her: his blue eyes unblinking, his jaw set?

"You're the one who knows about her family," he spits. "She told me everything. You were there the last time her dad—" He cuts himself off, shaking his head. "It doesn't matter anymore." He says it quietly, like he's trying to calm himself down.

"The last time her dad what?" I feel like Alice when she first lands in Wonderland: Nothing makes any sense today. Our school's rich princess was profiting off of black-market redwoods. A criminal was in love with her. She was scared of me, not the other way around.

"The last time her dad *what?*" I repeat, sitting up a little straighter. My heart is still pounding, but I'm not shaking anymore. I want to know what he's talking about too badly to back down.

"You honestly don't know?" Mack takes a step backward. I shake my head. "All that and she doesn't even remember." Again, the room fills with the sound of his sour laughter.

"What are you talking about?" My voice is shrill.

Instead of answering, Mack just gestures at the front door. Sam stands and pulls me toward it. Much to my surprise, I'm not ready to go.

"You're just letting us leave?" I ask incredulously. Riley told him to *take care of us*. I don't think he meant confuse the heck out of us and then let us go. "Won't you get in trouble with Riley?" Why do I care if Mack gets into trouble or not?

"He just wanted me to scare you into keeping quiet."

"We could still call the police and tell them about you."

Mack shrugs. "I guess you could."

"Aren't you scared of going to jail?"

Sam tugs at my arm but I hold firm. What's wrong with me? Why do I want to stay here?

"What did you mean this morning?" I ask quickly. "You told Riley that if Eliza had listened to you, she'd still be alive."

Mack shakes his head. His enormous shoulders begin to shake. He opens and flexes his fists.

"Elizabeth," Sam whispers. "Let's get out of here."

This time, when Sam yanks on my arm, I don't resist.

As we leave, I hear the sound of something pounding. I turn back and see Mack punching one of the bungalow walls. The entire house is shaking, a localized earthquake.

I think he's strong enough to knock the little house down.

ELIZA

dead trees

The cold never used to bother me. I wore flip-flops when it was forty degrees outside and hiked in shorts when the fog was so thick it soaked your skin and you could barely see three feet in front of you. But everything's different now.

It's not like I thought life and death would be the same, but still.

I was thirteen when I stopped trying to fall back to sleep after I woke up in the middle of the night. When I was still living at home, I'd study, read, watch TV. Anything to pass the time.

My sleeplessness got to be so reliable that I didn't even bother doing my homework the night before. I'd wait until my mixed-up internal clock woke me sometime after two in the morning and start working then, just to have something to do.

Living at Ventana Ranch changed everything: When I woke up in the middle of the night, I could leave the dorm and explore the woods. The first time I saw Mack and Riley, it was 4:00 a.m. and I was hiking.

The campus was quiet.

All my classmates were sleeping soundly.

It was dark, but I'd never been afraid of the dark.

When I reached the end of the Y trail, I used my ID to open the gate and kept hiking in the woods on the other side, public property. It was only October, and I'd already had enough restless nights to hike every trail on campus. It wasn't as safe as staying on campus, but I didn't care.

I didn't care about much of anything at that point.

The drought had been so bad that the pine needles were turning brown and falling off the trees. It looked like they were already dying.

Any other girl would've run when she heard the buzz saw.

But then, any other girl wouldn't have been there in the first place.

I watched them work. It was cold, but they were wearing only T-shirts, so soaked with sweat that I could see their muscles moving beneath the fabric in the light from their flashlights.

One of them—Riley, I was about to find out—kept his eyes on the forest around them instead of on the tree or the saw.

I recognized the look on his face: fear. He was scared of getting caught. He wanted to get this done as quickly as possible and get the hell out.

The other one kept his eyes narrowed in deep concentration, a look I would come to know well. He kept his gaze locked on the tree in front of him.

Later, he told me that of course he was scared of getting caught.

He was scared of getting caught at the same time that he was scared of the buzz saw,

at the same time that he felt bad about destroying the tree,

at the same time that he was adding up the amount of money he would need to buy a new surfboard and a new truck and a ticket to Hawaii and dreaming of taking his next wave.

I never knew a single person could hold so many different emotions at the same time. Not unless they were manic, and there wasn't the least bit of mania in Mack. His mood swings were normal: When he was happy, he smiled; when he was angry, he shouted.

There were times, later, when I was the one Mack was shouting at. His blue eyes would narrow to nothing more than slits. He'd stomp the ground or punch the nearest wall. He was so strong he could make the whole house shake.

Maybe I should've been scared of a boy like that. Maybe I should've run away in fear when he yelled at me.

But I could barely muster any emotion in those days, let alone enough fear to make me run.

So I stayed until the day Mack reached his breaking point.

But I'm getting ahead of myself.

That October day in the woods, Riley saw me first. The fear on his face stretched into worry: He was weighing his options, deciding just how far he'd be willing to go to keep me from turning them in.

He didn't have to worry.

I wasn't interested in reporting what I'd seen.

I was interested in the look in his eyes, the look in Mack's eyes.

In the emotions I'd never gotten to feel.

It was then that I had a revelation: Maybe the problem wasn't me after all.

Maybe the problem was just that in my sheltered, safe life, the stakes had simply never been high enough to make me really *feel* anything. Maybe I'd never done anything exciting enough to make me sufficiently tired to sleep through the night.

I'd read about people who had a higher threshold for stimulation—that's what happens when you're up half the night: You have time to read just about everything—people who skydived, who rock-climbed without a harness. They went big-wave surfing, or maybe broke the law. In between adventures, these people sunk into deep depressions because normal things weren't enough to make them feel happy or excited. They *needed* the rush that came with risking their lives just to feel normal.

Maybe I was one of them. Maybe an adventure was all I needed.

At first, Riley laughed when I offered to help.

Then I held up my ID. I insisted that it would be easier for them to do their work on campus: no chance of getting caught by a passing state trooper since they'd be on private property.

Why would a good little schoolgirl want to get involved in all this? Riley asked.

Maybe I'm not so good, I answered.

If I was good, I wouldn't have spent the entire summer fighting with my mother and avoiding making eye contact with my father. The look in my dad's eyes was nothing like the look in Riley's, nothing like the look in Mack's.

A few weeks later, Mack caught me sitting beside a tree we'd sliced open. Most trees could actually survive having their burls cut off—they usually grow bark over their wounds and heal—but this one didn't seem to be healing. I read that burl-poaching makes some trees more susceptible to disease and infection, as though their immune systems have been compromised. And trees whose burls have been robbed are more vulnerable to windthrow—to literally being broken by the wind.

Mack thought I felt sorry for the sick tree. To make me feel better, he pointed to the dozens of untouched, perfectly healthy trees around us. Trees that had lived for longer than even the oldest person I knew and would go on to live long after we were gone. That was when he still thought I'd gotten involved with him and Riley because—like him—I desperately needed the money.

Later, I found out he'd made up a whole backstory about me: that I was on full scholarship at Ventana Ranch and couldn't afford meals, had resorted to stealing food from the cafeteria. I laughed and told him that meals were included in our tuition. He'd blushed, and I'd felt—actually, really, for a split second, *felt*—bad about embarrassing him. It wasn't his fault he'd given me the benefit of the doubt. He didn't know that I shoved the cash he and Riley gave me under my mattress and never gave it a second thought.

I'm not as good as you think I am, I'd told him.

You're not as bad as you *think you are, either,* he replied.

I wasn't there because I felt sorry for the tree.

I wanted to watch it die. Wanted to know if I could figure out the exact moment when it turned from a living, breathing, photosynthesizing creature into a corpse.

That was the good thing about not sleeping: I had plenty of time to keep watch.

And now I'm still wide awake.

ELLIE

saturday, march 19

"We have to call the police," I breathe as Sam floors it, getting us out of Capitola as quickly as possible. My pulse is still so fast that I wonder if it's possible for a sixteen-year-old to have a heart attack.

"They took my phone."

"I still have mine." I pull it out of my sweatshirt pocket. My hands are shaking.

"What are you going to tell them?"

"That we found Eliza's killer!" I'm almost shouting.

Sam shakes his head. "I don't think that guy killed her."

I stare at my roommate, but he doesn't take his eyes off the road. "Are you crazy?"

"I think he really loved her."

I almost drop my phone. "That doesn't mean he didn't hurt her."

Maybe he saw her talking and laughing with one of our male classmates and got jealous.

Maybe she wanted out of the burl-poaching business and he said, *There is no out, you already know too much.*

Maybe she tried to break up with him and he said, *If I can't have you, no one can.*

I remember the way his ice-blue eyes flashed with anger when I called Eliza mean.

"He was practically punching a hole in the wall! He's obviously violent. Who knows what he's capable of?"

"Elizabeth, he was clearly upset about Eliza's death."

"Or he's upset because he's scared of getting caught."

"Then why would he let us go?"

Sam might have a point there. "Okay, so maybe it was an accident. Maybe they were fighting and she lost her balance and fell and he didn't do anything to save her."

"Julian saw them fighting a week before she died. Assuming it was even Mack Julian saw her fighting with."

"Mack is about Eliza's height, just like the person Julian saw. And anyway, they might have fought again."

"I know you're scared to talk to the police, but we shouldn't accuse an innocent man—"

"What are you talking about, innocent? The guy hacks trees into pieces for money! We already know he's not innocent." I'm squeezing my phone so tight that it's hot in my hand.

"There's a big difference between cutting a tree and killing a girl."

Mack practically said the same thing. "I know that."

I lean back in my seat and look out my window. We're going south on Highway 1. I watch the waves building in the Pacific Ocean. "We have to tell the police we found the burl-poachers, at least."

"A few days ago, I would've agreed with you."

"And now?"

Sam shrugs. "Now I think if we tell them we know who's killing the trees, they'll just assume that person killed Eliza."

"Is this more of your *judge not, that ye be not judged* stuff?"

"I'm not sure I'd call my belief-system 'stuff.'"

I feel myself blushing. "Sorry."

"And actually, no. I just don't want to point the police in the wrong direction."

"Sam, they're the *police*. It's their job to look at the evidence and put the pieces together. Mack *might* have killed her. He *should* be investigated."

Sam runs his palms over the steering wheel thoughtfully. "Do you really think he would have let us go if he'd killed her?"

I take a deep breath. My pulse has slowed to an almost normal rate. "I don't know."

"Just think about it for a little while before you do anything, okay?"

I hesitate. Won't it just make the police more suspicious of me if I have a suspect and don't tell them about him right away? I glance at my phone; it's 2:00 p.m. I'm being questioned in two hours.

Which means I have two hours to decide what to tell the police.

When we get back to campus, Sam's friend Cooper stops us on our way from the parking lot to the dorm.

"Did you hear?" Cooper is decidedly talking to Sam, not me. He doesn't even glance my way.

"Hear what?"

"They found, like, five thousand dollars in cash in Eliza's room." Sam's eyes meet mine. That must've been the money Eliza earned from working with Riley and Mack. *Blood money,* I think, remembering the way the rust-colored bark looked like it was bleeding. Sam and Cooper don't stop walking as they talk. They're both taller than I am and I rush to keep up with them.

"I heard it was ten," someone says, coming up the path behind us. Riya Dasgupta, a senior everyone knows got in early admission to Yale. She's wearing leggings with a sports bra as a shirt. Her perfect abs are glistening beneath a layer of sweat; she must be on her way back from the gym. I feel like a slob standing beside her in my bulky sweatshirt. Riya bounces on the balls of her feet and pushes her dark, stylish sunglasses up onto the top of her head.

Cooper whistles. "Maybe that's why they killed her." Now Cooper does look at me, hard. "*Whoever* killed her," he adds slowly, each word thick with meaning: *We still think it might have been you.*

Does Cooper know I'm on scholarship? Maybe he thinks I need the money.

I'm tempted to tell him about Mack, but I bite my tongue. If I'm going to tell anyone, it should be the police.

"Eliza was worth a lot more than ten thousand dollars," Riya counters. "I mean, if someone wanted money, why wouldn't they kidnap her and hold her for ransom? Everyone knows the Harts are loaded."

"Whoa, way to go dark, Ree." Cooper reaches out to muss Riya's black hair like she's a little kid, but she ducks out of the way. "Didn't know you had it in you."

"We all have a dark side, right?" Riya shrugs. "Anyway, I'm just being practical."

Is it just my imagination, or does she glance at me when she says *dark side*? Like she wants to lull me into confessing by admitting that she has a dark side, too? I have to remind myself that I don't actually have anything to confess.

"Did they know where the money came from?" I ask. Riya looks at me like I'm speaking Greek. Guess it never occurred to anyone to think the cash might have come from anywhere but her family. Like Riya said, the Harts are loaded.

"Did the police give her parents the money?" Sam asks.

161

Riya shakes her head. "They tried, but her parents want it donated to the school. The Eliza Hart Scholarship Fund, or whatever."

Cooper runs his hands through his sandy brown hair. "You know, I was supposed to be in San Diego this week," he moans miserably. "Look how pale I am." He holds a perfectly tanned arm out for Riya to judge.

Riya shrugs. "San Diego's not going anywhere."

Cooper ignores her. "I was supposed to hang with my cousin. He's a freshman at UCSD, and we were gonna party. Think about it. College chicks."

"I don't want to." Riya makes a face, feigning disgust at the idea of Cooper hitting on a bunch of college girls. "And you shouldn't call girls *chicks*."

Cooper just grins. "Being stuck on this campus makes me feel claustrophobic."

Like Cooper has any idea what it feels like to be claustrophobic.

Riya rolls her eyes. "You're not *stuck* on this campus. We're allowed to leave. And once the police interview you, you can drive down to San Diego. If you're so desperate to get out of here, have your parents tell the police to move you to the top of their list."

"Nah, I'll wait. There are people they have to talk to ahead of me. I hear Erin Smythe was in there all morning. She could barely answer their questions she was crying so hard."

"Well, good for you for having a sense of priorities at a time like this." Riya sounds genuinely surprised, like she really expected Cooper to think his vacation was more important than the police's investigation.

"But the minute they're done with me, I'm hitting the road. I'll speed the whole way and make record time."

Riya shakes her head, but she doesn't really seem annoyed. Cooper puts an arm around her as we walk.

"Apparently, Eliza had a boyfriend nobody knew about," Riya says without missing a step.

I lose my footing, tripping over my feet. Sam catches me before I hit the ground. "You okay?"

I nod quickly. "Fine."

Sam clears his throat and turns back to Riya. "Where'd you hear she had a secret boyfriend?"

"Arden Lin blabbed to the cops."

So much for keeping her secret. I'd have thought if anyone was going to let it slip, it would've been Erin.

"So who is this guy?" Cooper asks.

"Arden didn't know. Erin, either. They said he was probably in college or something." Sam and I exchange a look. "Eliza told them he was a little bit older. That's why she had to keep him a secret from her parents."

Would Cooper and Riya be impressed to discover that I know something about Eliza even Arden and Erin don't know? I'd be a hero, the girl who pointed the police in the right direction. Everyone on campus would like me for a change.

Or maybe they'd just take it as more proof of my obsession with Eliza. Only a stalker would know where her secret boyfriend lives.

I lag behind, letting Riya, Cooper, and Sam lead the way up the hill. Maybe I shouldn't tell the police about Mack. Not (just) because Sam thinks he's innocent, but because it'll only make everyone here that much more convinced that I'm obsessed with Eliza. The wind picks up as we get closer to the cliffs, to the spot still ringed with crime-scene tape. I shiver.

Suddenly, Sam stops walking. "I'm starving." He nods in the direction of the cafeteria. "Ellie and I haven't eaten since breakfast." He turns on his heel and heads into the dining hall. I follow, realizing how hungry I am, and grateful for the excuse to leave Cooper and Riya behind.

It's past lunchtime, but the cafeteria is crowded with students. I wonder how many of my classmates are as irritated as Cooper was about missing out on their spring break plans.

There are always snacks in the cafeteria. Little packets of organic peanut butter and West Coast bagels, a bowl of fruit and yogurt. I head for the coffee machines, lined up in a row facing the windows. This building is just yards away from the cliff where they pulled up Eliza's body. If I crane my neck, I can see a series of ledges built into the rocks.

Eliza died out there.

In fact, someone spotted her body from this room. Maybe that's why it's so quiet in here. Maybe the cafeteria will never feel like anything but the spot on campus where you can see the place where Eliza landed.

I've never liked cafeterias. I'm not the first (and unfortunately, I won't be the last) unpopular kid to suffer the misery of mealtimes at school, to feel the anxiety of having no one to sit with, no one to talk to.

In kindergarten and first grade, still living in California, I always sat with Eliza. Second grade through fifth, in Manhattan, the teachers made us sit with our class, so I always had people to sit with, even if I wasn't necessarily included in the conversation. At the time, I believed that sitting at a crowded table where no one includes you was even lonelier than sitting at a table by myself, than eating in the girls' room like the losers and loners did in the movies.

I was wrong.

Things got worse in middle school. In middle school, we were allowed to sit wherever we wanted.

I didn't exactly sit alone. Usually there were one or two other girls and even the occasional boy at my table in the corner of the cafeteria. But we didn't talk much. We mostly listened, even though we were too far from our classmates' chatter to make out much of what they were saying.

I thought it would be better here. I thought I'd have a bunch of friends at this small, inclusive school, and not only would I have people to sit with, but I'd participate in conversations. I thought I'd actually be part of the chatter.

Wrong again.

On the very first day of school, I gripped my tray and walked toward the table where Eliza was sitting. After all, she was the only person I knew, other than my roommate, and he and I hadn't done much more than exchange the occasional *hello* and *good-bye* at that point. (In fact, at that point, I could barely look him in the eye. I blushed every time I looked at him and remembered that I was sharing my living space with a *boy*.)

Eliza's back was to me, but I still think she knew I was coming, because she didn't look the least bit surprised when she saw me. Erin and Arden were sitting on either side of her, so I had to walk around the table to the opposite side.

"Mind if I sit with you guys?" I wanted to sound nonchalant, but instead it came out overeager.

Neither Erin nor Arden spoke. Now I wonder if Eliza had already told them her stories about me by then.

She shrugged, her wavy blond hair falling over her shoulders.

Not exactly a yes, but not technically a no, either. I sat. The four of us ate in silence for a few seconds.

"You all unpacked?" I asked finally. No one answered, so I repeated the question, louder this time.

"Finn!" Eliza called. A boy across the room headed

toward us. "Arden, Erin, I can't remember if you guys ever met Finn. We went to Sunday school together literally a thousand years ago."

"Well, not literally," I interjected brightly, hoping it would sound more like a joke than a correction. But Eliza kept her eyes on Finn.

Later, I actually wondered if that was why she hated me. Because I corrected her grammar.

Finn sat at our table. Then Cooper, with his suitemate, whose name was Tina. Then a couple more girls who lived in Harlan. They all talked. I tried to join in, but I couldn't think of things to say quickly enough—by the time I spoke up, they'd already moved on to another topic. They'd had all of middle school and the first two years of high school to learn how to talk to their peers. They hadn't spent all that time stuck at a quiet table in the corner like I had.

Eventually, I stopped trying to participate.

If I'd told this story to my mother, or to one of my old therapists, they'd have all encouraged me to try again the next day. To keep sitting at that table until I figured out a way to join the conversation. I can practically hear my mother telling me not to give up. *They just don't know you yet. You just have to make a little effort.*

But I never sat with Eliza again. In fact, I avoided sitting in the cafeteria whenever possible, grabbing snacks to take back to my room.

Now I shake myself like a puppy after a bath and grab a yogurt. I can't seem to stop myself from looking out the window at the cliffs where they found Eliza.

"Trying to remember the exact spot where she fell?" I spin around. Behind me, Arden Lin stands with an empty coffee mug. I step out of her way so she can fill her cup. (Hazelnut, no sugar.)

"Remember?" I echo just as Sam steps in, saying, "Don't be ridiculous, Arden."

Arden said *remember* because she thinks I was there when Eliza went over the cliffs. Sam calmly takes a bite of his apple, keeping his gaze casual, as though Arden just accused me of taking the last of the coffee, not of murdering her best friend.

Arden tosses her long hair over her shoulder. "It's not ridiculous. The police said in a case like this you have to consider all the possibilities."

"Elizabeth isn't a possibility," Sam says firmly.

"I think I know more about Eliza than you do," Arden counters.

I have to bite my lip to keep from shouting *No, you don't!* I know what Eliza was really doing when you and everyone else thought she was out hiking. I know her secret boyfriend's name and what he looks like and how his eyes narrow when he says her name because he has to concentrate to keep from crying.

Arden pours cream into her coffee and spins on her heel, so graceful that she doesn't spill a drop.

I may know more *about* Eliza, but that's not the same thing as having *known* her. Even if I told Arden about Mack, and even if she believed me (and she wouldn't), all this new information just leads to more questions, not more *understanding*. Eliza has become even more mysterious in the past twenty-four hours.

It's like she's not quite dead because there's still so much to learn about her.

The sound of a mug shattering draws me out of my thoughts. Across the cafeteria, Arden is staring at her phone. Her mug is in pieces at her feet, and she's covered in coffee.

"The police determined her cause of death," she breathes.

She's not really talking to Sam and me, or even to the handful of other students in the room, but someone shouts out "What?"

Arden looks up from her phone. Her eyes are bright with unshed tears. "Exposure," she whispers. "They think she died around five in the morning on Wednesday." It sounds like everyone in the room is gasping at the same time. I hear a student behind me start to cry. Someone puts an arm around Arden, leads her to sit at a nearby table.

"Let's get out of here," Sam says softly. Even though the hardwood floor is perfectly even, it reminds me of our hike this morning: I watch where he puts his feet, and try to put mine in the same place.

Just seconds ago, it felt like Eliza wasn't really gone. Like she was still dropping hints and leaving clues so that we could piece the real story of her life together. But there's no such thing as *not quite dead*.

She's gone. We just found out what killed her.

ELLIE

saturday, march 19

Dean Carson texts me again, explaining that in light of recent discoveries, they aren't available to speak with me at four o'clock anymore.

Please be at Professor Clifton's office tomorrow at 2pm Sharp.

Sitting on my bed, I stare at the capital *S* at the beginning of the word *sharp*.

Maybe I should text back that I need to see the detective today. I could say I have information that could lead them to Eliza's killer. My finger is poised above the letter *I*, just waiting to begin my response, but I can't seem to make myself start typing.

The sound of water running makes me look up. Sam must be getting in the shower. Sam, who doesn't think I should tell the police about Mack.

Exposure. It's what killed her, but it's not *how* she died.

Does *exposure* make it more or less likely that Mack pushed her over the cliffs? If he threw her with any force, she probably would've cleared the ledge, gone down to the sea, never to be found. That's what a smart killer would want: no body, no evidence.

If they were arguing and she just fell—an accident—she might have ended up on caught on a ledge.

But if it was an accident, wouldn't Mack have gone to the police—called an ambulance, search and rescue, the Coast Guard—immediately? If it was an accident, he wouldn't have left her there to die, no matter how mad he was at her.

Right?

Maybe he thought it was already too late.

I take my phone out of my pocket and Google: How long does it take to die of exposure?

Dying from exposure means death resulting from lack of protection over prolonged periods to extreme temperatures, environmental conditions, or dangerous substances.

Prolonged periods. If Mack had called the police the instant she went over, she might have survived. I keep reading.

The human body is very adaptable and is constantly balancing different things, from core temperature to water content. Too hot and it sweats; too cold and it shivers. But its capability to regulate itself has its limits, and death can occur, for example, by exposure to extreme heat or cold.

In some cases, it occurs by a combination of circumstances and stresses to the body such as a combination of hypothermia and starvation.

It's not cold in my room, but I'm shivering.

When Eliza descended—after tripping, jumping, being pushed—did she believe she was going to die? Was she expecting to hit the water hard, ready to have the breath knocked out of her on impact? Maybe she thought she could survive the fall. Maybe as gravity pulled her down she was already planning to fight against the waves crashing against the cliff wall. She was a strong swimmer. Maybe she believed she could swim to safety, or that she could stay afloat on her own until she'd be rescued by a nearby fishing boat or wash up on a sandy beach.

But then she landed on the ledge.

Was she awake while she lay there? Did she shout for help, her voice carried off on the wind? If Mack was at the top of the cliff, did she believe he would save her?

Was there finally a moment when she understood she was going to die?

I hope the impact of the fall knocked her unconscious. No one deserves to lie awake like that, just waiting to die.

Not even a mean girl like Eliza Hart.

Cooper texted Sam the results of the autopsy. It revealed that there were broken bones in Eliza's left arm and leg. The medical examiner couldn't determine whether Eliza broke her bones when she first landed on the ledge, or if she fell again, trying to climb the side of the cliffs.

I think she must have broken her bones when she first landed there. If Eliza had tried to climb out, she'd have made it.

Unless Mack was waiting on the top of the cliff to push her back down again.

My phone buzzes in my hands.

"Hi, Mom."

"Hi, sweetheart."

"How are you?" I ask.

"Exhausted," she answers with a laugh. She starts listing the errands she's been running and the meeting that went badly. But she doesn't actually sound exhausted. Maybe it's my imagination, but ever since I moved to California, I think there's been a lightness in her voice (as long as we're not talking about me). Like when I moved out, an enormous weight was lifted.

Mom pauses, then asks, "How are you?"

I roll over so that I'm sitting up with my back against the wall. I run my fingers over the bedspread, remembering when Mom and I went to Bed Bath & Beyond in August to pick it out, along with my shower caddy and robe and towels. She kept saying that Ventana Ranch was going to be a fresh start for me, and I smiled and nodded because at the time I believed it, too.

What if I told her the truth? Not just the truth about Eliza (the rumors, the whispers, the way they practically kicked me out of her memorial service), and not just the truth about what I did today (following trespassers away from campus, confronting them and almost getting myself killed, two claustrophobia attacks).

What if I told her that even though I haven't seen a therapist since I got to California, I haven't given up on curing myself, that I've been inducing attacks in an effort to overcome them?

But then she'd ask how it was going, and I'd have to tell her that I haven't made any progress at all.

I swallow a sigh, knowing that I won't tell her any of it. Ever since that attack in school last year, neither of us has wanted to talk about it. I don't want to disappoint her again.

"Ellie?" Mom prompts. The lightness disappears from her voice as the all-too-familiar Ellie tone takes over.

The sound of running water stops; Sam's getting out of the shower. With my thumbs, I pull the sleeves of my sweatshirt down over my wrists.

Here's another truth I'm not telling my mother: I want her to drop whatever she's doing, to miss Wes's basketball game, to buy a ticket and get on a plane and fly across the country to sit next to me and hold my hand while the police question me less than twenty-four-hours from now. I want her to explain that they can't question me in Professor

Clifton's office for perfectly legitimate and not-at-all-crazy reasons. I want her to stand up for me.

I want her to help me decide whether I should tell the police about Mack.

I want her to tell me that it isn't my fault that all the other kids hate me.

I want her to tell me that dying from exposure doesn't hurt.

Holding my phone against my ear, my hand is shaking. The truth is, she'd come if I asked her to. But she'd sigh and tsk and we'd both know she'd be happier staying at home with Wes and my stepdad, happier believing that Ellie has it all under control.

That Ellie is finally growing up.

That Ellie can handle it on her own.

I never told her that once I realized those girls—Sascha, Stacy, and Katie—weren't going to let me out of the bathroom, I closed my eyes and thought, *I want my mom*, over and over again like a mantra.

And now I know I'd rather face the police alone than face the disappointment in my mother's eyes.

So I add what I really want and how I really feel to the list of things I don't say out loud. Instead, I say, "I'm fine, Mom. I'm fine."

ELLIE

not even dawn on sunday, march 20

Eliza is falling, just out of my reach. I shout her name.

Eliza!

I lie flat on the ground, my arms dangling over the edge of the cliff.

Eliza!

She looks up. I hold out my arm. She's so close. All she has to do is reach up, and I'll be able to catch her. We lock eyes.

Eliza!

She reaches. Our fingertips brush against one another. Her fingers lace through mine—*got her!* But behind me, someone is wrapping his arms around me, his muscles like steel. He squeezes me tight, tighter. I can't breathe, the water is rushing in: I'm starting to have an attack. I twist my neck and see that it's Mack holding me, his eyes narrowed in anger. He doesn't even have to pull me back or pry my arms away. I can't hold on to Eliza when I can't breathe. My phobia has rendered me useless.

Eliza's hand slips out of my grasp. Her mouth twists into

an O of surprise as she falls back down toward the rocky ledge.

I hear her land with a dull thud.

———

"Ellie, wake up. Wake up. It was just a dream."

I feel the heat of Sam's body standing over mine, blocking the breeze coming through my always-open window. The sheets are twisted between my legs, my knees curled up to my chest, my jaw clenched tight.

"He wouldn't let me save her," I pant, trying to make my body relax. My muscles are sore from our hike yesterday: My quads feel like they're bound with ropes, and my abdominals protest as I uncurl myself from the fetal position.

"It was just a dream."

I shake my head fiercely. My eyes are still closed, but I can feel tears drip down my cheeks.

"I shouldn't be crying." I open my eyes to the dark room and pull the sheet back over me. I see my copy of *The Complete Short Stories of Ernest Hemingway* on the floor; I fell asleep with it on the bed. That must've been what I heard falling to the ground.

Just a book. Not Eliza.

"Why shouldn't you cry?"

"She wasn't my friend."

"There aren't any rules about these things."

Sam sits down on the edge of the narrow bed. His weight tightens the blanket over my torso, and I scramble away from him, smacking my back against the wall.

Sam must understand my panic, because he folds the covers back and adjusts himself on the bed beside me. For another girl, this would be romantic—the handsome boy getting into her bed in the middle of the night—but I'm sure Sam's just trying to ward off another attack. I may as well be his kid sister, the girl he has to protect from the monsters under her bed. The girl he puts his arm around only because it makes more room in the bed.

"What does it feel like?" Sam asks softly. He's not wearing a shirt, and my bare arm is touching his chest. His skin is warm despite the breeze blowing through the window. "When you're in a small space?"

I shake my head. "It's stupid."

"Does it feel like the walls are closing in on you? That's what I read when I Googled it."

"You Googled it?"

"Sure." Sam shrugs like it's no big deal. "What does it feel like?" he asks again.

I don't know why we're whispering. There's no one to overhear us. But I keep my voice low as I explain. "It feels like I'm underwater. It's not the walls that are closing in, but wave after wave of water, threatening to drown me."

"That's why you cough like that, gasping for breath?"

I nod. "I know it doesn't make any sense." I know it sounds crazy. Is this how schizophrenics feel, seeing people and hearing voices no one else sees or hears?

"I didn't say that," Sam says. "So that's what you're scared of? Drowning?"

I shake my head. "It's not actually the drowning that scares me. Even though I feel like I'm drowning, I *know* I'm on dry land. It feels awful, but deep down I *know* I can't actually drown."

"So what is it, then? What are you scared of?"

I pause. Eight therapists, and no one ever *really* asked me that. They all thought it went without saying: Claustrophobics are scared of being trapped. They may not have always agreed about *why*: a cry for help after the divorce, a bid for attention after Wes was born (even though the claustrophobia had been around longer than Wes). One therapist suggested that I'd felt trapped as a baby in the birth canal and recommended rebirthing therapy. (I only saw him once.)

"I'm scared that no one will find me. That I'll be left behind all alone."

Just like Eliza on the ledge.

"What do you think will happen if no one comes to save you?"

"I'll be trapped forever." Sam opens his mouth, but I speak before he can. I'm not whispering anymore. "I know it's irrational. Eventually someone's going to knock on the bathroom door. Sometimes I'm not even alone, like when I try to take the subway or an elevator." Or when there's a group of girls on the other side of the door, holding it shut.

Sam shakes his head. "I was going to say that you can find yourself. *You* know where you are."

"I'm not sure I do. I mean, obviously, I know where I am. But I don't *believe* I can get out on my own. And I'm not wrong—when I'm having an attack, I'm pretty much paralyzed. Turning a doorknob feels as complicated as long division."

"What if I promise to always come looking for you?" In the darkness, Sam's teeth almost glow when he smiles.

I smile back. No one—not the therapists, not my parents—has ever offered that before.

"This is the closest I've ever come to a sleepover," I say suddenly, surprising myself.

"What?"

"You know how girls start having slumber parties in the third grade? Where they stay up all night and tell each other secrets, that kind of thing?"

"Sure. I used to hide in my bedroom when my little sister and her friends took over the living room."

"I never went to one of those. Couldn't risk the whole sleeping-bag scenario."

Sam furrows his brow. "Couldn't the parents have found a way to make you feel comfortable? Let you sleep in a bed or something?"

I shake my head, but the truth is, I never asked.

"So you never told anyone your secrets?"

I shrug, feeling my left shoulder rise against his right one. "Therapists."

"They don't count."

"No," I agree. "They don't." I close my eyes, remembering the way Eliza, Arden, and Erin sat close in the meadow when they painted their nails, whispering to one another and giggling.

"Tell me a secret now," Sam says softly.

I open my eyes. "I wanted to be Eliza's friend." I guess it's not a secret if you believe the rumors Eliza spread: that I was a stalker, obsessed with her since kindergarten. But if you don't believe the rumors, you'd probably wonder why I wanted to be friends with a girl who was so mean to me. *I* wondered it, and I was the one wanting it.

"Your turn," I say. "You tell me a secret."

Sam adjusts beside me. I lean back, his arm like a pillow beneath my neck. Quietly, he says, "I didn't want her to die." It takes me a second to realize he's not talking about Eliza. "She was in pain constantly. The doctors had already told us it was hopeless, only a matter of time. My aunt prayed for her to be taken quickly, mercifully. But I just couldn't. A good person would've wanted it to be fast, wanted her suffering to end. But I—" Sam takes a deep, raspy breath. "I didn't care how much pain she was in—I mean, I cared,

I hated it—but I would've let my mom live with all that pain just to have her with me for another day."

"That doesn't mean you're not a good person."

"It doesn't?" Sam chuckles. It reminds me of Mack's laugh: sour and joyless. I suppress a shiver.

"Of course not. You loved her. You didn't want to lose her." Sam nods, but I can tell he doesn't entirely believe me. "What was wrong with her?" I ask finally.

"Cancer. Esophageal cancer."

"It sounds awful."

"It was."

"I'm so sorry."

"I guess these aren't the types of secrets they tell at sleepover parties."

I smile. "I wouldn't know."

He pauses. "What else did you miss out on because of your claustrophobia?"

"Let me think . . . actually, my parents stopped hugging me at some point. They were scared I might freak out."

"Your parents don't hug you?"

"Not really. I got a one-armed nonhug at the airport before I left."

"That sucks."

"My mom wouldn't let me hold Wes when he was a baby just in case I had an attack with him in my arms. And I never had a best friend, not since first grade." Suddenly, I can't stop listing my nevers. "Never had an inside joke. Never snuck out after curfew. My parents didn't even have to give me a curfew." Sam grins. "Never slow-danced. Never held hands with a boy. Never been kissed."

I feel Sam's arm stiffen beneath me. Even though it's dark in here, I'm sure he can tell I'm blushing because my skin is hot.

I started practicing kissing on the pillow when I was ten, after I saw a girl on a TV show doing it. Back then, I didn't know that my status as the class freak would keep me from getting kissed at school dances and parties in middle school and high school. I didn't know that I wouldn't actually attend school dances and parties. Back then, I still believed that one of my therapists was going to cure me. I still thought I'd be normal like everyone else by the time I turned thirteen. But thirteen came and went, and therapist after therapist came and went, but my phobia stayed, and the boys stayed away.

"Sorry," I mumble, looking down at the lump my knees make under the covers. "I didn't mean to make things super awkward."

Sam laughs, a real laugh this time. "You didn't. I'm just surprised."

Now it's my turn to laugh.

Sam sits up, bringing me with him. "No, I mean, now that you say it, it makes sense—I see how you must've worried it might bring on an attack, being that close to someone. It never occurred to me, that's all."

"What do you mean?"

"Well, you know . . ." Sam pauses, and now I feel *his* skin getting warmer. "Because you're so . . . because of how you look."

"How I look?"

"Come on, Elizabeth, don't make me say it." Sam groans. "Because you're so pretty."

I open my mouth to laugh again, but no sound comes out.

"I mean, I don't mean to sound sexist or anything. But I just mean, oddswise, I'd figured someone at your old school asked you out. You've got that long dark hair and your eyes—"

"Are nothing like Eliza's," I finish.

Sam furrows his brow. "What do Eliza's eyes have to do with it?"

I can't remember a time when I didn't compare my eyes to Eliza's. Mine are ringed with brown and hers are ringed with blue. "Hers are prettier," I explain simply.

Were prettier.

Sam shrugs. "Hers were different." A cool gust of wind blows into the room. Sam pulls the covers over us. "Not better."

"Anyway, it wasn't, like, a choice I made. I wasn't avoiding boys because I thought getting too close to them wouldn't bring on an attack. I'm close to you now and I'm okay." I bite my lip.

I feel Sam's muscles shift as he nods. "True." He pauses, then turns to face me suddenly, his mouth barely an inch away from mine. I feel his breath on my cheeks. "Maybe I can help you with another one of those nevers."

Before I can answer, his lips are on mine. Warm and soft, and gentler than I'd imagined. He moves slowly, waiting for me to open my mouth before he opens his. His left arm was already around me, but now he brings his right arm to meet it, keeping his grip loose just in case. He presses his hands onto my back, and I lean against him, letting him hold me up.

Sam shifts so that his hands are on my cheeks. The ends of his dreads brush my shoulders. They're softer than I thought they'd be.

Does this actually count as my first kiss? Sam's just doing me a favor, crossing one of those nevers off my list like he said. But I guess a favor-for-a-friend kiss is better than nothing.

Was this how Eliza felt when Mack kissed her? Did she feel his kisses in her belly? Did the skin on her fingertips tingle when she pressed them against Mack's chest?

Sam pulls away finally, leaning his head against the wall behind us. He falls asleep before I do, his arms still around me. The breeze keeps blowing through my open window, but I feel warm.

I roll over, my back against Sam's front. His arm drapes over me, loose and warm. Nothing like Mack's grip when he dragged me into his house this afternoon, nothing like Mack squeezing me so tightly in my dream.

Sam's breathing is steady and calm. I can feel his heartbeat.

But when I close my eyes, Mack's icy blue gaze is still there. I still see him looking over the cliff, watching Eliza plummet.

Sam might be right. It's possible that Mack had nothing to do with what happened to Eliza.

But *might* isn't a good enough reason to keep quiet.

ELIZA

reflexes

Why can't I sleep?

Why do I feel more and more awake?

To pass the time, I think about Mack.

The first time he kissed me, I didn't mean to kiss him back. He caught me by surprise. After all, until then he'd seen me mostly in the wee hours of the morning when I was in my pj's or workout clothes with my hair in a messy bun, using my ID to open the gate so that they wouldn't have to scale it, which made getting wood off the property significantly easier.

So much easier, in fact, that I managed to negotiate a 12 percent split with Riley, who'd offered me 5 percent to begin with. I didn't need the money, but driving up my price made me feel as though I'd done something productive.

On this particular day, I'd driven up to the guys' bungalow in Capitola to collect my share.

When I got to their house, Riley was nowhere in sight.

Mack's lips tasted like salt water and sunblock; he'd been out surfing before dawn that morning.

By the time I realized what he was doing, it was too late. I was already kissing him back and putting my arms around him, like my brain had no control over my lips or my tongue or my hands.

Though I guess I shouldn't have been surprised that my body was rebelling against my brain.

By that point, my brain had become completely useless.

Well, not completely.

I still managed to get out of bed every morning—even if I barely slept—and still got dressed and went to class and studied and hung out with my friends.

I still breathed in and out and ate at mealtimes and laughed at jokes and teared up at those ASPCA commercials with the underweight puppies in cages.

But all those things had become reflexive somehow, like the doctor knocking your knee with a hammer.

Was that why I returned Mack's kiss?

Was it just a reflex?

In the days that followed, I tried to undo what we did.

I laughed when Mack said I was special.

I told him I could line up a dozen girls from the junior class at Ventana Ranch exactly like me.

Girls who were just as smart and pretty and rich.

Mack said I was crazy if I thought that was why he called me special.

You might have me there, I said. I tapped my forehead. *Certifiable.*

Mack laughed, then kissed me again. And again, I kissed him back.

Still, over the months we spent together, I tried to show him all the things that were wrong with me. It wasn't easy because my disease didn't look like it did in the movies: I still went to class and got straight As and laughed with my friends and was the life of the party. I'd read enough on the subject to know that I wasn't the only person whose depression looked like this. Depressives like me were like highly functioning alcoholics: no one knew our dirty little secret, no one could have guessed the self-destructive thoughts that took root in our minds, the sleepless nights where our broken brains kept us endlessly awake.

It was so easy to hide in plain sight.

Sometimes I wonder how things might have ended up if my disease looked different from the outside.

Eventually I told Mack all about my family: my overly medicated dad,

and my shallow mom,

and the uncle running for Congress whose seat had practically been bought and paid for.

I told him that I hardly slept and sometimes didn't shower

for days at a time. (I'd told my roommates I was conserving water and soon they were skipping showers, too. They never knew that sometimes the simple act of showering seemed overwhelming.)

I told Mack I didn't care whether the trees we cut up lived or died and that I didn't need the money, hadn't spent a cent, had stashed it all beneath the thin mattress in my dorm room because money was meaningless to me, just pieces of paper that had always been there when I needed them. I didn't offer to share my cut with Mack, because I knew he'd interpret the gesture as more proof that I wasn't as bad as I said I was.

But no matter how selfish and screwed up I was, Mack didn't care. Or maybe I should say he didn't *mind*, because he certainly seemed to *care*.

About me, I mean. He cared about me.

He shook his head and laughed, hugged me tight and kissed me until I forgot what I'd been trying to tell him in the first place. Mack never complained when I called, wide awake, in the middle of the night, and he held my hand when we walked around Capitola, where I was spending more and more of my time, but he never asked to meet my friends or my parents.

Mack felt things so intensely: love and anger, right and wrong.

All the things that had always been fuzzy to me were clear to him.

Sometimes when he spoke, I felt like a visitor from a foreign land, frightened and disoriented because I didn't speak the language.

He was so surprised when I invited him to Christmas Eve dinner.

I would've hated myself then, if I cared about anything enough to hate it.

I hadn't introduced him to my friends, and suddenly I was inviting him to meet the parents. If he thought it was odd, he didn't say so. Maybe by then, he'd just accepted that I was a strange girl.

I couldn't stay with him: I would only hurt him.

But he had to be the one to break up with me.

He had to hate me so that he wouldn't miss me, wouldn't hold out hope that I'd change my mind, want him back.

It would be what I deserved.

After two months together, he still didn't believe I was as worthless as I insisted I was.

On Christmas Eve, however, I'd be able to show him.

I thought he'd see what my family was like, and finally run the other way like he should have before.

I thought he'd see how my parents had spoiled me— spoiled like *ruined*, like fruit left on the vine to rot—and finally understand why Riley always said I was a brat from a fancy school who had no business being with Mack.

I didn't think he would show up for Christmas dinner in

an ill-fitting sport coat instead of one of his usual ripped-up tees,

politely hand my mother a bottle of wine and a bouquet of flowers,

laugh at my dad's nonsensical jokes and praise my mom for the ham that had so obviously been cooked by someone else,

then finally pull me aside and tell me that he loved me when he thought no one else could hear.

I'd expected him to be disgusted, but instead he was trying to make a good impression.

That's when I realized I would have to do something really awful, something bad enough that he would storm out of the house in a rage.

Something to make him see that he was wasting his time, loving someone like me.

I didn't deserve his love.

I didn't deserve anyone's love.

I had to make him leave.

When my mother said, *You're dangerous for my daughter,* in her icy, deep voice, I saw my chance. Mack looked at his shoes then—work boots, the only non-flip-flop shoes he owned—dirty on our light-colored carpet. But I stood up and yelled and screamed, just like any other teenage girl. *You don't know what you're talking about!* I cried. *Since when do you know the difference between healthy and dangerous?*

I didn't give her enough time to tell Mack *why* she thought he was dangerous before we stormed out of the house. I already knew why and if Mack heard he might actually take her side and that wasn't how I wanted things to end.

If things ended that way, he might go on loving me, waiting for me to get better, believing I would get well enough that we could be together again.

I didn't want that for him.

I wanted him to give up on me.

I wanted him to hate me.

I didn't want him to miss me.

Did I already know, on Christmas Eve, that I wasn't going to get better?

ELLIE

sunday, march 20

When I wake up, late-morning sun streams through the window and Sam is gone. Maybe I dreamed the whole thing. Maybe I'm still dreaming now—otherwise how can I explain his scent on my sheets?

I pinch myself. Definitely awake. Awake and alone.

Well, what did you expect, Ellie? It was a pity kiss, a favor-for-a-friend kiss, a check-something-off-your-to-do-list kiss. Just because *you* felt something doesn't mean he did.

Get it together, Sokoloff. It was No Big Deal. People kiss all the time, and it doesn't always mean something. They kiss at parties playing Spin the Bottle and Seven Minutes in Heaven (according to movies from the 1980s) and then they're just friends afterward. (Okay, in the movies they usually fall madly in love, but I'm not in a movie. Or if I am, it's definitely not a romantic comedy.)

People kiss, and then they move on. It happens all the time.

Besides, you've got more important things to worry about. Like getting questioned by the police and maybe accusing a man of murder. What are you doing worrying about a kiss?

Get your priorities straight, Elizabeth!

Now Sam even has me calling myself Elizabeth.

I roll over, grab my phone, and pull up my most recent text message. I hesitate for a second, then send a text to Dean Carson, just like I made up my mind to do before I fell asleep last night.

The detective tells Sam to wait in his room while he talks to me. Dean Carson sits beside me on the scratchy couch. (I try to imagine that in the catalog: *Our dean is so devoted to his students that he spends his Sundays at their side while the police interrogate them. Come to Big Sur, where your dean can act as proxy for your parents!*) The policeman—Detective Roberts, he introduces himself, and anyway I recognize his voice from the night after they found Eliza—stands, a notepad in his hand just like in the movies.

Other than the notepad, Detective Roberts doesn't look like detectives in the movies or on TV look. He's not wearing a uniform, just jeans and a tweedy sport coat. He looks more like a college professor than a hardened cop. I stare at his hips, trying to make out the bulge where his gun must be.

"I wish you'd told me about your claustrophobia sooner,"

Dean Carson admonishes. "It's school policy that students disclose any medical conditions on their applications."

Is Dean Carson saying that if they'd known about my claustrophobia they wouldn't have let me into Ventana Ranch?

"I never really thought about it as a medical condition," I answer slowly, and I don't take my eyes off Detective Roberts.

"I'd never have asked you to come to Professor Clifton's office had I known."

This morning, I texted the dean to explain why I couldn't come to Professor Clifton's office. He offered to conduct the interview here instead.

I hear voices in the hallway beyond the closed door to our suite. Someone must've seen the dean and Detective Roberts knocking on my door. They're probably all wondering why I'm being questioned in my room instead of in Professor Clifton's office like everyone else. I bet they think it's something much worse than a fear of small spaces. They probably think this is proof that I'm a suspect.

If I admitted I was claustrophobic now, I bet they wouldn't even care.

It would be far from the worst thing they believe about me.

Detective Roberts flips his notepad open. "It's come to my attention that you and Eliza Hart had something of a history."

I don't say anything. It's not exactly a question.

Dean Carson nods furiously at my side. "This was brought to our attention by—" He pauses, as though considering whether to say which of my classmates confided in him. He must decide against it, because he finishes, "By a few of your peers. I've been wanting to ask you about it, Ellie, but—" He gestures toward the detective, as if to say *but I'm not the one asking questions here.* He looks frustrated, like he thinks he should be the one in charge. His turf, his students. *As do I.* His suspicions.

"Would you agree with that assessment, Elizabeth?" Detective Roberts asks. "That you two had a history?"

"It's Ellie."

"I'm sorry?"

"Everyone calls me Ellie." Everyone but Sam.

"My mistake. Ellie. Would you agree that you and Eliza Hart had a history?"

"We went to elementary school—" I pause, correct myself. "Kindergarten and first grade together."

"When did you discover that you would be attending Ventana Ranch together?"

"The day we moved into the dorms. I saw her name on her door." I try to say it like it's no big deal. Like I wasn't excited to reunite with my long-lost best friend.

"You didn't know she was coming here before that?" Dean Carson interjects. Detective Roberts looks exasperated at another interruption from the teacher.

"No."

Dean Carson frowns dubiously. I imagine the questions he's not asking: *Even with Facebook and Twitter and Instagram and whatever the heck else you kids are up to nowadays?*

And the answer I don't give: *We were seven years old the last time we saw each other. I didn't exactly have a Snapchat account back then.*

"No one would blame you if you wanted to be near Eliza," he says finally. "She was a very special girl."

Of course they would blame me. They've blamed me since I got here.

The dean continues, "She was the kind of girl everyone wanted to be friends with." His Adam's apple bobs up and down as he swallows.

My stomach sinks. I imagine another line in the catalog: *Come to Big Sur, where the dean of students will almost, sort of accuse you of stalking the most popular girl in school!*

Detective Roberts taps the end of his pen against his notepad.

This isn't how I thought this interview would go. Last night, in addition to deciding to tell the dean about my claustrophobia, I made up my mind to tell the detective about Mack. I imagined he would sprint out of the room and into a police car, sirens blaring, speeding up Highway 1 all the way to Capitola.

"Ellie?" the detective prompts. "Can you answer my question?"

I look at him blankly. He repeats, "Why do you suppose your classmates thought you had some kind of problem with her?"

I open my mouth to tell him about Mack, but the words that come out instead are: "I don't know."

Detective Roberts scribbles something in his notebook. He's probably not supposed to let the person he's questioning see when he's frustrated, but it's written all over his face. I wouldn't want to be the detective assigned to sort out the difference between teenage gossip and the truth, either.

I imagine how he'd react if I told him that Eliza spread rumors about me. Maybe he'd roll his eyes at more teenage nonsense.

Or maybe he'd think that one girl spreading hurtful rumors about another girl was enough to give that other girl a motive for murder.

"The girls I spoke with seemed pretty convinced that there was something going on between you two. One in particular said that you were . . . *interested* in Eliza."

I bet it was Arden. And I bet she said *obsessed*, not interested.

"Any idea why she would say that?"

"I don't know," I say again. It's the truth. I don't know why Eliza told everyone on campus that I'd followed her to Ventana Ranch. It's not like she needed to invent a reason to be the center of attention. Everyone already paid attention to her.

Again, the detective taps his pen against his pad. "Don't you think it's strange that one of your classmates would say that if it wasn't true?"

I have a name. *Two* names. Mack and Riley. I've seen their faces. I could describe them for a police sketch artist. I have an address. Eliza's fingerprints are probably all over that bungalow. Maybe there's a lone strand of her hair still twisted in the sheets of Mack's bed.

"I have to tell you something," I begin. The words come slower than I expected.

"Yes?" Detective Roberts asks eagerly. Dean Carson's eyes are lit up in expectation, like he's waiting for a full confession.

My mouth is dry; I get up and walk to the kitchenette, pour myself a glass of water, take a few gulps, then turn back to face the detective and the dean. Sweat pools at the back of my neck. Why is it taking me so long to tell them about Mack?

Then it hits me: I haven't said anything yet because *I don't want to do that to Eliza.*

Once I tell, they'll know Eliza helped steal the redwood burls.

They'll know her secret boyfriend wasn't a Stanford football star, but a thief.

It will change the way her parents and her friends and her teachers will remember her.

They might stop saying things like *She was a very special girl.*

Why do I care what they say about her? I should only care about putting her killer—her *real* killer, not me—away. What's *wrong* with me?

Another answer hits me, as sudden and shocking as a slap: *I want Eliza to like me.*

Even now, even after all the rumors she spread and the fact that she's, you know, no longer with us, I'm still holding out hope that maybe we'll pick up where we left off in kindergarten and be friends again.

"Ellie?" Dean Carson says. "What is it you'd like to tell us?"

"I know Arden told you about Eliza's boyfriend," I begin. Despite the water, my mouth is still sticky and dry. "But she didn't know his name." I swallow. "I do."

"Oh?" Detective Roberts asks.

"Yeah, it was Mack—I don't know his last name, but I know what he looks like and where he lives."

The detective narrows his eyes. "And how do you know that?" Now he thinks I'm obsessed with Eliza, too. This is all wrong.

"Yesterday Sam and I were hiking on the Y trail. We heard voices. At first we thought it was other students, but then we realized it was a couple of strangers. They were talking about Eliza. They used her ID to get onto the property so they could get to the redwoods."

Detective Roberts nods as if to say *keep going.*

I squeeze my hands together. My palms are sweating. Why am I so nervous? I didn't do anything wrong. "Sam and I followed them off campus—"

"You did *what?* Do you have any idea how dangerous

that was?" Dean Carson interjects, but the detective shoots him a look, shutting him up.

"To a town up the coast called Capitola. They said Eliza worked with them, letting them on campus—that's what the money in her dorm room was. And Mack said they were a couple, sort of."

Detective Roberts is unfazed. "We're already aware of Eliza's relationship with Alexander McAdams, more commonly called Mack."

I let out a breath. The police already found Mack.

They already know more than I do: They know Mack's real name.

The police will arrest him.

The police will find out what really happened.

"Do you think he hurt Eliza?" I ask breathlessly.

"I can't share the details of our investigation," Detective Roberts answers finally. "However," he continues, his gaze fixed on me, "the sort of vigilante investigation you and your roommate engaged in yesterday is foolish." *Vigilante* sounds like something out of a movie, like Superman and Batman. I definitely didn't feel like a superhero, crouched in the driveway of that bungalow. "I need you to promise me you won't do anything like that again."

Now, when I rub my hands together, it's not because I'm nervous. I'm *frustrated*. I just handed the police the name of a suspect—they already knew about him, but still—and the detective is acting like the fact that I followed Mack to Capitola matters more than the fact that he killed Eliza.

Maybe killed her.

Probably.

Possibly.

I never knew that doubt was physically uncomfortable. My skin actually itches with it.

Detective Roberts gestures for me to sit back down on the couch, across from where he's standing. I can practically hear him thinking, *Stupid kids.* He shifts gears, asking the more obvious questions: Did I see anything strange in the days before Eliza's body was found? (No.) Did I notice anyone unfamiliar on campus? (No.) Did I hear anything suspicious—the sound of a struggle, a girl shouting for help? (Again, no.)

He doesn't ask whether I fought with Eliza last week, even though Erin and Arden must have told him they thought I was the person Julian saw.

He doesn't ask anything like *where were you at eleven p.m. on March fourteenth* because they don't know exactly what time Eliza went over the cliffs. Not that I would have much of an alibi: I was in my room, studying, alone.

I squirm in my seat, crossing and then uncrossing my legs, picking imaginary pieces of lint off my sweater.

If Eliza were here, she'd probably have Detective Roberts eating out of her hand by the time it was over. When he left, he'd probably apologize for taking up so much of her time.

Eventually, Detective Roberts flips his notebook closed. "I guess that's all for now."

That's all? "What about Mack?" I ask. My voice sounds small.

"As I said, we're aware of him."

Being *aware* isn't enough. "Aren't you going to investigate him? Arrest him? Interrogate him?" My voice is high-pitched, desperate. "I could describe him. Tell you where he lives." Though if they're already aware of him, they probably already know what he looks like and where he lives.

"As I said, I can't divulge the details of our investigation." He flips his notebook back open. "Why don't you ask your roommate to come in?"

I shake my head in disbelief, momentarily frozen with shock and disappointment. Finally, I get up and walk across the room, knock on Sam's door.

I haven't actually talked to him today. Avoiding him was easier than I expected, considering that we live together. I just stayed in my room until Dean Caron and the detective got here, and then *they* asked Sam to leave.

"Come in," Sam shouts. I open his door. Sam's lying on his bed with his long legs crossed, holding a textbook above his head. It's the first time I've ever seen him studying.

I linger in the doorway. I'm not sure I've ever actually stepped inside his room, though I know other girls have from time to time—like Sam said, the walls are thin.

Sam probably doesn't even know exactly how many girls he's kissed.

"Detective Roberts is ready for you." Six words.

Sam swings his legs over the side of the bed and stands. His dreads are pulled into a tight bun at the base of his neck.

"I told the detective about Mack," I blurt quickly. Alexander McAdams.

Sam nods. "Thought you would."

"He already knew about him. He wouldn't tell me if they think he did it."

If this were a movie, they'd have arrested Mack by now. Put him under hot lights and sweated a confession out of him.

If he did it. My itchy doubt feeling is back again.

Sam gives my hand a tiny squeeze as he walks past me, then takes my place on the couch.

"You can leave now, Ellie," the detective says. "If I have more questions, I'll be in touch."

I nod, heading into my own room. I sit on the edge of the bed and look at the hand Sam just squeezed. At first I thought he was squeezing it to reassure me—a silent sort of *everything's going to be okay*—but now I'm not so sure. Because his palm—always so warm and dry—was sweaty.

Maybe my roommate is even more nervous about getting questioned by the police than I was.

ELLIE

sunday, march 20

"I'm sorry," I say as soon as Detective Roberts and Dean Carson leave.

"What for?"

"I was so caught up in how scared I was about getting questioned that I forgot you were nervous about it, too."

Sam shrugs. "Let's just say it wasn't my favorite part of the day." He reaches up and undoes the elastic holding his dreads, then leans back on the couch.

I nod. "I'm still sorry. I'm new to this whole . . ." I pause, searching for the right word. Then I worry that Sam thinks I'm pausing because of our kiss last night, like I think it means something more than it did and I'm about to call him my boyfriend, so I rush and say, "To this whole *friend* thing. I haven't really had any in a while."

Sam nods. "I know what you mean."

All this time, I thought Sam was effortlessly friends with everyone. I mean, he's the kind of person that people are drawn to: cool, nonchalant, smart. But he doesn't seem to consider any of our classmates *real* friends.

"Do you have a lot of friends back home? In Oakland, I mean, not Mill Valley."

"I didn't really stay in touch after Mom died." Sam shrugs. "Or maybe they didn't want to stay in touch with me once I left."

"Do you miss them, though? Your old friends?"

"Sometimes. It was easier with them. They knew me my whole life, you know what I mean?"

I shake my head. "Not really. It wasn't easier for me with the kids from my old school, and they'd known me almost my whole life. It's easier with you," I add shyly.

Sam doesn't say anything. I decide to change the subject. "How do you think the detective knew about Mack?"

Sam shrugs again. "The police could've found his name in her phone."

"Oh, right."

"Or maybe he went to them himself after he heard Eliza died."

"What do you mean?"

"It's less suspicious than waiting for the police to track him down themselves, right?"

"I guess." Should I have been more forthcoming with Detective Roberts? Maybe I should've opened by telling him that Eliza and I hadn't gotten along here at Ventana Ranch. "Do you think they arrested him?"

Sam shakes his head. "I think if they'd made any actual arrests, it would be on the news. I don't think they can keep that kind of thing secret."

"But he should've at least been arrested for the tree stuff." I'm so frustrated I want to stomp my foot.

"I know. I don't get it, either."

"What do they know that we don't?"

"I guess a lot. I mean, he *is* a detective." Sam grins.

And I'm obviously not. My first try at detective work—following Mack and Riley to Capitola—and I didn't even have anything worthwhile to share with the police. "All that for nothing."

"Not nothing," Sam counters. "We learned something from Mack."

"Nothing useful."

Sam shakes his head. "He said Eliza was scared of you."

I take a step back. I assumed Sam thought—like I did—that Mack was lying. What reason could Eliza possibly have had to be scared of me?

Or does Sam think talking to Mack was useful because Mack has some secret ammunition against me, proof that I am all the things Eliza said I was? Maybe I had it backward: Maybe *Mack* told the police about *me*.

Man, was she scared of you.

Detective Roberts certainly seemed more interested in learning about my relationship with Eliza than about Mack's.

Sam continues, "Mack said you were there when something happened. When *what* happened?"

Maybe Sam told the police he suspected me, too. Maybe he's been pretending to be my friend this whole time, strategically gaining my trust so that I'd confess.

"Mack said whatever it was had to do with Eliza's father, right?"

Maybe he promised the police he'd get something out of me. Maybe they told him what to say. I shake my head.

"What do you mean, no?" Sam asks. "That's what Mack said."

"I mean, I can't believe that after everything that's happened, you actually think I hurt Eliza!"

Sam knits his eyebrows together. "What are you talking about?"

"I hate to disappoint you, but I have no idea why she'd be scared of me. I don't remember anything that happened with her dad." I mean, I remember some things. Fingerpainting in the playroom. The fight he had with his wife while I hid beneath the dining room table. "I was just a little kid, Sam. What do you expect me to remember?"

Sam crosses the room and takes my hands in his. His skin is warm, like he's been lying out in the sunshine, not hanging out in our dorm room.

"It's easier for me, too," he says finally.

"Huh?" I ask dumbly.

"It's easy for me. With you."

"Oh." I exhale.

Quietly, he explains, "I know you were only five years old when you met Eliza. It's not your fault you don't remember." He pulls me to sit beside him on the couch so that we're facing each other. "But I do think there's something Eliza remembered, something you saw that she didn't want you to see."

I swallow the lump rising in my throat. "But I don't remember—"

"I know," Sam agrees. "But *she* didn't know that. The way I see it," he continues, "Eliza must have spread those rumors to try to keep you quiet—right? I mean, why say you're a pathological liar unless there was something she thought you might say that she didn't want everyone to believe?"

Oh my God, could *that* be why she started the rumors?

"But if she'd just told me—" I can't finish the sentence, not out loud; the lump in my throat is too big and the end of the sentence is too sad. If she'd just told me, I would have kept her secret. I could've been her friend. Maybe I could have helped her. I drop my head and press the heels of my hands into my eyes.

I have to stop trying to befriend her. She's gone.

Sam says, "We need to find out what she thought you knew."

I raise my head. My vision is blurry. "But I told you I don't remember."

"I know," Sam concedes. "But somebody else does."

"No way," I say after Sam shares his idea with me. "That's nuts."

Sam shakes his head. "I'll admit it's desperate, but it's not crazy."

"They don't want us at the funeral."

"They can't stop us. They invited the whole school to attend." The administration sent the student body an email with all the details.

The police released her body to her parents after they determined her cause of death. The funeral is scheduled for three days from now, at a Catholic church in San Francisco, the only place big enough to hold the enormous crowd the Harts are expecting. In the email with all the information about the service, the administration said they were even providing buses to take students and faculty to and from the church.

There's a wake, too, between now and then, but the school isn't providing transportation to that. I had to Google what a wake was: It's a vigil held by friends and family the night before a Catholic funeral.

"They may have invited the whole school, but that doesn't mean they want *me* at the funeral." I shudder, remembering what happened at the memorial service. "And Detective Roberts said we shouldn't do any more investigating on our own. We could get into trouble."

"I'm not talking about going all Batman and Robin. You're just going to ask the man a few questions."

"Erin and Arden won't even let me in the door, let alone close enough to her father to ask him about something that happened over a decade ago. Besides, I'm really not okay with ambushing a grieving father at his daughter's funeral."

I've only been to one funeral before, when my grandfather died. I was fourteen and Mom didn't think a funeral was a place for children, but Wes insisted on going, which meant I had to go, too.

I gasped when I saw the plain pine casket at the front of the sanctuary. My grandfather hadn't been a big man—only five foot six inches tall, and he'd probably shrunk a little as he got older and his bones compressed under the weight of gravity—but the box seemed so small. Too small.

I froze halfway down the aisle, even though everyone was looking at me. I tugged at the collar of my black dress, at least half a size too tight. My lungs felt wet. Was it possible to have a claustrophobia attack by proxy?

"Pull it together, El," my little brother admonished. "You're the only person in the world who goes to a funeral and makes it all about her." He was nine years old at the time.

Now Sam gets up and starts pacing. I have a sudden urge to touch him, to reach out and grab his hand, interlace our fingers while we work this out. I roll my shoulders down, and slide my hands beneath my legs.

It was a pity kiss, Ellie. And anyway, that's not what you should be thinking about right now!

My mouth still feels dry. I clear my throat.

"I have an idea," I announce finally. Sam stops pacing. "There's a sort of reception after the service, right?"

Sam reaches for my phone—he still has to replace the one Riley stole—and pulls up the email from the dean with the details. "It says mourners are welcome at the Hart house in Menlo Park to pay their respects to the family."

"What if we just showed up a little bit early? Like, we couldn't make it all the way into the city for the service, but we didn't want to miss our chance to share our condolences."

"But what for?" Sam asks. "If Eliza's dad's still at the funeral—"

"Mack said I saw something. Whatever it was, I probably saw it *there*, at the Harts' house, right? Maybe being there will help me remember."

After ten years and eight therapists, I know all about going back to the scene of an event to try to bring back blocked memories. My first therapist (Dr. Shapiro) took me to the building on West Seventy-Eighth Street where I had my first attack. She had me close my eyes and take in the smells—the sense of smell is the sense most related to memory, she said—and try to remember why I panicked, exactly what had scared me. But when I opened my eyes and saw that she'd led me into the elevator, I ran for my life and refused to talk for the rest of the day.

Sam tucks his dreads behind his ears, a gesture I've come to recognize: He's thinking. "Who will let us in, if everyone's at the funeral?"

"There will probably be someone there—a friend, a housekeeper, a caterer—setting up for all the guests they're expecting." The Harts wouldn't invite all those people over without offering food and drink, even at a time like this. "But other than that, we'd have the place to ourselves."

I wonder if the carpet in Eliza's room is that same champagne color. She had a full-size double bed, not a narrow twin like mine. Her sheets and blankets were cream—no little flowers or teddy bears dancing along the edges. It was all so grown-up. I climbed under that bed when we were playing hide-and-seek once. Of course, Eliza found me almost as soon as she shouted, *Ready or not, here I come!* Eliza always got to be It when we played and so I never won; it was her house, after all. She knew every nook and cranny better than I ever would.

How can I remember that and not remember whatever it was Eliza claims I saw? Did my ridiculous brain—the brain that thinks *closets* are dangerous—block it out for some reason, bury it under all the things I do remember? It feels like it's my mind I'm playing hide-and-seek with.

"That's not a bad idea," Sam concedes finally.

I just hope it works.

ELLIE

wednesday, march 23

I'm staring into my closet (standing safely outside of it) when the phone rings. "Mom, I'm kind of in a hurry." Sam and I are leaving in ten minutes, and I still haven't figured out what to wear.

"Oh, are you going to the funeral?"

I nod, even though obviously she can't see me. Sam and I thought it would be best if we left at the same time as everyone else. That way, if they see us at the Hart house later, we can just say we stood in the back of the church during the service because we didn't want to be in the way. It won't even look weird that we're taking Sam's car. Plenty of kids are driving their own cars instead of taking the buses.

Yesterday, a tow truck came onto the campus and picked up Eliza's car from the student parking lot. Maybe it'll be sitting in the Harts' driveway when we get there.

"Ellie?" Mom prompts.

"Yeah, Mom. I'm going to the funeral."

"Well, please pass my condolences along to the Harts."

"I will, Mom."

It's a lie. Of course I won't. And I wouldn't, even if I was going to the funeral for real. My mom knows that I'm not the kind of kid who feels comfortable doing things like passing along condolences. Not like Wes. Once, a teacher at my old school was out for a week when her father died, and Wes left a card on her desk saying how sorry he was for her loss. Later, she stopped me in the hallway to tell me how lucky I was to have such a considerate little brother.

Mom says, "I hope it won't be too hard for you, seeing your friend like that."

In our last conversation, she was quick to point out that Eliza wasn't my friend, but I don't remind her now. "I won't have to see her, not really."

"She was Catholic, wasn't she? Sometimes Catholics have an open casket."

Mom doesn't know, of course, that I'm not going to the church. I lean against my open closet door, looking at my clothes hanging neatly (messes make spaces look even smaller than they are).

I look down at my toes; the polish I painted on last week is chipped. I rub my forehead. Maybe I *am* a stalker, just like she said. I painted my nails a different color every week because that's what she did, too.

I wonder what color her nails are now.

"You've never seen a dead body before," Mom continues. "It might be tough on you."

My mom doesn't know that I saw Eliza's body when they pulled her up over the cliffs. In a casket, someone will have dressed her and done her makeup, brushed her hair and tried to make it look like she was just sleeping.

But no one could've mistaken the body on the cliffs for anything but a dead body.

Sam calls my name.

I reach into the closet and grab the first black thing I find. "Mom, I gotta go."

"Of course, honey, you don't want to be late."

"No," I agree. I close my eyes and imagine Eliza lying in a casket at the end of a long aisle, in between row after row of church pews. It looks like she's waiting for me. "I don't want to be late."

I'm wearing a black sleeveless dress that I picked out last summer, imagining I might wear it to a school dance one day—but that was back when I thought that California would cure me, when I still believed I might be popular here. I even thought there would be a boy who'd want to dance with me. That was before I remembered that it gets cold here and a summer dress won't last you all year round. Before I found out that no one at Ventana Ranch dresses up for school parties and before I knew that no one here would invite me anyway. The dress is at least an inch shorter on me than it was when I bought it last summer.

Eliza's clothes always fit perfectly. She probably cleaned out her closet every time she grew a centimeter. Sitting in the front seat of Sam's car, I tug the dress down past my pale knees. I'm so cold that I'm covered in goose bumps.

I glance sideways. Sam is wearing black pants and a light gray button-down shirt with a charcoal-gray tie. He seems just as at ease in these clothes as he does in the jeans and sweatshirts he usually wears. I wonder if his dad bought him a black suit for his mom's funeral. Maybe he wore this same tie.

"Can I ask you something?" Sam keeps his eyes on the road.

"Of course."

"Why do you give yourself claustrophobia?"

That's not the question I was expecting. But maybe he doesn't want to think about funerals. Maybe he's trying not to think about the last funeral he went to.

"I didn't give it to myself. It just happened to me."

"No, I mean—why do you induce your attacks sometimes?"

Oh, right. The thin walls between our bedrooms.

"One of my therapists practiced immersion therapy. I guess I think that if I make myself stand in the closet long enough, I'll just get used to it."

"Why would you want to get used to feeling that way?"

"Oh, I don't know, so that I can live a normal life?" Despite the cold, I roll down the window and feel the breeze off the Pacific fill the car. Driving north, we're on the inside of Highway 1, closer to the mountains than to the ocean. "I want to be able to ride on the subway and drive through tunnels and take elevators to high floors and kiss"—I blush wildly but keep talking, hoping he won't notice—"without worrying about feeling smothered."

"Did I make you feel smothered?" Sam sounds genuinely concerned. "I didn't mean to."

"No," I answer quickly.

"You could've told me if I did."

"I know," I say softly. Suddenly, I feel like crying. I bite my lip and stare out the window. The breeze blows my hair across my face. "I just don't want to be a freak anymore." I can barely make the words fit around the lump in my throat. I'm surprised Sam can hear me.

"I don't think you're a freak."

I laugh, but it comes out sounding like a cackle, the same sour sound I heard from Mack and Sam. I think about our classmates in the buses up ahead of us, heading to a funeral like it's a field trip. "You're in the minority," I say finally.

Sam shrugs. "I'm used to that." He takes his eyes off the road long enough to turn to me and grin.

I smile back. The lump in my throat shrinks.

ELLIE

wednesday, march 23

Food is laid out on tables set up in a row across the dining room. It's warm in here—there's a skylight letting the sun in—and the cheese is sweating under plastic wrap. They're waiting for more mourners to get here before they open the containers, though the housekeeper says we're welcome to help ourselves if we'd like. We apologized for being early. Sam explained that we must've mixed up the time, and she nodded warmly, as if to say *no one expects you to remember those details at a time like this.*

I don't recognize her. Maybe the Harts had a different housekeeper when I knew them. Or maybe she's just a temp, hired for the day to help out with all these guests. Maybe this woman never even met Eliza.

I recognize the dining room table, even though it's been pushed off to the side. I run my hands across the smooth dark wood. This table looks like something that should be in a mansion in England. It feels utterly out of place in this bright, sunny California home.

"Please excuse me." The housekeeper gestures to a few blank spots on the table, indicating food that has yet to be prepared. "I'm afraid there's still so much to do in the kitchen. Will you two be all right by yourselves until the others arrive?" She sounds so kind that I almost feel bad. Because we'd like nothing more than for her to disappear into another room, leaving us free to explore.

When the housekeeper is out of sight, Sam nods in the direction of the living room. The walls aren't the same color I remember; they've been painted a sort of dusky gray with cream-colored trim. Instead of the terra-cotta tile floors that cover so many California homes, the floors are hardwood, with an enormous antique-looking rug in the center of the room. I don't remember if this is the same couch, but I do recognize a carved ivory end table.

"Remember anything?" Sam murmurs.

"Just the end table."

Eliza once left a glass of apple juice on that end table and it left a water ring. Cassie, her babysitter, was worried that we'd get into trouble, but Eliza wasn't. She just moved a lamp so it covered the ring and told Cassie it was okay. I remember thinking that I'd never be as grown-up as Eliza. Even now, a decade later, I'd still be scared of getting yelled at by my mom if I ruined a piece of furniture. And none of our furniture is as nice as that end table.

At home—back in Manhattan—our living room walls

are littered with family photos. Framed pictures of Wes and of me as a baby, of my mother's parents, of her grandparents, whom she never met, who never made it out of Poland during the Second World War. The walls in the Hart living room are blank except for one enormous piece of modern art. I wonder how much it's worth.

We're not ostentatious, I remember Eliza saying to me once.

What's ostentatious?

It means we don't show off.

I nodded. Our kindergarten teacher said that nobody likes a show-off.

There are no knickknacks on the surfaces; at home, our end tables are covered in Wes's basketball trophies. (Mom is too proud of them to let Wes keep them in his own room. She wants them on display for everyone to see.)

The living room opens up into a more casual room. The den, I guess. Or maybe they called it the family room, I don't remember. I do remember sitting on the carpeted floor, staring up at the TV screen and watching Disney princess movies. Eliza had every princess movie, even the old ones that my parents thought were too boring. They were never boring (though now I shudder to think of Snow White encased in that glass coffin). Cassie brought us cookies and made us promise not to get crumbs on the carpet. I close my eyes and picture myself eating my cookie holding my paper towel up around my face like a bib, ready to catch any stray crumbs.

The cookies were store-bought, but not from a package like the cookies at my house. These cookies had come from a local bakery.

When I open my eyes, Sam is looking at me expectantly. I shake my head. Cookies aren't the kind of memories we're looking for.

We walk past a wall of sliding doors that lead out to the backyard. The deck where Eliza would drive her oh-so-cool electric car.

We turn into a long hallway.

"Bedrooms," I whisper, surprised by how certain I am. I remember Eliza's parents' room is at the end of the hall, behind double doors. But there are three doors between here and there: Eliza's room, a hall closet, and a third door that I don't remember. A guest room, maybe.

We head toward the first door. That's Eliza's room. Or it was, the last time I was here. For the second time today, I feel like I am stalking her, just like she said. Who else but a stalker would sneak into her room the day of her funeral?

"Sam," I whisper. "Is this—are we doing the right thing?"

"What do you mean?"

"It seems so . . . disrespectful. Going into her room like this. Without her permission."

Sam's face softens. "I know," he agrees, hesitating. "It's your call."

Finally, I turn the knob and open the door. I can tell Sam is holding his breath as we cross the threshold. He thinks my memories will come flooding back the instant we step inside.

It's more of a trickle than a flood. I remember Eliza's full-size sleigh bed, the wood as shiny and polished as it was when we were little. I remember the creamy wallpaper with subtle pink splashes that look sort of like abstract flower petals, and the thick champagne-colored carpet that was so soft Eliza once told me it was made of rabbit fur. For one whole day, I believed her.

But I don't think any of these memories explain why she was afraid of me.

"Still nothing?" Sam can't hide the disappointment in his voice.

I shake my head. "Nothing important."

I rub my hands up and down my bare arms. "Do you think Eliza's parents have come in here since she died?"

"I don't know. The police have probably been in here at least, right?"

I nod, imagining Detective Roberts in his tweed jacket, combing through the room in search of some insight into Eliza's life, some clue into her death.

I open the door to Eliza's bathroom. (En suite, of course.) The floor is covered in tiny white tiles, and her sink is the old-fashioned kind that doesn't have a cabinet beneath it. Luckily there's a window facing the front yard, so I don't have to hesitate before stepping inside. There's a shiny glass medicine cabinet, and I bite my lip when I open it, not sure what

225

I think I'm going to find. I try to think of something scandalous that might be hiding in there: Midol? Birth control pills?

But the medicine cabinet is empty. I mean, *empty*. There's not so much as a bottle of Advil. Was Eliza so perfect that she didn't even get headaches? Or maybe her parents already cleaned it out.

I go back into her room and open one of her drawers. It's full of clothes. Maybe her parents will wait months before they get rid of her clothes, her books, her belongings. Maybe next year they'll turn this into a guest room or a gym or a luxurious walk-in closet. Maybe it's only a matter of time before these four walls aren't *Eliza's Room* anymore.

Someday it will become just a room.

I step back into the center of the room and look around like a tourist taking in the streets of Manhattan.

"There aren't any pictures." It's even more bare than the living room.

"What do you mean?" Sam asks.

"No pictures of her with Arden and Erin or with the swim team. No posters of her favorite bands or school banners or—or anything."

"Maybe she didn't want to mess up the wallpaper."

I shrug. Maybe she didn't care enough about her friends to display photos of them. After all, she kept secrets from them, right? They didn't know about the trees, didn't know about Mack.

Didn't know the truth about me.

"Maybe . . ." I head for a closed door on the other side of her bed. Her closet. I remember it was a walk-in closet and not very practical for hide-and-seek because it was so big that even if I tried to hide behind her clothes she could see me.

There's a small round window at the end of the closet up by the ceiling, kind of like a porthole. Not much, but it's enough that maybe I can step inside without having an attack. If I leave the door open. And Sam comes with me.

The rods and shelves are stuffed with clothes. There's a big unopened box in the center of the closet. I see it was shipped from Ventana Ranch—someone must have packed up the belongings from her dorm room. I wonder if Erin or Arden kept an item or two for themselves before everything was sent away. A favorite sweater or T-shirt, something to remember their best friend by.

I point to a rod filled with dresses. "I used to hide there," I say. "Behind her clothes. But we were so little then that her clothes weren't long enough to cover me up." I get on my hands and knees. The closet is covered with the same champagne carpet. I breathe in: It smells the same, like cedar and lavender. Suddenly, I'm a first grader again, and listening for Eliza to call out, *Ready or not, here I come!* I used to press myself flat against this wall. I push aside the dresses.

"What the hell?" Sam says.

The wall where I used to hide isn't blank. It isn't even covered in wallpaper. It's covered in pictures. Some look like printed photos that Eliza took herself and some look like they've been ripped from magazine and newspaper articles. There are even a few drawings in there, sketches that maybe Eliza did herself.

There must be a hundred pictures here, layered on top of one another like a collage. Page after page, image after image of the woods around our campus.

Some of the pictures show tall trees, healthy, strong, and untouched. But others are pictures of butchered trees—the trees Eliza helped Riley and Mack gain access to. There are old-fashioned Big Sur postcards and one black-and-white picture of a tree with a tunnel carved into the bottom big enough for a car to drive through. There are pine needles and pinecones taped to the wall so the collage is three-dimensional.

"Wow," I breathe. "It must've taken her months to collect all this."

"Why do you think she did it?"

"No clue." In the center of the college is a row of photographs. An enormous tree, healthy and strong. The same tree with a burl gouged out of the center of its trunk, I guess after Riley and Mack did their dirty work. Another photo: The same tree's pine needles are turning brown, and the wound at its center is dark with sap. Another: The tree's branches are dipping downward, collapsing under their own weight, the weight they'd held up for decades before. Another: The wound is dry now, the wood so pale it looks almost like bone. The branches that dipped down are completely bare, unable to sustain even the life of a pine needle.

And a final photo, a selfie of Eliza with the tree behind her. She looks different. I mean, she's still beautiful blond Eliza, but she's not smiling. She isn't looking at the camera, but looking past it. Her eyes are completely blank, like she was trying to make her face look like the tree behind her.

Before I can stop myself, I reach out and pull that photo from the wall.

"What are you doing?" Sam asks.

I don't know. It's not like this is a particularly good picture of her. It's nothing like the pictures people pasted to their *Rest in Peace, Eliza Hart* posters back at school, nothing like the pictures people have been posting to social media since she was found: Eliza in between Erin and Arden with her arms overhead after a swim meet or grinning in the sunshine at the beach.

I slip the photo into my bag. I feel like I'm supposed to have it.

ELIZA

the butterfly effect

It's still cold but not as bad.

The air feels soft, like it's made of silk.

The pain isn't as sharp. It's dull, like I'm covered in bruises and someone or something is pressing against them.

And I'm tired. Not actually *sleepy*, but not so very wide-awake, either. Not quite so wired. More like a normal person feels around 3:00 p.m., when they need a hit of caffeine or a snack to make it through the afternoon.

My dad was on the Stanford swim team. I can't imagine him caring about something consistently enough to work as hard as he'd have had to work to make it on to the team, but I know it's true. I've seen pictures of him at meets and came across a box of medals in the closet in his office.

I started swimming because I thought it would make him happy, back when I still believed that anything I did made a difference. I was good, so good we thought maybe I could swim for Stanford one day, too.

Dad used to come to my meets. He didn't stand up and

cheer. He never argued with the coaches about how they were teaching us or complained that we'd been cheated when we lost. He just sat in the bleachers quietly. I'm not sure he even watched me swim. But he was always there. That was the most he could muster.

For him, it was a lot. He knew I was doing it for him, and showing up was as close as he could come to saying thank you.

But I'd failed. My swimming didn't make him happy.

When he was sick, nothing did.

Unless he was the other kind of sick. The kind that made him care so much it was scary. The doctors prescribed pills called mood stabilizers—I always thought that sounded more like some groovy recreational drug left over from the 1970s than a medically prescribed pill packed with chemicals—but he didn't like to take them.

I wonder what would've happened to me if I took the pills that were supposed to keep a patient calm. Can you care *less* than not at all?

I don't know if it was a trick of genetics or the result of growing up the way I did or some pernicious combination of the two, but I only ended up having half of what was wrong with him. I never had the caring-too-much problem.

Lucky me.

Not that I blamed him. I always believed it was my mother's fault.

She married him.

She had a child with him.

She stayed with him.

She kept his secrets.

And I did, too.

If I felt things, I think I'd feel sorry for what I did to Ellie Sokoloff at Ventana Ranch, making everyone hate her. It wasn't her fault she was at the house that day.

If Ellie Sokoloff hadn't been at the house that day, maybe she and I would have stayed friends.

We might have hatched a plan to keep her parents together and her family living in Menlo Park, just like kids in the movies.

Ellie and I could have made our way through elementary school hand in hand.

In middle school, she would've stood up and cheered at my swim meets.

She might have sat next to my dad and pointed out my lane in the water.

Maybe everything would have turned out differently if Ellie and I stayed friends. The butterfly effect and all that.

Maybe not.

I said I didn't plan this, and I wasn't lying.

I wasn't one of those angsty teenagers who sat around plotting and planning her death.

I didn't have a fascination with razor blades and I didn't dream of drowning—I didn't sleep enough to dream.

I didn't romanticize jumping off a bridge or driving my car into a tree.

But I did spend a lot of time thinking about sleep. I used to tiptoe into my roommates' bedroom in the middle of the night and watch them, their eyes blinking to show that they were in REM sleep and their chests rising and falling at a steady pace.

Sometimes I even made a small sound,

opened the window,

turned on the light,

just to see if they would wake up. But they went on sleeping and dreaming through the night, eight hours and more.

I don't know why I watched them.

Maybe I thought my brain could learn something,

or perhaps I was just jealous,

or I suppose I was just holding out hope that my poor brain would get some rest though osmosis.

It took me years to understand why Dad avoided half his meds. For a long time, I thought he was just careless. I didn't realize he was doing it on purpose.

He was willing to crash if it meant he got to fly first.

He loved the mania more than he loved me,

more than he loved my mother,

more than he loved anything at all.

He took up all the space in the house, breathed all the air. We watched him, waiting to see what was coming next: up or down or some tightrope walk in between.

I didn't want to be like him.

At first, I told my mother she was just being paranoid.

Just because I'm his daughter doesn't mean I'm like him.

But I was lying. I knew what it was. I just didn't want to admit it.

Mom got me pills. Sometimes I took them, but they never helped. She said I didn't give them a chance; they needed time to kick in. I said she'd never given me a chance.

Or maybe I just never had a chance.

ELLIE

wednesday, march 23

We close Eliza's door behind us. "Where to next?" Sam whispers.

"Maybe we should head back to the living room before the housekeeper catches us."

"You're giving up?"

"No, it's just . . . if Eliza's room didn't jar my memory, what will?" This is starting to feel hopeless.

"Mack said it had to do with her father, right?" Sam asks, and I nod. "Maybe we should head to his room. His and Mrs. Hart's, I mean."

Sam heads toward the double doors at the end of the hall, but I don't follow. *His room. His room.*

It was probably technically his office or his study, but Eliza called it *his room.*

We weren't allowed in there, but she showed it to me once, opening the door slowly like it was a secret passageway.

The third door, the one I thought might be a guest room—that was it. I rest my hand on the doorknob, cool and smooth beneath my skin. I hesitate. Mr. Hart's room was *off-limits*.

I open the door. There's no carpet in here and no area rugs, just the shiny hardwood floor. In the center of the room is an enormous wooden desk, but there's nothing on top of it, not a paper or file in sight. Not even a desk lamp.

"Elizabeth," Sam hisses from down the hall. "What are you doing?"

I don't answer. I'm not sure I *can* answer. It feels like my limbs have taken on a life of their own, like they're stepping into the room of their own accord and I don't have any say over it.

Sam slips inside, shutting the door behind us.

And the water rushes in.

I gasp desperately for breath. Sam puts his hands on my shoulders, trying to lock eyes with me, but I can't make my gaze be still.

"Shhh," Sam coos. He's trying to comfort me, but there's an edge to his voice.

I'm scaring him. I'm scaring *me*.

What's happening? *Why* is this happening?

I turn my head frantically, taking in every corner of the room. Mr. Hart's study isn't small. There are enormous floor-to-ceiling windows overlooking the backyard, framed by gauzy lace curtains.

Windows. Air.

I twist myself from Sam's grasp and head for the windows. I try to wrench one open, but my hands are trembling too hard. Finally, I rest my forehead against the smooth, cool glass.

I try to use my internal voice to self-soothe, try to think, *There, there, you'll be okay, you're safe.* But I can't hear the sound of my internal voice over my ragged attempts to breathe.

My knees go so weak that I start to slide down the glass. As I fall, my cheek brushes against one of the lace curtains.

They didn't used to be made of lace.

They used to be heavier, velvety.

I thought they were soft, softer even than the carpet Eliza claimed was made of fur.

I rubbed them against my face.

When? How could I when this room was off-limits?

My uneven breaths fog up the glass.

"Elizabeth?" Sam whispers. He reaches for me, but I smack his hands away.

The memory floods my mind:

It was spring. First grade was almost over, and I'd had dozens of playdates here at Eliza's house and had yet to win a single game of hide-and-seek. I was determined to find a hiding spot where Eliza wouldn't find me. Not beneath the dining room table or under Eliza's sleigh-shaped bed.

I rushed down the hallway, hearing Eliza's voice counting. *Ten, eleven, twelve . . .*

I had to hide before she got to twenty.

I can see my seven-year-old fingers gripping the brass doorknob. Can remember my decade-old logic: *She'll never find me in here.*

I shut the door and dove behind the curtains. I barely heard it when Eliza shouted *Ready or not, here I come!* but I could hear her feet shuffling across the carpet as she walked right past the door without so much as pausing. She must have looked for me in her room first, then her parents' room. Her footsteps faded as she made her way toward the living room.

I was so pleased with myself. Until I heard the door open. *How did she find me so fast?*

I stayed frozen in place, holding my breath so she wouldn't hear me.

But then it wasn't Eliza's bare feet I heard against the wooden floor. These footfalls were heavier. This person was wearing shoes.

I shifted so that I could see out through a gap in the curtains. I swallowed a gasp. It was Eliza's father.

I was going to be in so much trouble.

But *he* was the one who wasn't where he was supposed to be! He should have been at work. My dad never came home before dinnertime.

Except . . . sometimes Eliza's dad did. Like that time the year before when he came home and we all painted in Eliza's playroom.

But that day, he'd been laughing and smiling. Now his mouth was pressed into a straight line.

I decided to stay hidden. He'd leave eventually, and then I'd run into the hallway and tell Eliza that I'd been hiding under her bed the whole time, that she must've missed me when she looked under there. I'd even let her win if she insisted that it didn't count since she'd looked in my hiding place.

I just had to wait until Mr. Hart left the room.

It was warm behind the thick cloth. I peeked out and watched him remove his jacket and carefully hang it on a hook on the back of the door. He unbuttoned then rolled up the sleeves of his white shirt, revealing long white stripes going up and down his wrists. He poured himself a drink from a cart on the other side of the room. The liquid Mr. Hart swirled in his glass was about the same color as apple cider, but I could tell it was the type of thing Eliza would call a grown-up drink. He sat down on the high-backed leather chair behind his desk and opened the top drawer. He pulled out what I thought was an oversize ciga-rette—a cigar, I realize now—and held it under his nose, taking a deep breath. He put it in his mouth, but he didn't light it. He set his drink down on the desk and didn't drink it. Instead, he pressed his hands to the surface of the desk and traced the wood like he was reading Braille.

Then there was a flash of silver as he moved his hands, and suddenly there was red, red, red, everywhere.

Mr. Hart held up his arms and I saw deep, horrible cuts going longways on either side of his arm like the white lines on his wrists had come open.

I didn't scream. I still thought he would leave soon and I would be able to make it out without giving myself away, without getting in trouble.

Anyway, Mr. Hart looked so calm that it almost didn't seem like anything was wrong. He was a grown-up. Grown-ups were the people we were supposed to go to when we hurt ourselves.

It didn't actually look like he was in pain. He leaned back in his chair and closed his eyes. He laid his arms, wound side up, on his armrests. He looked completely relaxed, like was falling asleep.

And that looked very, very wrong.

I started to shake.

I wanted out. Out of my hiding place and out of this room as quickly as possible. Blood was dripping from the chair onto the floor; a long, slimy path of it was headed right toward me. The moment it touched the curtains, I knew they were ruined because once, at a classmate's birthday party, I'd skinned my knee while wearing a party dress and my mom was so upset. *Bloodstains,* she told me. *We'll have to throw that dress away.*

The blood kept coming, soaking into the cream-colored curtains. The red was so close to my light blue sneakers. I shuffled out of the way as best I could, pressing my back flat against the window. I couldn't take my eyes off the red liquid spreading across the floor.

I didn't care if I got in trouble. I had to get out.

I tried. I really tried. But somehow I got twisted up in the curtains. The more I struggled, the tighter they became. The curtains had turned into ropes, and I felt like a character from one of the fairy tales I liked so much, the princess who opened the forbidden door and lived to regret it.

I wanted to turn to face the window so that I wouldn't have to see the blood, but the curtains were so tight that I couldn't. It was hard to breathe. I stayed still and held my breath. I didn't want Mr. Hart to hear me. I wasn't scared that I would get into trouble for being in this room anymore.

I was scared of Mr. Hart.

I was scared he would do to me whatever he'd done to himself.

I don't know how long I hid there. I couldn't see anything anymore—somehow the curtains had fallen across my face—but I heard the door open and the scream when someone (the housekeeper? Cassie?—it didn't sound like Eliza) saw Mr. Hart. Whoever it was must've called an ambulance because soon I heard sirens and EMTs rushing into the room. I heard them shouting words like *gauze* and *pressure* and groaning as they lifted him off his chair and onto a gurney.

They didn't see the little girl hiding in the corner.

Eliza found me after he was gone.

"Where's Cassie?" I asked.

"In the kitchen on the phone with my mom." Eliza's mom didn't have a job like mine did, but she always had errands or meetings or volunteer groups. "I told her we were in my room."

It took Eliza a long time to unwrap the curtains. They were twisted and knotted between my arms and legs, pinning me against the window. My legs had fallen asleep from being wrapped so tightly, and I fell onto the floor, onto Mr. Hart's blood. Some of it got on my face. I could taste it.

"Don't!" Eliza warned when I started to gag.

It felt like I was choking, but I managed to swallow. I imagined the throw-up going backward down my throat and spreading through my body, soaking my insides.

Eliza helped me up. We crept down the hall to her room, where Cassie thought we'd been all along. Eliza walked on her tiptoes, so I did, too. There were long black streaks on the hall carpet from the wheels of the gurney. I kept my eyes focused on the lines like they were arrows telling me which way to go.

"Elizabeth?" Sam's whispering, but it sounds like a shout.

I turn around to answer my roommate. But apparently, I've gone too long without taking a real breath.

Because the next thing I know, the world goes black.

ELLIE

wednesday, march 23

I wake up with Sam's face hovering over mine. For a second I think he's going to kiss me, but then I realize he's checking to see if I'm breathing normally.

"I'm okay," I say softly, and Sam sits up, pulling me up along with him.

"You hit your head pretty good when you fell."

I put my hand to my head. A bump is already blossoming. "I'm fine."

Sam pulls me up to stand. "Maybe you should splash some cold water on your face." He leads me toward the bathroom off the study and turns on the water, closing the door behind us. I lean over the sink and duck my head beneath the faucet and drink from the faucet like it's a water fountain, suddenly parched. The end of my ponytail falls into the water, but I don't bother holding my hair back.

Eliza made me take off my shoes to walk from her father's study to her room so that I wouldn't track blood on the carpet. When we got to her room, she took off my shirt and my pants and put me in her bathtub just like my mom did every night at home. She ran the water hot and held a spray nozzle over my face until I thought I would drown. She didn't speak, but the rust-colored water in the tub and my ruined clothes on the bathroom floor explained what she was doing. I was covered in blood and she was washing it off.

She held the water over my face and I couldn't speak.

Now I start to cough, sputtering, gasping for breath. Sam turns off the water.

"Elizabeth." His voice is stern, somber, lingering over each syllable. "Tell me what's happening."

I close my eyes and more memories come:

Eliza toweled me dry and gave me some of her own clothes to wear: leggings and a T-shirt with a rainbow on it.

"What about my clothes?" I asked.

"I can throw them away."

I shook my head. "My mom will be mad."

Eliza shrugged. The wallpaper in her bedroom had long since been replaced after our painting party with her dad months earlier. There were no traces of the horse I'd drawn, of the flowers Eliza had painted.

I reached for my sneakers. You could barely see that they used to be blue. I loved those sneakers.

"Maybe if I tell her—"

Bright with tears, Eliza's gray eyes looked particularly blue, changing color the way I'd always been so jealous of.

244

"You can't tell!" she shouted, kicking my shoes out of my reach. "You can't ever tell."

"Why not?"

Eliza didn't answer. Instead she said, "Maybe it was a bad dream." She sounded almost hopeful. She didn't look at me when she spoke. It was like she wasn't really talking to me. "You napped in your hiding place and had a bad dream."

I shook my head. If it was a dream, then how did my clothes get ruined?

"I won't tell," I promised.

"You'll be in trouble if you do." Eliza sounded like a teacher, not a seven-year-old girl.

"I won't," I repeated.

"Good."

"What was your dad doing?"

"He does that sometimes," Eliza said, like that answered the question.

"Why?"

"He just does, okay?" Eliza was really shouting now. "And if you don't shut up about it I won't let you come over ever again."

I bit my lip. At that moment, I wasn't sure I ever wanted to come over to Eliza's house again.

"I'll let you drive the car," Eliza offered, her face softening. "Just please don't talk about it anymore."

Sam pulls me up so that I'm facing the mirror above the sink. He presses a towel against my face, wiping off all the makeup I'd put on so carefully this morning, pulls my hair out of the ponytail I'd methodically brushed it into. My face is blotchy, and my eyes are bloodshot. The neckline of my black dress is soaking wet. I pull at the hem. I feel sick, like I have the flu and a fever and food poisoning all at once.

My hands are still shaking. I place them on either side of the sink, trying to steady myself.

"I remembered something," I explain finally.

Somehow, I *know* it's a memory. Just like I remember having Cheerios for breakfast this morning or that I slept in my favorite flannel pj's last night.

I study my reflection in the mirror: the gray-brown eyes, the messy hair, the sweat on my forehead. The lips that Sam kissed a few nights ago. There are tears running down my cheeks. I brush them aside. I wish I could see through my face and into my brain, figure out where that memory had been hiding all these years.

"Is that why you had an attack?" Sam asks. "Because of what you remembered?"

I tighten my grip on the sink, begging my hands to stop shaking. "I guess so."

I wish my seven-year-old self were here somehow, that I could give her a hug, explain to her what she saw, tell her everything would be okay.

But of course, everything wasn't okay. It still isn't.

I saw a man try to kill himself.

He does that sometimes.

The long white stripes I saw on his wrists were *scars*. Which means that day in the study wasn't the first time he cut himself like that. Had Eliza seen it, when it happened before? Maybe that's how she knew what to do: wash away the blood and then promise never to talk about it.

A promise I took so much to heart that somehow I made my brain forget what it had seen altogether.

"It wasn't always perfect at Eliza's house," I say finally. I reach up and tuck my wet hair behind my ears. I already knew that. That day in Capitola, I remembered hearing her parents fight.

"What are you talking about?" Sam asks. "Is it perfect in anyone's house?"

Maybe not. But I *thought* it was perfect here. That's all my dysfunctional brain allowed me to remember: Eliza's perfect dollhouse and her perfect toys and her perfect electric car and the perfect cookies that Cassie gave us as an after-school snack.

But now I can recall that Eliza's father wasn't always fun. He didn't always come home and offer to finger-paint with us. Sometimes, he came home and walked right past Eliza's room without saying hello (something my own father never did). Sometimes, he yelled at Eliza to clean up whatever mess we'd made, and sometimes his wife screamed at him to clean up his own messes while he sat in a chair in the living room like he couldn't move if he tried.

I keep staring at myself in the mirror. Maybe if I had X-ray vision, I could see why my brain works the way it does.

At once, I'm so sick of looking at my own reflection that I open the medicine cabinet just to have something else to look at.

Sam whistles when he sees what's inside. "I don't think I've ever seen that much medication. And my mom had *cancer.*"

I reach out and grab the nearest bottle. "Risperdal."

"What's that for?"

I pull my phone from my pocket and Google the name. "It's an antipsychotic."

I reach for another bottle, careful to put the Risperdal back where I found it. "Lithium. I've heard of that one. Mood stabilizer."

Another bottle. "Zoloft."

"Antidepressant," Sam supplies.

Another bottle. "Klonopin."

Sam grabs my phone and looks it up. "That's for anxiety," he supplies.

Another bottle. "Diazepam."

"That's Valium. Also for anxiety. They gave it to my mom to help her sleep."

Another bottle. "Lorazepam."

Sam Googles it. "A sedative."

All the bottles are labeled with the same name: George Hart.

"What do you take all these medications *for*?" I ask.

Sam shrugs. "Depression?" he guesses.

"But then why the antipsychotics?"

"Bipolar disorder?" he suggests. "They give you mood stabilizers for that, right?"

I don't know, but I nod anyway.

"Is depression hereditary?" Sam asks suddenly. "Bipolar disorder?"

"I'm not sure."

"Either way, living with a sick parent isn't easy. It can really mess with your head."

I put the last bottle back and close the cabinet, making sure the latch catches. "Just because her father's sick doesn't mean Eliza was. It's not like inheriting your dad's eye color or your mom's hair." I try to sound certain but the truth is, I don't know. Maybe it's like height: you can inherit the genes to be over six feet tall but without proper nutrition, you'll never get there.

I turn my back on the mirror and the medication hiding behind it. "I mean, no one at school—her friends, even Arden and Erin—ever guessed she was depressed. They'd have told the police by now if they thought there was the slightest chance she could've killed herself."

Sam cocks his head to the side, his dreadlocks falling over his shoulder. "Why is it so important to you that she didn't do it—kill herself? You're acting like she let you down or something."

"She didn't let me down," I insist. "She didn't *owe* me anything."

"Then why do you sound like you're disappointed in her?"

I run my fingers roughly through my wet hair. "I don't know," I whisper.

Depressed girls don't sit in the meadow painting their nails and gossiping with their friends. They don't swim laps in the pool, winning medal after medal for their school.

Do they?

Just because she didn't *seem* depressed doesn't mean she wasn't. She was an expert at keeping secrets: Erin and Arden didn't know the truth about her secret boyfriend, didn't know about Eliza's part in butchering the trees. And no one at school knew the real reason she hated me.

Not even me.

The picture I stole from her closet feels like it weighs a thousand pounds in my pocket. She looks sad in that photograph. Broken.

I take a deep breath and tell Sam what I remembered. I don't leave anything out: I tell him about the blood on the floor and the curtains that trapped me.

"Maybe that's why you feel like you're drowning," Sam suggests when I tell him about wanting to throw up, about the shower Eliza forced on me.

"Maybe," I agree. I take a deep breath. My hands are still shaking, but the feverish feeling is fading. "So that's why she hated me? Because I saw something she didn't want me to see?"

Sam shakes his head. "Don't you remember what Mack said? She didn't hate you. She was scared of you. She must've been scared you were going to tell everyone about her father. About what happened that day."

"But I didn't remember what happened that day until about five minutes ago."

"*She* didn't know that."

I press one of my trembling hands to my forehead.

Eliza wasn't a mean girl. She was a *frightened* girl.

"I promised her I wouldn't tell. Why didn't she believe me?"

A decade of therapy and no one ever unearthed this memory. That's how deep I buried it. How much I wanted to keep my promise to Eliza.

Sam shrugs. "Maybe she didn't think she could count on a promise you made when you were seven years old."

"Maybe," I agree, but there's a lump rising in my throat. Things could've been so different. We could've been friends. If only I'd remembered sooner, reached out to her, renewed my promise.

"You have every right to cry," Sam says, noticing that I'm blinking my tears away. "She was your friend, and you miss her."

Oh my God, he's right. I miss her. I've been missing her since I was seven years old. Sam holds out his arms and I put my head against his chest. And I cry. I cry for the little girl

251

who kept her promise and the sixteen-year-old who didn't understand why her old friend rejected her. I cry for the sophomore who got locked in the bathroom and the ten-year-old who didn't get invited to any sleepover parties.

And I cry for the girl who grew up in this house. The girl who is still a mystery, but who's becoming clearer to me now than she ever was while she was alive. The girl I still wish I were friends with. The girl who didn't know that I would always keep my promise to her.

"Listen," Sam says suddenly, lifting his chin off the top of my head.

Outside, cars are pulling into the driveway. Voices are filling the hallway, footsteps sliding across the carpeted and hardwood floors.

The funeral must be over. The mourners are here.

I wipe my eyes. "We better leave."

ELLIE

wednesday, march 23

"Let's go," Sam agrees. "We found what we were looking for, right?"

I follow Sam down the hall. I want to get out of here before any of our classmates see us and make a scene like they did at the memorial on campus.

"When are they going to bury her?" I ask suddenly. "Don't they usually bury the body right after the funeral?"

"The email from the dean said the burial was going to be private. Maybe the family is going to do it later."

But then, where is she now? Did they leave her in the church? Is her casket en route to the cemetery as we speak, where it—*she*—will wait until her parents get there to be buried?

The thought of Eliza alone in a box somewhere makes me shiver.

"Come on, Elizabeth." There's urgency in Sam's voice. He's heading for the front door, still hoping we can get out without being seen. "You've been through enough today."

The foyer is ahead of us, just before the family room. The hum of voices speaking in quiet, respectful tones grows louder as we get closer. I look at the tile floor and focus on Sam's feet, the same way I did when we were on Hiking Trail Y.

Which is why I almost walk into him when he stops abruptly.

"Look," he breathes.

I follow his gaze, and my heart starts to pound when I see what—who—Sam's looking at. At the end of the hallway near the front door, Mack is leaning against the wall. He looks into the family room, then drops his eyes, like he can't decide whether or not to step inside. He's wearing what must be the closest thing he has to a suit: dark jeans and a wrinkled sport coat. The clothes look unnatural against his tan. He should be wearing board shorts on the beach. There's a bandage around the knuckles of his right hand, not yet healed from when he punched the wall the other day.

"I can't believe he'd come here when the police are investigating him," I whisper.

"We don't know if he's actually a suspect, remember?"

I peek into the family room and see Erin and Arden sitting together on the couch. Erin reaches into her purse and hands Arden a tissue; Arden doesn't even have to ask. But for once, I'm not jealous of how close they are. It takes me a second to realize it, to identify the absence of a longing tug in their direction.

254

I don't have to be jealous that they have each other and I have no one. I have Sam. I reach out and squeeze his hand.

Before Sam can lead the way out the front door, someone else walks into the foyer, her heels clicking against the hardwood. We linger in the hallway, just out of sight.

"What are you doing here?" Mrs. Hart hisses angrily. I spin around. Is she talking to me?

No. Mrs. Hart is talking to Mack.

Wait a second—Mrs. Hart *recognizes* Mack?

"I'm saying good-bye," Mack answers. "Just like everyone else here."

"I told you that you weren't welcome in this house." Eliza's mother is wearing a black suit. The color is harsh against her pale skin. Her straw-colored hair is pulled into a tight bun at the nape of her neck. "You were dangerous for my daughter."

My heart beats faster: Mrs. Hart thinks Mack killed her, too. That medication we found doesn't mean what Sam thinks it means. I look around, hoping that Detective Roberts is here. Maybe he can finally arrest Mack right now, on the spot. But the detective is nowhere in sight.

"I'd say that things are a lot different than they were at Christmas." Mack sets his mouth into a straight line, his anger written plainly on his face.

Eliza brought Mack home for Christmas? But she told Erin and Arden to keep their relationship secret. Why bother, if she was going to introduce him to her family?

Mrs. Hart steps back as though Mack slapped her. Finally, she says, "You don't know my daughter like I did. I suspected all along that she was only with you to get a rise out of me."

"Well then, I guess I served my purpose." Mack steps forward, closer to Mrs. Hart. "And don't forget that you didn't know your daughter like *I* did, either. Maybe if you hadn't been so concerned with keeping up appearances, she'd still be alive right now." Mack keeps his voice low, but his anger comes through loud and clear.

Mrs. Hart narrows her eyes. "What are you talking about?"

Mack continues, "If you'd just let Eliza get the help she needed instead of worrying about your precious reputation—"

Is Mrs. Hart the reason Eliza wanted to keep me quiet?

Did Mrs. Hart tell her daughter to make sure I didn't tell anyone what I'd seen?

Because she wanted to keep up appearances?

"We don't know exactly what happened." Mrs. Hart's voice is tight. She's speaking through gritted teeth, concentrating hard on every syllable. Is she angry, or trying not to cry? "It's not as though she left a note."

Mack thinks Eliza killed herself—and Mrs. Hart knows that he does.

Mack squeezes his hands into fists, and I think he might start punching the wall in this house, too. "How can you still be in denial now?"

"I've known my daughter a lot longer than you have."

"I went to the police," Mack continues. "I told them what I knew. Told them I was the one fighting with Eliza last week—and I told them why."

Mack went to the police? They didn't have to track him down; he showed up and *volunteered* to be interviewed, just like Sam thought he should?

That's how the police were aware of him: not as a suspect, but as a source of information.

That's why Detective Roberts didn't ask me whether I'd been the one Julian saw fighting with Eliza. By the time the detective interviewed me, Mack had already admitted it was him.

"I know you spoke with the investigators." Mrs. Hart keeps her voice low, almost hissing. "Why do you think you haven't been arrested yet?"

For the first time, Mack looks confused. He unclenches his hands. "What are you talking about?"

"There are advantages to being associated with the Hart family. I called in a favor so that no charges would be pressed against you and Riley for that mess with the trees."

Mack looks incredulous. "Do you expect me to thank you for that? Just another cover-up so the world wouldn't know what Eliza was really doing?"

"You can't prove anything," Mrs. Hart says. "Even with your evidence, the police can't prove anything, either. They'll believe me before they believe you."

Another set of footsteps crosses the hardwood. Mr. Hart. His black suit is nearly as wrinkled as Mack's. He looks as though he just woke up from a nap and can't wait to get back to sleep.

I shudder at the sight of the man from my memory, staring at his wrists as though I think I'll see his scars through his sleeves. Like I think he might still be bleeding under there.

He stands behind his wife and puts his hand on her shoulder. Mrs. Hart stiffens at his touch. Her husband's hand is shaking. He wasn't trying to steady her. He wanted to be steadied.

"I'd like you to leave," Mrs. Hart says finally. Mack opens his mouth to argue, but before he can say anything, Mrs. Hart adds, "Please." Her voice sounds desperate and cracked.

Mack's shoulders rise and fall as he takes a deep breath. "Fine," he says. "I've said what I came here to say." He turns on his heel—I notice he's wearing the same work boots he wore the day we met him—and disappears through the front door. His boots leave a trail of dry, dusty dirt.

"Let's go," Sam whispers. Mr. and Mrs. Hart don't seem to notice when we walk past them.

It's colder outside than it was when we arrived in Menlo Park. How long were we inside that house? It's dusk, and clouds are gathering. It's starting to rain, just a sprinkle at first, but it feels like a storm is coming. A breeze twists my dress between my legs. Sam walks toward his car, parked down the street. There are dozens of cars crowded onto this residential block. The bus that drove our classmates from Ventana Ranch is parked on the next block. The driver leans against it, smoking a cigarette.

Across the road, Mack's back is to us. His hands are planted on the hood of his truck, but his shoulders are shaking with sobs. Before I know what I'm doing, I've crossed the street and put my hand on his back. "I'll meet you at the car," I call over my shoulder to Sam. A few days ago—a few minutes ago—I would've been scared to face Mack by myself. But I'm not scared of him anymore.

Mack turns to look at me, trying to wipe away his tears, but they keep coming.

For the first time in my life, I know exactly what to say. It's so obvious and so simple, but it never occurred to me to say it before now.

"I'm sorry for your loss."

Mack swallows, his Adam's apple bobbing up and down. "Thank you."

"Can I ask you something?" Mack nods. "Last Saturday, in the woods—Sam and I overheard you talking to Riley. He said Eliza might still be alive if she'd listened to you. What did he mean?"

Mack takes a ragged breath. "For months I'd been begging her to get help. Find a therapist, go on antidepressants, anything that would make her feel better. But she always said her mother wouldn't let her." Mack blinks, glancing back at the Harts' front door. "What kind of mother doesn't let her daughter get the help she needs?"

I follow Mack's gaze, imagine Mrs. Hart greeting her guests somewhere inside, not one hair out of place. "I don't know," I answer finally, turning back to Mack. "It's terrible."

But the truth is, I *do* know, at least a little bit. After so many years of sending me to so many therapists, my own mother was worn out. She and I stopped talking about my problems because it was easier than trying (and failing) to solve them for the millionth time.

Maybe Eliza stopped talking about it and her mother chose to believe she was getting better. Maybe Mrs. Hart didn't ask because she didn't want to hear the answer, just like my mom.

And yet . . . my problems were never life-threatening.

The rain picks up, landing in fat droplets on my face. I fold my arms across my chest and squeeze, trying to keep warm.

"I told her she could come live with me. We could spend everything we made off the trees on her treatment. I was ready to take her away from all this, but she said no." He kicks at the ground. "So I thought if I ended our relationship, she might see that she needed help. Tough love—I read about it online. But even then . . ." He chokes on the last couple syllables and falls silent.

He thought letting her go could save her. Instead he lost her for good.

That fight Julian saw must have been the night Mack broke up with Eliza.

It was probably the last time Mack saw Eliza.

It was the exact opposite of *If I can't have you, no one can.* He was willing to let her go to save her.

"It wasn't your fault," I say softly. "I'm sure you did everything you could."

"I *know.*" Mack's voice sounds dry, cracked, just like Mrs. Hart's did. He gazes at the Harts' driveway, the front door out of sight behind a hedge. "You have to believe you're worth something to get help. And Eliza . . ." He pauses. He looks like the wind's been knocked out of him. "Eliza didn't think she was worth anything in the end."

I reach into my pocket and pull out the picture I stole from Eliza's room. "Here," I say, using my hand to shield it from the rain. It's so cold now that I can see my breath. "I shouldn't have taken this."

As Mack reaches for the photo, I notice that there's a word scribbled on the back. I look closer, squinting in the rain.

Twins.

"What do you suppose she meant by that?" I ask. What could Eliza Hart possibly have had in common with a centuries-old, hundred-foot-tall tree with a gash in the center of it?

Mack looks at the photo and shrugs before slipping it into his inner-jacket pocket to keep it dry. "No clue," he answers.

261

"But I'm beginning to think there was a lot about that girl I'll never understand."

I nod, then turn and head toward Sam's Camry.

"Hey!" Mack calls. I spin around. "I'm sorry for your loss, too."

I swallow and nod. "Thank you."

ELIZA

already dying

I can't remember ever having felt so tired.

Yet sleep is still out of reach.

When I was a little kid, I sometimes pretended to sleep.

I used to tell myself that fake sleep was better than no sleep at all.

The first day back at Ventana Ranch after Christmas break, I walked into the woods and checked on the tree I'd started to think of as my own. I didn't wait until the middle of the night. I wanted to see it while it was still light. This tree was the first one I'd helped Mack and Riley rob. I'd been visiting it since October.

The bark around the burl we'd sawed off had started to grow over with moss so dark it was almost black. Above, half of its branches were bare. It looked like the tree was going bald. Like it had aged a decade in just a few months.

Did you know that burls might be key to the redwoods' survival? It's part of how they reproduce: the seeds from pine-cones aren't likely to get enough light to grow on the forest floor, but burls bulge from the roots and base of the tree, sprouting clones of the original tree, soaking up the nutrients and water it provides. Then, when the tree dies, a burl sprout shoots up, claiming the real estate its parent left behind.

That's what the scientists in the article I read called the original tree—the *parent* tree.

I wasn't trying to look like the parent tree when I took the picture.

I didn't have to *try*.

We already looked alike.

We were both already dying.

By January, I was still swimming and hiking, but my muscles were shrinking. My appetite was gone, and even though I made myself eat with my friends at mealtimes, I was losing weight.

And the sleeplessness was getting worse. Before, I couldn't *stay* asleep: I woke up in the middle of the night buzzed with energy. Now I couldn't *fall* asleep at all. I didn't tell my mom, but she gave me pills for it anyway, the same pills my dad took, the ones that made him sleep like the dead, sleep through a fire or an earthquake.

I read more than once that sleep deprivation is a form of torture.

Still, I didn't take the pills.

Death seemed better than that kind of sleep.

Then again, death seemed better than a lot of things by then.

There were circles under my eyes, visible beneath my tan. I bought cover-up for the first time, but the effort of brushing the creamy flesh-colored liquid on my skin felt enormous.

I printed the photo in my dorm room while Arden and Erin slept. I would be home again, back in Menlo Park in a few days, attending an event to celebrate my uncle's November win before he got sworn in in late January. I took the photo home with me on Friday and added it to the growing collage in my bedroom. I couldn't stop pasting things to the wall. The collage reminded me that I had the power to hurt living creatures, things that had lived in peace for longer than I ever would.

I thought it would make me feel more alive, having that kind of power over something so enormous.

But instead, I found myself thinking: *If I'm capable of irreparably damaging a tree that had lived on this earth for a century, imagine what I could do to myself.*

My right hand shook when I wrote the word *Twins* on the back of the photograph. Both my hands shook constantly by then. I could barely paint my nails anymore. I told Erin and Arden it was too much caffeine, and they believed me. Why shouldn't they?

My hands weren't the only things that were shaking by then: My breaths were shallow; my heartbeats felt unsteady.

How much longer would I be able to keep up the facade? If I waited too long, everyone would know. And I mean *everyone*. If only I'd had the good sense to be unpopular. But popularity was part of the lie, part of being normal.

It wasn't my mother's shouts that finally drove Mack away.

You're dangerous for my daughter.

Eliza shouldn't be with a boy like you.

When she said those things, my mom didn't even know that Mack was a high school dropout who cut up trees so he could make enough money to spend the rest of his time surfing.

But she could tell just by looking at him that he was nothing like *us*.

Nothing like the safe boys at Ventana Ranch who were destined for Ivy League colleges,

who would go on to work on Wall Street or to found the newest tech start-up,

who wore socks with their shoes and never drove barefoot.

But none of that was why my mother thought Mack was dangerous.

My mother cared because Mack was intense. She was terrified of what an intense relationship would do to her already-damaged daughter.

She didn't want me wasting any of my very limited energy.

She was scared of Mack for the same reasons I'd been scared of him. Mack had more emotion in him than we were used to seeing in a healthy man.

After my mother told him to leave, Mack said I could come live with him in Capitola. He said we could use all the money we'd earned to get me the help I needed, and he shouted that if that wasn't enough, he'd sell his surfboard,

his Jet Ski,

he'd rip into a thousand more trees if he had to.

Standing in our driveway on Christmas Eve, Mack begged me to leave with him.

I said no.

I looked at the sky. It was nearly midnight. In the houses around us, children were probably struggling to stay awake, hoping to hear Santa's reindeer clip-clopping on their rooftops.

The children were nestled all snug in their beds, while visions of sugarplums danced in their heads.

I'd never believed in Santa Claus. I'd never believed in magic.

There was no magic in the house where I grew up.

Mack stomped his feet and threw out his arms in frustration. It was so cold that I could see his breath coming in shallow puffs, and he reminded me of a racehorse champing at the bit.

I told him my mother would never let me go to therapy. Said she would hate me if I shared the family secrets with some stranger, even one who was bound by doctor-patient confidentiality.

There were things I hadn't even told Mack.

He knew about my dad, but he didn't know about my dad's mom, who'd self-medicated with alcohol until cirrhosis set in.

Mack didn't know that my uncle—the same one who'd been elected to Congress—had been to rehab three times and still wasn't sober. (Even I wasn't supposed to know about that.)

Mack didn't know that depression doesn't always make you sad. Sometimes it just makes you numb.

Mack didn't know that this wasn't my first bout with darkness. He didn't know that halfway through sophomore year, my mother saved my life.

I'd taken a bottle of Valium from Dad's medicine cabinet, then tiptoed across our backyard. I thought I would take the pills and then slip into the pool. I knew that if the drugs put me to sleep instead of killing me, chances were I'd drown.

But my mother found me first. She stuck her own fingers down my throat until I threw up. I told her I was just trying to get some sleep. I'm still not sure I wasn't telling the truth.

She cried. I told her I was sorry. I told her I wouldn't always be so much trouble.

I didn't want to be so much trouble.

I think my mother let me go to Ventana Ranch after that because living in Big Sur would keep me far away from the pills in Dad's medicine cabinet.

I read somewhere that forty thousand Americans kill themselves each year, and nearly half a million attempt suicide seriously enough to require medical attention.

Seriously enough. Suicide requires effort. You have to work at it to get it right.

Or get it wrong, depending on how you're looking at it.

I also read that about a third of people who try to kill themselves will try again within a year.

I read about something called "spontaneous suicide," when someone decides, for no apparent reason, that today is the day. Or anyway, for no reason apparent to the living people who've been left behind.

Here I am, just another statistic.

At Christmas, when I turned down Mack's offers to help, he looked as though I slapped him. I was seventeen years old, he insisted. Why was I letting my mother run my life?

When I didn't answer, his face shifted from anger into something else. Disappointment.

Do you really care about what people think as much as she *does?*

I didn't answer. The conversation had already exhausted me. I just wanted to go back inside, lie down, and not sleep for yet another night.

Mack stormed off, his boots pounding against the pavement of our driveway.

It took him a few more months to break up with me, but he finally did it, the week before I died.

He probably thought he was helping. Tough love and all

that. Like kicking an addict out of the house for refusing to go to rehab. Like a person could be addicted to feeling the way I felt. You can't be addicted to feeling nothing at all.

Or maybe you can. I don't remember.

He snuck onto campus—he could climb the fence easily when he wasn't weighed down by a burl—when everyone else was sleeping. We fought, and he lost because I refused to do what he said. Or maybe I lost, because in the end, he left me alone.

This time, he didn't yell. This time, his voice barely went above a whisper. That's how I knew he'd reached his breaking point. That's how I knew it was the end.

He said: *You're going to die if you keep this up.*

Like I said, he saw it coming before I did. His muscles were tensed so tight he shook when he spoke.

He was so alive.

I threw my ID at his back. A parting gift. He looked up at me as he knelt to lift it off the ground. His face was twisted like he was in pain.

Memory is funny. You don't get to choose which moments you remember and which ones you forget. I'd trade every memory of fighting with Mack for just one more memory of spending time with my dad in between his bouts of darkness and mania and medication.

I remember exactly how things ended between Mack and me. You'd think it would get fuzzier now, but it hasn't. It hurts just as much as anything else.

Sometimes I think that I must have believed I would survive the fall. Or maybe I was testing myself: If I survived, then I *deserved* to live, like how they used to nearly drown witches to determine their innocence.

Sometimes I believe that I didn't really intend to die.

But then why did I wear my mother's dress?

I read once about a kind of altitude sickness that affects mountain climbers on major ascents like Everest and Kilimanjaro. It makes them stop walking, even though they know if they don't keep moving they will likely die of hypothermia. They *know*, but their brains aren't getting enough oxygen for them to *care*.

It's as good an explanation as any for the last months of my life.

ELLIE

wednesday, march 23

"I'm freezing," I say as Sam turns onto the freeway.

Sam turns up the heat and reaches into the backseat, never taking his eyes off the road. "Here." He tosses me a rumpled sweatshirt. I pull it up to my neck like a blanket.

I can still see Mack's shoulders shaking when he cried, the look on his face when I handed him the picture. I curl my hands into fists beneath my chin and press my lips together, remembering the feel of Sam's mouth against mine.

Will anyone ever love me the way Mack loved Eliza?

Oh my God, what's wrong with me? All this time, with everything I've learned, and I'm still jealous of a dead girl.

"I don't think I've ever seen anyone look at someone the way Mack looked at Mrs. Hart," Sam says suddenly. "He blamed her for Eliza's death." He doesn't add, *Not the other way around*. He doesn't have to.

I nod. "He said she cared more about how things looked than how they actually were."

That's why Mack went to the police. He wanted them to know the way things really were.

Eliza Hart wasn't murdered.

Mack didn't hurt her.

Mack loved her.

Mack wanted to *save* her.

I wonder what it was like to grow up in that house. To be seven years old and already know about suicide.

To be seven years old and already believe you're not supposed to talk about it.

To be seven years old and already know how to keep such an enormous secret.

Is it any wonder Eliza kept her own struggles secret? That's what she'd been taught to do. She even kept secrets she didn't have to, like continuing to hide Mack from her friends after she'd introduced him to her parents.

I tried to keep my claustrophobia a secret for just a few months, and I failed—Sam knew about it all along.

I lean my head against the window and watch the rain drip down the glass. Even now, I can't imagine Eliza jumping off that cliff. I can only picture her tripping and falling. Losing her footing. Getting hit with a freakishly strong breeze.

How can we know for sure? Like Mrs. Hart said, Eliza didn't leave a note. Maybe her illness wasn't really *that* bad: It didn't keep her from making friends, from kissing boys, from being popular and doing all the other things I never got to do.

Mack's words echo through my brain: *How can you still be in denial now?*

And: *Eliza didn't think she was worth anything in the end.*

How could Eliza—beautiful, bright, sociable—believe she was worthless? Her whole life was ahead of her. She could have done anything.

Her brain played an even bigger trick on her than mine did on me.

For the first time ever, I feel luckier than Eliza.

What her father did that day scarred me, but unlike Eliza, I got to leave that house behind. My mother may hate what's wrong with me, but she never stopped me from getting help. Just the opposite.

I drop my head into my hands. My hair is still damp. The rain. No, not just the rain. It was wet before I left the house. It got wet when I drank from the tap in Mr. Hart's bathroom.

Oh. My. God. "Sam?"

"Yeah?"

"I didn't have an attack."

"Are you kidding? I was seconds away from calling 911 when I dragged you into the bathroom."

"Exactly!" I shout. Sam looks at me like I'm losing it. "I had the attack in his study, but it stopped once you got me into the bathroom." The small, windowless bathroom.

When Sam closed the door behind us I didn't feel the water rushing in. I felt it falling back, like a wave sliding away from the beach.

I almost start to laugh. All that therapy, even hypnosis, and no one ever figured out what was hiding in my brain the whole time. I think about all the friends I didn't make, the parties I didn't go to, the boys who didn't want to kiss me. All the times my mom looked at me and wished I could be more like Wes.

Would it all have been different if only I'd visited the Harts' sooner?

Now I'm not laughing, I'm crying. Why am I crying? I just found the memory that probably caused my claustrophobia. I've finally figured out where all my problems originated. That's *good* news.

Isn't it?

"I'm pulling over." Sam turns on his blinker and heads for the nearest exit.

Knowing doesn't make up for the past ten years.

Knowing doesn't erase the snide comments and the girls who didn't invite me for playdates and sleepover parties.

Knowing doesn't mean that my mother never looked at me with disappointment in her face and *knowing* doesn't mean that I haven't been terrified, every day since before I was in second grade, that I would be trapped and lost forever.

And *knowing* isn't necessarily a cure.

I shake my head and catch my breath, wiping away my tears. "I'm okay," I promise.

"You sure?"

"I'm sure." I nod at the road ahead. "Let's go home."

Sam shifts back into the left lane. The views are spectacular when you're driving south on Highway 1. When we get to Monterey, I watch the waves crash in the rain. The coastline looks blurry, a picture out of focus.

Just like Eliza.

Mrs. Hart and Mack argued about who knew her best. Maybe all of us—Mack, her parents, her best friends, her teammates, her teachers, me—maybe we only got to know the parts of her that she allowed us to see. The troubled girl. The dutiful daughter. The fun friend. The champion athlete. The good student. The popular princess.

Maybe not one of us actually knows *all* of her.

I wanted to hide my problems from everyone at Ventana Ranch, just like Eliza hid hers.

But I failed and Eliza succeeded.

And I'm alive and she's dead.

ELLIE

friday, march 25

The police ruled Eliza's death an accident. Dean Carson announced it at breakfast in the cafeteria this morning. Sam and I weren't there, but Sam got a text from Cooper telling him the news. They couldn't find any evidence of foul play, there was nothing connecting the fight Julian witnessed with her death, and—they didn't say this, but it was implied—they found no proof that it was a suicide. The police are packing up to leave campus, abandoning their post at the front gate and taking down the crime-scene tape from the cliffs.

"Case closed," Sam said when he told me. He leaned against my doorframe.

"Guess so," I agreed. Then I asked him to close the door behind him because I had a paper to work on. My computer is still balanced on my lap. This essay was due before break began, but I didn't hand it in and apparently Professor Gordon forgot to ask me to. I could still send it to her by Monday.

Back on schedule. Back to normal.

Except I can't stop staring at my closet door.

In fact, I've been watching the door almost nonstop for days now. When I try to read, I end up gazing over the cover of my book and looking at the door instead. When I go to sleep at night, I lie down with my back to the door and wake up facing it in the morning.

I haven't tried locking myself in there yet. Haven't tested whether what happened—or really, what didn't happen—in the bathroom off Mr. Hart's study will happen again.

I close my eyes and imagine myself someplace small, the same way I spent years trying to imagine myself someplace big. Will my heart start to pound when I picture elevator doors sliding shut with me inside? When I imagine one of those bathrooms on the plane, the reason I didn't drink water the entire day before I flew from New York to California?

My heartbeat stays steady. Then again, visualizing never worked when I was trying to calm it, so why should it work now that I'm trying to jumpstart it?

I open my eyes and sigh. There's only one way to find out, and I'm not ready to try it yet.

Sam knocks, letting himself in before I can answer. He just got back from driving up to Carmel for a new cell phone. He invited me to come with him, but I said I had work to do. Now he says, "Let's go for a hike."

I shake my head. "I have to finish my paper."

"You haven't gotten out of that bed since we got back from Menlo Park."

That's not entirely true. I've gone to the bathroom a few times. I've eaten food from our kitchenette. I've even walked across the room and put my hand on the closet door. I just haven't actually gone inside, like Alice hesitating before going down the rabbit hole to Wonderland.

Sam sits on the edge of the bed. I try not to think of what happened the last time he sat on my bed and I definitely try to ignore the way my body shivers at this close proximity.

I want to ask Sam whether *back to normal* means that he'll be back to his old tricks. Back to hanging out with our classmates and sneaking (other) girls into his room after curfew.

I want to ask, but I don't because I'm scared of what the answer might be.

"Come on, Elizabeth." Sam crosses his arms as if to say *I mean business*, but he's smiling. "An easy path this time, I promise."

I shove my laptop out of the way and swing my legs over the side of the bed. I pretend not to notice Sam offering his hand to help me to my feet.

There isn't a cloud in the sky as we walk past the pile of candles and flowers that's been growing outside Eliza's dorm over the past week. Moisture from the fog made the ink on the signs run, blurring the words. The wind knocked a bouquet into the path; I bend down and pick it up. They were yellow roses, but the petals have turned almost entirely brown. Gently, I place the flowers next to the fake candles; only half of them are still flickering. I guess the rest of the batteries have burned out.

"I heard they're going to take all of this away and put up some kind of permanent memorial instead," Sam says. "A bench, I think. There's going to be a vote to decide what the marker on it should say."

I reach out and touch one of the posters, run my finger along the words *Rest in Peace, Eliza Hart*. Her life must have lacked peace, for her to do what she did. I follow Sam down the path toward Hiking Trail B. It's warmer than I expected, so I take off my sweatshirt and tie it around my waist. The trail narrows and the trees close in around us.

But it's not silent. A group of our classmates—all girls, I think—is headed right toward us from the other direction. From far away, they look exactly like one of the pictures in the school catalog: friendly and smiling in the California sunshine.

Erin and Arden are at the head of the pack. It's my first time seeing them since the funeral, and I'm surprised to discover how much I feel sorry for them. I mean, I always felt bad that their best friend had died (though they didn't exactly make it easy after months of having been mean to me and then more or less accusing me of murder), but it's different now. Now I know so much about Eliza that they don't.

Maybe I could tell them *I'm sorry for your loss*, just like I told Mack. I know better than to expect them to say it back like he did. Still, it's a place to start.

But as the girls get closer, I see Erin's eyes narrow in anger. She plants herself in the center of the path, blocking our way. Sam and I stand side by side. "You sure are lucky," she says.

I glance sideways at Sam. It would've been luckier if we'd stuck to Hiking Trail Y.

"*Accident* is an awfully convenient word," Arden adds, just behind her friend.

I twist the knot holding my sweatshirt in place. "You still think I had something to do with what happened to Eliza?"

Erin crosses her arms. "I don't have any reason not to."

"But the police—"

"Just because the police couldn't find any evidence doesn't mean that you didn't do it."

"I'm not the one Julian saw her fighting with."

"I *know*," Erin huffs impatiently. "You think the police didn't tell us? Her boyfriend came forward, said they had a fight when they broke up."

From the way she says *her boyfriend* instead of *Mack*, I can tell that the police haven't actually told her much. She probably still believes Eliza's secret boyfriend was a college student.

"So then you know it wasn't me—"

"I don't know anything about you." She turns to face Sam. "And don't let her trick you into thinking you know her, either. Eliza said she was an excellent liar."

"Yeah," another girl jumps in. Jenn Marten. "She *always* said so."

Jenn wasn't even friends with Eliza. Erin and Arden never used to hang out with her, and I doubt Eliza ever said two words to her. But Eliza's absence leaves an open slot among the popular girls and it looks like Jenn is vying for it. And apparently, the fastest way to bond with Erin and Arden is to join them in hating me.

"Ellie." I'm surprised to hear Sam use my nickname. "Maybe you should just tell them the truth."

"Yeah, Ellie," Erin coaxes, "tell us the *truth*." She thinks Sam wants me to confess. Arden puts her hand on Erin's arm. Arden's usually the one who does the talking. She looks surprised by Erin's outburst.

I'm not. Or anyway, I shouldn't be. What was I thinking, that I'd tell them, *I'm sorry for your loss* and wipe the slate clean? These girls have hated me for months. Why would they stop now?

Erin must lose her patience with my silence because the next thing I know, she's shoved me to the ground. I land hard, pine needles pricking my palms and fingers. I bite my tongue as I fall, tasting blood.

"Hey!" Sam shouts. He reaches down to help me up, but for the second time today, I don't take his hand. I stay on the ground, crouched on all fours, trying not to cry.

"Like I'd believe a word coming out of her mouth anyway," Erin spits.

Instead of looking at the ground, I look up at her. Erin's face twists so that she looks exactly like one of the girls who locked me in the bathroom at my old school. For a second, I think she's going to kick me.

Except Erin's face has something the other girls' faces never had. Genuine sadness. Erin is struggling with the loss of her best friend.

I finally understand why Erin needs to believe that I hurt Eliza. Because the alternatives are accepting that it was just a freak accident—which hardly seems like a good reason for someone you love to die—or accepting that the girl she lived with—studied with, ate with, gossiped with—was depressed enough to kill herself and Erin never saw it.

"Let's go," Erin says finally, gesturing for her friends to follow her. I sit back on my heels and watch them leave.

When they're gone, Sam kneels on the ground beside me.

"They still hate me," I manage finally. Understanding *why* doesn't make it feel any better. "And don't say that they don't know me well enough to hate me because they don't *have* to know me to hate me for something I didn't do."

"I'm sorry, Ellie."

"They wouldn't have believed me if I told them the truth."

Sam tucks his dreads behind his ears. "Probably not."

I'm worried that if I talk about it any more I'll start crying, so I say, "You've called me Ellie twice today." I manage a weak smile. "You must really feel sorry for me."

Sam shakes his head. "Actually, I'm starting to like the way it feels to call you Ellie."

I push myself up to stand. "Let's go home."

Sam nods and leads the way up the trail. Without turning around, he says, "At least now we know why you felt the way you did."

"Yeah. There's a straight line from what happened that day to my phobia."

"Yeah, but I mean the way you felt about Eliza."

I stop in my tracks. "How did I feel about Eliza?"

"How obsessed you were with her, you know?" The word *obsessed* comes out easily, like it's been on the tip of his tongue all this time. "It's like your subconscious was trying to tell you something. To point you in the direction of the memory you lost." Sam keeps walking, like the words he's saying are no big deal. I start walking again, but I don't try to match his strides.

There's still traces of yellow crime-scene tape stuck to the trunks of the trees beside the cliffs. "Cooper said they're going to put up a fence here." Sam walks toward the edge of the cliff, pointing. "All along here, and down on the other side of the dorms and the cafeteria, too. They don't want any more *accidents*." Sam stretches his arms out wide, looking out over the ocean, his back to me.

At once, I realize something. "You lied to me about being afraid of heights."

Sam spins around gracefully and without fear. "What?"

"After the memorial service, when you told me you knew about my claustrophobia, you said you were afraid of heights."

Sam looks sheepish. "Ellie, I was just trying to—"

I don't give him a chance to finish. "You must've thought I was a freak just like they did." I wave vaguely at the buildings up the path, dorms where our classmates study and sleep. I gesture back at the path where Erin pushed me to the ground. "The crazy girl with the phobia, obsessed with her former best friend."

"I don't think you're a freak."

I shake my head and say softly, "I don't believe you."

I run away before he can say anything else, sprinting up the path so fast that my chest hurts, so hard that my knees scream in protest with each footfall. The pine needles that were stuck to my leggings fall off, trailing behind me as I run.

I don't want him to see me crying again. I don't want him to know that this time, *he* made me cry.

ELLIE

friday, march 25

I take the stairs in our dorm two at a time, huffing and puffing as I go.

Sam didn't just lie about being afraid of heights. All this time, he believed I was obsessed with Eliza and he never admitted it.

A lie of omission is still a lie.

And Sam's omission isn't nearly as big as *hers*.

Her lie is the reason that everyone here still thinks I might have pushed Eliza over those cliffs.

Her lie is the reason they hate me.

If *she* would just come clean, everything would be different.

Everyone would finally understand that I had nothing to do with what happened to Eliza.

She's probably relieved that Eliza's death was ruled an accident. Maybe she even bribed the police to ensure their conclusion, just like she got Mack and Riley off the hook.

If she'd only let her daughter get the help she needed.

If she'd only let Mack help.

By the time I reach our floor, I can't catch my breath. I've never been so angry in my entire life. Not at Wes for making fun of me, not at those girls who locked me in the bathroom, not at Eliza for starting those rumors. My heart is pounding, and sweat is pooling at the nape of my neck. My hands itch as I ball them into fists. I'm grinding my teeth so hard it's giving me a headache.

I feel trapped. Not, like, attack-trapped, but trapped on this campus. Just like Eliza said I'd be. I'm sick of the trees and the trails. I miss asphalt and honking horns and the ability to stick my hand out to hail a cab that will take me anywhere.

I could borrow Sam's car. I mean, I don't have a license, but driving doesn't look that hard. One pedal for go and one pedal for stop and blinkers for changing lanes. Right? The 107-mile drive to Menlo Park (I looked it up before the funeral) is plenty of time to become an expert driver. How else do you learn, anyway?

I throw the door to our suite open and head for Sam's room instead of my own. I hesitate for a split second before stepping over the threshold. I've never actually been in his room before. I take a deep breath. It smells like salt water and soap, spice and boy sweat.

The keys to his Camry are on his dresser beside a framed picture. I recognize my roommate even though he looks like he's only about six or seven years old in this picture. He's next to a woman whose skin is a few shades darker than his. She's holding his hand. He's already up to her chest, and I wonder if she knew even then how tall her son would be.

Another framed photograph sits beside it. A more recent picture of Sam towering over two little kids. His sister and brother from his dad's second marriage. I never asked Sam what their names were, how old they are. They must be important to him if he displays a picture of them next to a picture of his mom.

I take another deep breath, let it out slowly.

This is crazy. I'm not going to *steal* Sam's car. I can't even drive. Instead of picking up the keys, I lift the frame off the dresser and sink onto Sam's unmade bed, my shoulders slumped.

I hear the door of our suite open and shut. When Sam sees that I'm in his room, he stops in the doorway, like he's the one who shouldn't be here, not me.

"Avery." He nods at the picture in my hands. "That's my little sister. She's eight now. And my brother is Matt. He's six."

"They're really cute."

Sam grins. "You don't know the half of it."

"Do you miss them?"

Sam nods. "It's the only part of living in Mill Valley that I miss."

"That's nice. I mean, not that you miss them, but that you love them that much." I wonder if Wes and I will ever feel that way about each other.

Sam crosses his arms and leans against the doorframe. "What are you doing in here, Ellie?"

I stand up and put the frame back where I found it. "I need a ride," I say finally.

"Where?"

"I have to talk to Mrs. Hart," I explain.

Sam presses his lips together. I can see him struggling to find the right thing to say, the thing that will stop me: *What are you thinking?* (Too vague.) *Are you sure that's a good idea?* (Too open to interpretation.) *Leave the poor woman alone.* (Too accusatory.)

Or maybe, *Like I said, you're obsessed with Eliza.*

"Please, Sam. I know you think I'm just obsessing—"

"I didn't say—"

"But I need this," I interject. "It's important to me."

Sam nods, then reaches up and toys with his hair. I can tell when he makes up his mind before he says anything because he pulls a couple of dreads from the front and knots them around the back to hold his hair in place.

There's no talking me out of this, and he knows it. I'm going to Menlo Park even if I have to hitchhike all 107 miles.

But that won't be necessary because my roommate's going to give me a lift.

ELIZA

nine lives

I told Mack more of the truth than I had anyone else:

the truth about my dad,

the truth about the lies I spread when Ellie Sokoloff came to Ventana Ranch.

But I couldn't tell him the whole truth.

He wouldn't have understood, no matter how hard he tried. Unlike me, he didn't grow up in a house where the word *Depression* was always spoken with a capital *D*.

Mack never lived with a father who went to a dozen therapists and tried more medications than a cancer patient.

Most people who don't live with it think that therapy and pills will fix it. I believed that the first few times we sent Dad off to get his medication adjusted: Just a little tune-up and a little time off, and he'd be back better than ever.

Surely that's what Mack believed when he begged me to go to therapy and take meds.

Do it for me, he said.

Mack didn't know that I'd said the same thing to my

father when I was younger: Didn't he love me enough to be well for me? Wasn't I enough to make him happy?

Get better for me.

It was years before I understood that treatment for mental illness isn't that simple. It's like living with cancer that goes into remission after a course of chemotherapy: It's under control, but it could still metastasize.

And like a cancer patient, Dad underwent a succession of treatments. We tried ECT (electroconvulsive therapy) and TMS (transcranial magnetic stimulation). Every time the doctors suggested something new we were optimistic. There were good periods, times when he must have found the right therapist, the right pill.

But eventually, his meds would need to be adjusted. Or we discovered he hadn't been taking his meds at all. Or a therapist called the house to tell us he'd missed two sessions in a row.

Mom always said it wasn't his fault.

I read books about depression and studies about suicide. I was surprised to discover there was such a thing as the American Association of Suicidology. I was surprised that *suicidology* was a word.

In fifth grade, I read somewhere that the life expectancy of a person with mental illness is twenty-five years shorter than someone without it.

I memorized that particular fact without even trying.

If people knew what I was really like, they wouldn't feel sorry for me. *Popular pretty rich girl,* they'd say, *what does she have to be depressed about?*

The thing they don't understand is that I agree with them; I *don't* have any reason to be depressed. I could have a terrible day or a great day, and I'd end up feeling just as bad the next morning.

That's the worst thing about this disease. It feels like there's no way out. I'm trapped, stuck feeling like this.

There were plenty of good things in my life, even toward the end.

I got into Ventana Ranch.

My SAT scores were high.

My parents got me a shiny new car for my sixteenth birthday.

I won gold medals for swimming,

ate delicious food,

hiked through the woods on gloriously sunny days,

met a boy who loved me.

But Mack would never understand that none of those things felt good to me anymore.

None of those things felt *anything* to me anymore.

I'm wide awake again. Wired. Buzzing.

In tenth grade, we read a poem called "Lady Lazarus" by

Sylvia Plath. I don't remember the whole thing. Just bits and pieces.

Like this:

I have done it again.

And like the cat I have nine times to die.

When would my dad's ninth time come?

Kindergarten began just a week after Dad's first attempt. Maybe there had been other attempts before. But that was the first one I saw.

Dad was still in the hospital—a mental institution that was more like a fancy hotel except for the locks on the doors—when Mom dropped me off on the first day of kindergarten. Her floral dress rustled when she walked, and I concentrated on the sound of it: *Swish, swish. Swish, swish.*

When Mom kissed me good-bye, she told me that everything would be all right, and I believed her. Her long blond hair—she still wore it down back then—tickled when it brushed against my face.

By recess, Ellie Sokoloff and I had decided that we were going to be best friends. When our mothers came to pick us up after afternoon snack, Ellie and I insisted that they arrange our first playdate. I leaned against my mom's legs and felt the smooth material of her dress on my cheek.

"Feel how soft," I said, holding the dress out for Ellie to touch. Our moms laughed.

When we got home, my dad was there, a surprise just for me. I ran to greet him, shouting, *Daddy!* just like I knew he and my mom expected me to.

It wasn't that I wasn't glad to see him. It was just that our house seemed so much heavier with him in it.

Like the cat I have nine times to die.

We were silently waiting for his ninth time.

I grew up both with and without a father. He was present, physically healthy, but absent at the same time.

There was a girl in my class whose father had congestive heart failure, and sometimes I recognized the look on her face because I'd seen it on my own. Our fathers were alive, but their presence was fragile. One wrong step—a missed dose, a skipped beat—and we could lose them forever.

I read a lot about girls without fathers: girls whose fathers left before they'd been born, girls whose beloved fathers had died when they were young, girls whose fathers turned out to have a secret family on the other side of the country. In all the books and essays and articles I read, I couldn't find anything written about girls like me.

Girls whose fathers tried to leave, and failed.

My father stayed alive, he went to therapy, he (mostly) took his meds. But the house stayed heavy.

For a long time, I blamed my mother.

In the beginning, I asked: *Why can't you make him better,*
find him better doctors,
adjust his meds,
make him happy?

She sent him to new therapists and new psychiatrists. Sometimes he got better, for a little while. Sometimes he got worse.

Eventually, I stopped asking her to find him new therapists or better medication.

Instead: *Why don't you leave him?*

Then: *Don't you love me enough to leave him?*

Finally: *I'm not going to end up like him.*

And I didn't.

ELLIE

friday, march 25

My heart is pounding when I ring the doorbell to the Harts' sprawling ranch house. I'm going to give this woman a piece of my mind. She's going to admit what she did. She's going to tell everyone.

She *has* to.

When she answers the door, she looks different than the last time I saw her. Instead of a black suit, she's wearing a cream-colored blouse with ill-fitting wrinkled tan slacks. Her hair isn't pulled back into a tight bun at the nape of her neck, but falling across her face in blond waves. It's not nearly as long as Eliza's was, and maybe a shade darker, but you can still tell that Eliza got her hair from her mother. There are dark circles under her eyes, which are bloodshot, as though she's been crying. She's holding a tissue tightly in her left hand.

"Ellie Sokoloff." She even *sounds* different. Her voice sounds thinner, as though the woman speaking isn't a person at all but a balloon that's slowly deflating. She doesn't even

look surprised to see me. Maybe mourners have been showing up for days to pay their respects. Or maybe she's just too
tired to muster something as frivolous as surprise.

I spent the drive to Menlo Park silently rehearsing what
I'm going to say to Mrs. Hart:

I know about Eliza.

I know what you did to her.

You have to come clean.

You have to tell the truth.

This is all your fault.

But now that I'm standing in front of her, I feel tongue-
tied. "Mrs. Hart," I begin slowly.

"Who's that?" Mrs. Hart cuts in, putting her hand up
over her eyes like a visor. She nods at Sam, still sitting in the
driver's seat of his car in the driveway.

"That's my roommate, Sam."

"Why don't you both come in?" She waves Sam out of his
car and gestures for us to come inside. This is nothing like I
expected: no angry confrontation, no tearful confession,
no doors slamming in my face. I take a deep breath and step
across the threshold.

I don't think the living room has been cleaned since the
funeral. Plastic plates litter the coffee table, the couch cush-
ions are crushed and out of place, the light carpet is dotted

with footprints, and there are stray napkins wadded up on the end tables. It looks like Eliza's mother told the caterers to pack up their stuff and leave, sent her housekeeper away, and closed the doors.

Now she drops onto a chair as though she weighs a thousand pounds and the effort of being on her feet has exhausted her. Sam and I sit on the couch across from her. Her eyes are closed. She looks *smaller* than she did before. Her clothes look too big, like maybe she hasn't eaten in days.

"I should offer you something to drink." She opens her eyes. "I'm so sorry."

"No, we're sorry," Sam responds before I can. "It was rude of us to just knock on your door out of the blue like this."

She doesn't answer, just fixes her gaze on me. Her eyes are exactly the same color as Eliza's. The dark purple circles beneath them bring out the blue.

I know about Eliza. I know about Eliza. I know about Eliza.

She fiddles with her necklace. A tiny cross on a gold chain. "What brings you here, dear?"

I flinch when she calls me dear. It's hard to hate someone who calls you dear.

"I wanted to ask you about Eliza," I say finally. My mouth feels sticky. I swallow. "Do you think she might have been . . . I mean, Mack told us she was—I mean . . ." I swallow and gaze at the ceiling. "I remembered something that happened in your husband's study when I was in first grade."

Mrs. Hart doesn't ask *what* I remembered. In fact, she shudders like she knows exactly what I'm talking about.

"I'm sorry to bring it up," I stutter. I don't look at Sam. I know the expression on his face will tell me to *be quiet, just let this poor woman grieve.* "I just—well, I know Eliza struggled with depression like her father did."

"Not exactly like her father," Mrs. Hart corrects. "My husband is bipolar. Eliza was diagnosed as a unipolar depressive when she was fourteen."

I'm taken aback by how easily she offers up this information after she went to such lengths to conceal it while Eliza was alive. I've never heard of unipolar depression. I consider the word: If bipolar means two opposite moods—the lows of depressions and the highs of mania—then unipolar must mean that you get trapped in just one of the moods. Depression, obviously.

"Well," I continue tentatively, "I was thinking that if she'd just gotten some help—"

Mrs. Hart opens her mouth like she's going to laugh, but no sound comes out. "I used to think the same thing."

The question slips out of my mouth quickly, like the words are slippery: "But then why didn't you let her get the help she needed?"

"Dear, I *begged* that girl to get help. I sent her to therapists, but she refused to talk to them. Made appointments with psychiatrists who prescribed her medicine she refused to take. For a few months there, I actually crushed up her medication and tried to feed it to her in ice cream like she was a naughty puppy."

I shake my head. "But Mack said—" I cut myself off before I can finish the thought.

Eliza must have lied to Mack, too.

Finally, I say, "I don't understand. If you were willing to get her the help she needed, then why did she—" I can't bring myself to finish the sentence, but it doesn't matter. The words I don't say seem to hang in the air between us.

Why did she kill herself?

Mrs. Hart shakes her head, tears hovering in the corners of her eyes, making them even bluer. "Eliza didn't want help. She took her illness as proof of her worthlessness instead of the thing that tricked her into feeling worthless."

"I don't understand."

Mrs. Hart smiles faintly. "Did you know my husband still prefers to say that the scars on his wrists are from the time he broke a scotch glass?" She doesn't wait for an answer. "It took me years to realize that it wasn't me he was lying to. He was lying to himself." She shakes her head. "Eliza learned from him. As though shame could be genetic."

Eliza was the one who worried about saving face, not her mother.

"But Mr. Hart got help," I say finally. "He takes medication."

Mrs. Hart doesn't ask how I know this. "Sometimes," she says sadly. She blinks, and a few of her tears overflow.

She doesn't wipe them away. "And not always as instructed by his doctors. Eliza saw that her father didn't exactly get better as the years went by—he had good periods and bad periods. He didn't always take his meds when and how he should, and they had side effects—weight gain, weight loss. Sleepiness, sleeplessness. He took medication *for* the medication." She almost laughs.

"I had no idea."

"Most people don't. Most people see commercials for the latest antidepressant and assume that the only people struggling with mood disorders are the ones who haven't taken a magic pill yet."

"You make it sound like Eliza was right. Like she never had a chance."

Mrs. Hart shakes her head. "No. Treatment can work wonders. But it has to be administered properly. By the time I understood how sick my husband was, he'd wreaked havoc on his body. He'd spent years mixing medications, taking them improperly, self-medicating with alcohol, skipping therapy—you name it. Sometimes I thought even his doctors gave up on him. How can I blame Eliza for losing hope?" She sighs. "I should have taken her from this house years ago. I should have protected her from all that hopelessness."

"But then . . ." I stop myself. I've already asked so many personal questions.

But Mrs. Hart finishes for me. "Why didn't I leave?" I nod. "I thought it would be worse. I was scared that he might do more damage without us here." She takes a deep breath. "And . . . I suppose I thought I could save them both.

"I tried to stop her from going back to Ventana Ranch in January," Mrs. Hart adds suddenly, urgently, like she needs us to know this. "We argued all through the holidays. She promised that it wasn't as bad as I thought it was. Insisted she would be *sadder* if I kept her out of school. That it would be worse if everyone there knew about her. I said we'd come up with a cover story, but she said it was no use, they'd find out, and everything she'd worked so hard for would be ruined."

Mrs. Hart shakes her head. "I gave in. I never could say no to her, whether it was a new dress or a new car." She swallows. Over the years, there must have been so many toys, so many clothes, so many gifts she gave her daughter, wondering which would be the one that finally made her little girl happy.

"I told myself as long as she's under eighteen, I can intervene if I need to." Mrs. Hart's voice is hoarse, as though she can't quite believe that intervention isn't an option anymore. I read once that denial is the first stage of grief, but I don't think I ever really understood what that meant before. It's not that Mrs. Hart doesn't know Eliza's dead—of course she knows it, the detritus from the funeral reception are right in front of her—but she doesn't quite *believe* it.

"I could have forced her into a treatment center. I *should* have forced her. Now she'll always suffer."

"Her suffering is over now," I suggest softly. It's the kind of thing people say. It's the kind of thing we *want* to believe. But then I remember what Sam told me: He didn't want his mother to die, even if that meant prolonging her suffering. I wince, not sure whether I've said the right thing.

Mrs. Hart shakes her head. "No. She died without hope. She'll never live long enough to have the chance to feel better." Her voice gets quieter and thinner with each syllable. I have to lean forward to hear her.

"Maybe it was an accident," I say, my voice still quiet. "That's what the police think. You told Mack—"

Mrs. Hart flinches at the sound of Mack's name, though she doesn't ask how I know about him. "I think I was wrong about him," she says.

I stiffen. Wrong to tell the police to let him go?

She says, "I thought he was dangerous for my daughter, that their relationship was too intense. But maybe intense was what she needed." She stares at the wall behind me before refocusing her gaze on my face. "I told the police that I believed it was an accident. That she'd never been suicidal before. They believed me. They didn't even pull her medical records. Or perhaps my brother-in-law pulled some strings to keep them from digging too deep." Mrs. Hart sits up straight, smoothing her shirt over her torso. "But I know the truth."

"What's the truth?" My question comes out as a whisper.

Mrs. Hart's voice sounds even smaller. "They found her wearing my dress. It was her favorite when she was little.

Even after it went out of style, she never let me throw it away."

"I remember that dress," I say softly. "You wore it the first day of kindergarten."

"Did I?"

I nod. Mrs. Hart shrugs like she can't understand what was so memorable about it. "It was just a plain little day dress. Entirely out of fashion nowadays. But Eliza always said she was going to wear it herself when she was big enough. You'd have thought it was my wedding dress or something."

"She could make anything stylish," I say.

"Yes, she could," Mrs. Hart agrees. "I gave her the dress when she turned sixteen, but she never wore it. She said she was saving it." Mrs. Hart pauses, almost choking on her next words. "For a special occasion." She takes a ragged breath. "It was her way of leaving a note."

I don't think I really *believed* Eliza killed herself until this moment.

Mrs. Hart told Mack, *You can't prove anything.*

Mack couldn't. But she could.

I lace my fingers through Sam's and squeeze.

"Why didn't you tell Mack the truth?" I manage to ask finally. "He thinks you didn't let her get help."

"My daughter had her reasons for telling Mack what she did."

"And you're not going to tell the police what really happened?"

"No."

"Why not?" I'm not asking for myself, not anymore. I'm asking for Eliza now.

Mrs. Hart closes her eyes again. "Because I think that's what Eliza would have wanted me to do. And because keeping her secrets is the last thing I can do for my daughter." She opens her eyes and looks at me. She doesn't say anything, but it feels like she's asking a question:

Will you keep her secrets, too?

ELLIE

friday, march 25

"What are you going to do?" Sam asks as he merges onto Highway 1. The Pacific Ocean stretches out to our right, sparkling in the fading sunlight and unimaginably big.

"I don't know."

Mrs. Hart offered us tea again, and again we said no. We apologized for disturbing her and excused ourselves. For a split second, I wanted to invite her to come with us. It seemed almost cruel to leave her in that house. The air inside was thick with grief. But then, I guess Mrs. Hart will take her grief with her wherever she goes from now on.

I can't believe I ever thought she might turn Eliza's room into a gym or a closet. For Mrs. Hart, no matter if they clean out the drawers or get rid of the clothes, the first room off the long hallway in her house will probably never be anything but Eliza's room.

She will always be Eliza's mother.

She will never stop missing her daughter.

She will always wonder if there was something she could have done differently, something that would've kept Eliza alive.

With each turn of the wheels, we're getting closer to Ventana Ranch. Closer to the students who hate me.

"I would back you up if you wanted to tell," Sam says. "They might believe it coming from the both of us."

"Do you think I *should* tell?"

Sam doesn't answer.

I say, "It might help people to know that even someone like Eliza Hart had issues. I mean, if Eliza hadn't been so determined to keep her problems secret, she might have gone to treatment instead of coming back to school in January."

"Maybe."

"Maybe someone else has secret problems, and maybe if they knew about Eliza, they wouldn't be so ashamed."

"Someone like you?" Sam's voice is gentle.

"I've gotten plenty of help. Eight therapists, remember?"

"You kept your phobia secret from everyone at Ventana Ranch."

"Not from you."

"That doesn't count."

"Why does it have to *count*?"

It's dusk as we round a cliff in Monterey. The ocean is getting dark. Soon, the water will look black instead of blue.

"Ellie," Sam says softly, and I know he wants to talk about the fight we had earlier. "I don't think you're a freak. I *never* thought that."

He continues, "And I didn't mean you were obsessed with her in a bad way. I just meant—you seemed to care an awful lot about a girl you barely knew."

It never felt like I barely knew her. Not while she was still alive, anyway. It was only after she died that I realized how little I—how little any of us—really knew about her.

"I couldn't help it," I answer finally. "On some level, it still felt like she was my best friend, you know?" I never stopped picturing her the way she was at age seven, the only best friend I'd ever had.

Sam nods. "My mom's been gone for years, and I still think of her as my best friend."

"That's different."

"Not completely."

We drive in silence for a few miles. "So you think I should tell?" I ask finally. "Because mental illness is nothing to be ashamed of?"

"Yes." Sam nods. "But I don't think you should tell about Eliza."

"What do you mean?"

"That's *her* secret, and maybe it never should have been a secret, but she wanted it to be."

I nod.

"But," Sam adds, "I do think you should tell about you."

We drive in silence until Sam pulls into the student parking lot an hour later. "You know, I could teach you to drive," he offers. "That way, next time you want to confront a grieving mother about her daughter's suicide, you won't need me to play chauffeur."

I groan. "That's a terrible joke."

"I know." Sam grins. "But one of us had to say *something*." He opens his door and gets out of the car, so I do the same. I close the door behind me and lean against the Camry.

"Let me ask you something," I begin. Sam walks around to my side of the car and stands in front of me, less than an arm's length away. "If you don't think I should tell the truth about Eliza, why did you offer to back me up if I did?"

Sam steps toward me. The sun has set completely now. It's cold but my roommate's breath is warm against my face when he speaks. "Because I want to help you."

"But they'd hate you, too. You wouldn't be able to go back to normal—back to hanging out with Cooper and . . ." I bite my lip, swallowing the rest of my sentence: *back to hooking up with other girls.*

"Do you really think I care about going back to normal more than I care about you?" He sighs. "I know you think it's easy for me to fit in, but—" Sam pauses, running his hand over his face and running a thumb across his lower lip. Suddenly, my roommate looks very tired. Finally, he says, "I don't want to go back to the way it was before."

He leans down, his face hovering above mine. I slide along the side of the car so our faces aren't lined up anymore.

"I don't need your help." It comes out sounding harsher than I want it to. "I mean, not in *that* department. In kissing. I don't want you just to kiss me because you want to help me."

Sam straightens. "What are you talking about?"

"I mean the next time someone kisses me, I don't want it to be because they feel sorry for me. I want it to be real."

"You think I want to kiss you because I feel sorry for you?"

"The other night you said you were just trying to help me cross something off my list."

"And here I thought that was kind of a smooth line." He's trying not to laugh.

I fold my arms across my chest. "I don't think it's funny."

Sam sidesteps so we're face-to-face again. "I'm not laughing at you." He tries to set his mouth into a straight line but he's still struggling not to smile. "I kissed you because I wanted to."

"Wanted to help me, you mean."

Sam shakes my head, and now he looks truly serious. "No." He bends so that his face is just centimeters above my own. "Because I *wanted* to."

"But then why haven't you kissed me since?"

Sam looks sheepish. "I wasn't sure you wanted me to. I mean, you had a lot going on. It didn't seem . . . appropriate to make a move."

"And *now* it does?" We just left a grieving mother behind in her empty house. We know our classmate really did kill herself. These aren't exactly romantic revelations.

"Not really," Sam admits. "I guess I just got tired of waiting."

All at once, the gap between our faces seems huge, and I'm desperate to close it. I stand up on my tiptoes until my mouth is pressed against Sam's. His arms snake around my waist, and I lean back against the car. Butterflies dance across my stomach.

This time, I'm not thinking about Eliza. I'm not thinking about favors and checklists and all the nevers I have yet to complete. This time, when Sam kisses me, I don't think about anything but Sam, and me, and this kiss that I never want to end.

We hold hands as we cross the parking lot and ascend the stairs that lead to the dorms. We pass the spot where they brought up Eliza's body. I stop and gaze out over the cliffs. In the darkness, there's nothing to see.

Eliza stood here less than two weeks ago. She was still alive. She chose to jump.

I shiver. Sam puts his arm around me.

"I *was* obsessed with Eliza. Not in a bad way, not like she told everyone. But still. I cared about her too much."

Sam shrugs. "Who's to say how much we should care about anything?"

I nod. We resume walking up the path.

"Hey—why did you lie to me about being afraid of heights?" I ask.

"I'm really sorry about that."

"I know," I say softly. "But why did you?"

He plays with his dreads. "I just wanted you to like me."

"You think phobics only make friends with other phobics?"

Sam laughs. "I was desperate! We'd been living together since September, and you hadn't made friends with me yet. I guess I was just trying to find some common ground."

I reach out and pull Sam's face toward mine, kissing him right here in the middle of the path between the dorms, where anyone might see us.

"I can't believe Eliza thought she didn't deserve this," I whisper. Suddenly, I feel like crying.

"What do you mean?" Sam's fingers play with my hair.

"I mean . . ." But I'm not sure exactly what I mean. Maybe when Mack kissed her, she couldn't really *feel* it. Maybe Eliza couldn't feel how good it feels to fall for someone. "It must be terrible," I say finally. "To believe you don't deserve love."

Sam takes my hand again and leads the way past Eliza's dorm. We pause at the spot where they're going to build a bench for her.

"Have you decided if you're going to tell them about Eliza?" Sam gestures at the dorms around us, our classmates inside.

Before we left the Hart house this afternoon, I asked Mrs. Hart why she told us about Eliza. After all, she said she wanted to keep her daughter's secrets. Mrs. Hart looked surprised by the question. "Because you already knew about us," she answered finally. "I thought you were the only one of Eliza's friends I didn't have to hide it from."

Eliza's mother still thought of me as Eliza's friend—just like I did, despite everything.

Eliza's mother hoped that the right treatment could help her daughter, just like my mother did.

Eliza was ashamed of her illness, just like I've always been ashamed of mine.

Shame is a funny thing. Right now, I can't quite remember why I wanted to keep my claustrophobia a secret from my classmates here.

But I would be ashamed if I broke Mrs. Hart's trust, if I didn't grant Eliza her dying wish.

So I answer, "I'm not going to tell about Eliza."

Sam squeezes my hand and leads the way up the stairs toward our suite.

Maybe Eliza needs her struggles kept secret in order to rest in peace.

I'm beginning to think that the only way I can *live* in peace is to be more open about mine.

ELIZA

sleep

You should know, I understand that I was luckier than a lot of people. My family could afford to pay for treatment and medication. My mom didn't spend late nights on the phone with our HMO or begging Medicaid for more coverage. When my dad had to be hospitalized, he went to a private institution where they served organic vegetables grown in a local garden and where we could visit him and sit on fluffy couches instead of hard folding chairs. The floors were hardwood and clean, not linoleum and dusty. Treatment looked nothing like it did in the movies. Not if you spent enough money, anyway.

But the place still smelled like plastic and despair. Not enough money in the world to cover that up.

I remembered more from "Lady Lazarus":

Dying
Is an art like everything else.

I do it exceptionally well.

There were so many things I did exceptionally well when I was alive.

I swam faster than my classmates and competitors.

I dressed better and made it look effortless, and I knew how to style my hair so it looked like I'd just gotten out of the shower that way.

I got good grades and had lots of friends, none of whom knew about my broken-down sorry excuse for brain chemistry.

I didn't give up.

I tried to pull myself together.

I even took the pills Mom gave me.

But I was my father's daughter. I never took the pills for long.

How many times could they adjust my meds and try again? How many therapists' couches could I sit on, complaining about a life that seemed so good on the outside?

How many arguments could my mother and I have?

How many sleepless nights could a person survive?

I'd run out of fresh starts.

I'd had enough.

Pouring me a glass of milk after school, my babysitter used to trill, *When you've had enough, say when.*

WHEN.

It's not cold, and it doesn't hurt.

The only thing I feel now is tired.

Not the awful kind of tired I got used to when I was alive: the sort of tired that keeps you awake, that keeps your eyelids glued wide open.

This tired is different. This is the kind of tired other people talk about.

This is the kind of tired that lets you sleep.

So I sleep.

ELLIE

sunday, march 27

I can hear my heartbeat. I feel phantom water dripping down my throat and into my lungs, but it's just a trickle, a stream instead of a rushing river.

"You okay in there, Ellie?"

Even though Sam can't see me, I nod. He's waiting on the other side of the closet door. At first, I wanted to test myself without him, but Sam suggested that I try it in stages: once with him just outside the door, once with him in the next room, and once with him out of our suite altogether.

"Ellie?" Sam prompts.

"I'm okay," I answer. "I'm okay," I repeat, talking to myself this time.

I hear Sam move to the common area between our bedrooms just like we planned. My pulse quickens but I can still breathe.

When the front door of our suite opens and shuts, my breathing grows more labored, but I'm still able to inhale enough oxygen to fill my lungs. I'm able to do the things that my therapists told me to: I tell myself that it's okay, I'll get out of here, I'm not in any danger. But I don't try to picture myself on a mountaintop like Julie Andrews in *The Sound of Music* or floating over the rooftops of London like Mary Poppins.

Instead, I picture myself as I am: Elizabeth James Sokoloff, safe and sound.

This isn't the kind of activity the catalog was talking about when it promised parents *the Ventana Ranch School will help your child learn and grow* alongside pictures of students learning how to sail, hiking the Santa Cruz Mountains, surfing big waves up the coast.

I take a deep breath and open the closet door. I'm covered in sweat, and my heart is pounding. I brush my hair away from my face with my fingers and wait patiently for my lungs to function normally, for my pulse to slow. Sunlight streams through my open blinds.

"They should put this in the catalog," I say out loud.

"I could stay with you if you want." Sam sits beside me on my narrow bed and takes my hand in his.

I shake my head. "I have to do this on my own."

"I'll be right next door if you need me."

I smile. "I know."

I watch him walk out of my room and close the door behind him, listen to the sound of his footfalls as he goes into his own room, the sound of his bed squeaking as he lies down and picks up a book to read. But I know he's not going to be able to concentrate. He'll be thinking of me. Rooting for me.

I pick up my phone. She answers on the third ring.

"Is everything okay?" There it is. Her Ellie tone. I guess I can't blame her for assuming something is wrong. I almost never call her. She's usually the one who calls me.

There was something familiar about the look on Eliza's mom's face. Behind the grief and the sadness, there was something else, something I recognized: exhaustion. I'd seen it in my mother's face every time she got called into school or took me to yet another therapist.

And I'd seen it in my own reflection.

My mother wasn't the only one thinking, *Why don't you ever get better?* Not the only one who said, *You've gone to therapy, gotten you all the help you need—and you're still sick.*

I thought those words myself a thousand times. I was just as disappointed as she was after every therapy session and every attack.

"Ellie?" Mom prompts.

"I'm fine," I answer quickly. Too quickly. I'm so used to telling her that everything is fine that it's become a reflex. "Actually"—I take a deep breath—"it's not fine. I mean, I'm okay and everything, but things haven't been fine here."

"What do you mean?"

Butterflies flutter in my belly. I could just tell her that I've been sad about Eliza. It wouldn't be a lie. But it wouldn't be the whole truth, either.

So much of Eliza's life was a repeating loop of secrets and shame. Even if everyone who knew her got together and combined what we know, I still don't think we'd be able to uncover everything she kept hidden. She had too many secrets. She never let anyone see all of her.

Secrets can be fatal.

And I don't want to die.

"I haven't wanted to tell you, but I've been having a hard time here. Most of the kids don't like me and I've still been having attacks."

"Why didn't you call Dr. Solander?"

"I didn't want to admit that I needed help."

I hear her take a deep breath. "Ellie, sweetheart, you've always needed help." The tone in her voice makes my heart ache.

"I wanted you to be proud of me." I hurry on before she can contradict me. "I mean, I know you were proud of me for getting into Ventana Ranch and coming to California by myself, but you always seemed so disappointed, too."

"Ellie—"

"No, let me finish," I interrupt. "You were disappointed every time I had an attack, every time a therapist didn't cure me. Every time I couldn't just get over it and be more like Wes."

Mom doesn't say anything. I think I hear her breath catch, like maybe she's trying not to cry.

"But something happened after Eliza died. It's complicated." I thought long and hard about whether or not to tell my mother what I remembered in Mr. Hart's study. If I told, would I be breaking the promise I made to Eliza so long ago?

But if I kept it secret, I'd be breaking the promise I made to myself more recently: I'm through with secrets.

So I tell her. I say it fast, so that she doesn't have a chance to break in. When I finish, Mom sounds furious. "I can't believe Laurel never told me what happened. I have half a mind to call her and—"

"Don't," I cut her off.

"But all these years, all the pain it caused you—"

"No," I say firmly. "She has enough to worry about."

Mom doesn't argue.

I know I'll probably never be all the things Eliza was, all the things I admired her for. I'll probably never show up in just the right clothes, or be the girl who always knows the right thing to say, the girl who draws people to her like a magnet, always the most popular, the most beloved.

I'll probably never understand how Eliza lost hope so completely that she killed herself.

I'll probably never stop wondering whether there was something I could've done or said that would have changed her mind.

I picture Eliza's gray-blue eyes, her long wavy hair, the perfectly painted nails on her hands and feet.

I'm going to tell my mother the truth about Eliza's death eventually. I promised myself: *No more secrets.* But I won't tell her today—not because it's a secret, but because right now I need her to hear me when I say something else.

"The claustrophobia wasn't my fault," I begin.

"I never said it was," Mom insists, but even she must know the words sound hollow.

"I want to start going to therapy again."

After all these years, Mom doesn't exactly have the highest opinion of therapists. "All that therapy and none of it helped you. You uncovered this memory yourself."

"Maybe," I agree. "But I still need to work through it."

"All right." Mom takes a long breath. "I'll call Dr. Solander."

"No," I say firmly. "A specialist. Someone who knows about repressed memories and claustrophobia."

"So what are you saying, Ellie? Do you want to come home?"

"I'm not sure," I answer honestly. Everyone at Ventana Ranch—except for Sam—still hates me. And Big Sur is kind of in the middle of nowhere. It'll be a whole lot easier to find a specialist in Manhattan.

I walk to the window and look outside. Someone threw

away the flowers and electric candles outside Eliza's dorm, clearing a space for the bench that's going to go in its place. As always, my window is open, and I can smell the ocean and the redwoods. I don't need to see the rest of the world to know that Sam was right: This is the most beautiful place on earth.

At least, it is to me.

That night that Sam and I spent together, I told him that I'd never had a sleepover because I was scared of sleeping bags, but the truth is, I was scared to ask the grown-ups to accommodate me.

It would've been too embarrassing if the grown-ups did try to make it work, leading me off to a special bed while everyone else slept snugly in their sleeping bags on the floor.

It was easier to stay home than face that.

It would be easier to go home, now.

Finally, I say, "I'd like to try to stay. With therapy. See if things get better." Because it seems like Mom deserves some good news I add, "The claustrophobia is already a little better."

"It is?" Mom's voice sounds a little bit lighter, the Ellie tone receding.

"It is," I promise. "But I still need help."

"All right, then," Mom says firmly, and I imagine she's sitting up straighter. "We'll get you help."

I'm still looking out the window when Mom and I hang up. I open it wide and stick my head outside. I feel the ocean breeze, smell the moss on the ground below. The sun's setting and the fog's rolling in, making my hair wet. There's still a chill in the air, but it's already warmer than it was a few days ago.

It's spring.

I don't say it loud enough that anyone will hear me. They'd probably shout at me to be quiet, insist that I have no right to wish her well. But I know the truth, and wherever she is, I hope she knows how much I mean it when I whisper:

Rest in peace, Eliza Hart.

Rest in peace, Eliza Hart.

Rest in peace, Eliza Hart.

AUTHOR'S NOTE

When I first had the idea for this book, it was Eliza's voice I heard: sharp and biting, brief and to the point, even a little bit funny. The truth is, I just really liked her.

I knew the story would include Ellie's perspective as well, so I began researching claustrophobia. Personally, I've always found small places more comforting than terrifying, so I wanted to make sure I could understand someone like Ellie.

Over time, it got harder and harder to write Eliza's chapters. I researched her illness, reading books about people who'd experienced depression, people who'd attempted suicide, people who'd lost family members to suicide.

I struggled especially as I got to the end of the novel. How could I convey Eliza's hopelessness without actually conveying hopelessness? How could I give her the peace she'd been seeking without suggesting that suicide was the only way she could find peace? How could I show the devastation Eliza's death wrought on her family and friends without blaming her for what had happened? She'd been sick, and it wasn't her fault. Like so many people who attempt suicide, she hadn't been acting out of selfishness; she genuinely—though mistakenly—believed their lives would be better without her in it.

Writing this story was a balancing act—I just wanted to tell Ellie's and Eliza's stories in the way that felt the most true. At the end of her story, Ellie knows that there are things more dangerous than small spaces—like not asking for help when you need it. In fact, she knows that sometimes asking for help is the bravest thing you can do.

If you or someone you know is considering suicide, please call the National Suicide Prevention Lifeline at 1-800-273-TALK (8255) or visit SuicidePreventionLifeline.org for free and confidential emotional support.

ACKNOWLEDGMENTS

Thank you to my wonderful editor, Emily Seife, and thanks also to David Levithan, Nancy Mercado, and the team at Scholastic; thank you to Maeve Norton for the striking cover, to Melissa Schirmer in production, to my copy editor, Jackie Hornberger, and to Jennifer Powell in the sub-rights department. Thank you, Tracy van Straaten, Lauren Donovan, Isa Caban, Vaishali Nayak, to my dear friend Rachel Feld, and to everyone in the sales, marketing, and publicity departments.

Many thanks to my marvelous agent, Mollie Glick, to the lovely Joy Fowlkes, and the teams at CAA and Foundry.

Thank you to my writing group: Caroline Gertler, Jackie Resnick, and Julie Sternberg for their patience, support, and sage advice; and thank you to Jocelyn Davies, Anne Heltzel, and Danielle Rollins for long talks and the occasional late nights.

Thanks to Samantha Schutz, and thank you to my teachers—especially the writers whose stories helped me tell this one, including (to name just a few) Jill Bialosky, Carrie Fisher, Marya Hornbacher, Andrea Perry, William Styron, Amy Wilensky, and Elizabeth Wurtzel.

Thank you to my sister, my parents, and my friends. And once again, thank you, JP Gravitt, for everything.

"I thought a dog would be the key to perfect happiness. And I was right. We are perfectly happy."
—Ann Patchett, "This Dog's Life"

To learn more about the redwoods and burl-poaching, visit www.savetheredwoods.org.

ABOUT THE AUTHOR

Alyssa Sheinmel is the *New York Times* bestselling author of several novels for young adults, including *Faceless* and *Second Star*. She is the co-author of *The Haunting of Sunshine Girl* and its sequel, *The Awakening of Sunshine Girl*. Alyssa grew up in Northern California and New York, and currently lives and writes in New York City. Follow her on Instagram and Twitter @AlyssaSheinmel or visit her online at alyssasheinmel.com.